The Nap-Away Motel

The Nap-Away Motel

Nadja Lubiw-Hazard

Palimpsest Press
1171 Eastlawn Ave.
Windsor, Ontario. N8S 3J1
www.palimpsestpress.ca

Printed and bound in Canada. Cover design and book typography by
Dawn Kresan. Edited by Aimee Parent Dunn and Malak El Tahry. Copy-
edited by Ginger Pharand.

Palimpsest Press would like to thank the Canada Council for the Arts and
the Ontario Arts Council for their support of our publishing program. We
also acknowledge the assistance of the Government of Ontario through
the Ontario Book Publishing Tax Credit.

LIBRARY AND ARCHIVES CANADA CATALOGUING IN PUBLICATION

TITLE: The Nap-Away Motel / Nadja Lubiw-Hazard.
NAMES: Lubiw-Hazard, Nadja, 1965–author.
IDENTIFIERS: Canadiana (print) 2019004604x
　　　　　　Canadiana (ebook) 20190046163

ISBN 9781989287170 (SOFTCOVER) | ISBN 9781989287187 (EPUB)
ISBN 9781989287194 (PDF) | ISBN 9781989287200 (KINDLE)

CLASSIFICATION: LCC PS8623.U215 N37 2019 | DDC C813/.6—DC23

The Nap-Away Motel sits hunched low to the ground: an L-shaped row of rooms facing an empty parking lot; a grey-shingled roof that slumps downwards; peeling yellow paint on the exterior walls. It looks as desperate and weary as its occupants. Once upon a time it was an inviting rest stop for travellers, back when the Kingston Road motel-strip flourished, before the construction of Highway 401 into Toronto. Back then, Nap-Away had a pool, a small rectangular shimmer of blue at the edge of the parking lot. Aluminum lawn chairs, webbed with strips of plastic the colour of watermelon, gathered in small clusters around the pool deck. Fringed patio umbrellas shaded circular tables, and brilliant burst of red geraniums grew in large planters along the fence. The freshly painted walls of the motel shone in the summer sun. The cars driving into the city would slow, the signal lights would blink, and the visitors would arrive, spilling out into the sunshine, pointing at the pool, delighted to find this charming and cheerful roadside motel. Years ago, Nap-Away was desired.

Now, Nap-Away's sign never boasts that it's occupied. Instead the word VACANCY blinks intrepidly, offering prostitutes a place to exchange sex for money on the worn beds, against the mildewed bathroom walls, kneeling on the threadbare carpets; offering a night's sleep to the refugees and the runaways; offering temporary housing when the shelters are overflowing to the weary mothers, who arrive with runny-nosed babies on their hips and kids trailing behind, carrying their clothes in plastic grocery bags; offering a working place for shifty-eyed drug dealers and desperate junkies.

The green spring dandelions push through the cracked asphalt in the parking lot, where a rusty tricycle lies abandoned on its side. A pigeon struts across the lot, puffing up his purple neck feathers, turning in a perfect pirouette towards his mate, a small white bird with mangled toes on her left foot. The graffiti-tagged door to Room 11 bangs open and both birds take flight, the stiff feathers of their wings clapping together on the upswing. They land on Nap-Away's sloping roof, their scaled red toes seeking purchase on the crumbling grey shingles, as they look down at the person who has emerged.

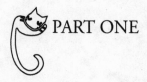

PART ONE

ORI

Sometimes I'm a girl and sometimes I'm a boy. Today's a girl-day, so it's Orianthi. Red skinny jeans, my brother's old Blundstone boots, a black tee, no logo, purple hair chalk. Back story on the boots—I was wearing them the day Carter took off, three months after our seventeenth birthday. Otherwise they'd be gone too. They're awesome, all worn out and scuffed up and vintage-like. Orianthi. It's a cool name, right? Rockin' guitarist and all.

Carter ran away, and I followed. We're tethered, but I guess he forgot. I miss his quirky hyena laugh, his tenderness, his viciousness. Raspberry pie at midnight, single fork. *Ori*, whispered, sing-song, reverent. All that science shit he used to teach me: trilobites, coprolites, dendrites. Ukulele punk—humble, badass. Whatever. Short story, he's gone.

I'm kind of wondering how I ended up here, Room 11, Nap-Away Motel. Bed shaped like a hammock, stink of cigarette smoke and mouse piss, stain on the carpet that looks like blood, cracked mirror in the bathroom. Bleak. Dubious beginning for a lost-twin quest.

I waited for Carter to come back, for thirteen days. At first I was disbelieving. I sent him jokey texts with stupid emojis that I knew he would hate and waited for him to respond. Then I got really pissed. Stopped texting him. But I kept looking for him at all the places we hung out. Around the sixth day I spiralled down into a blacker place. Soundtrack "Cosmic Love," Florence + the Machine, all that darkness when the stars go out. On the seventh day I found his cell phone. Smashed open, all its intricate circuitry exposed. The screen was shattered into a million little pieces of cracked ice. I cradled it for a moment in my cupped palms. Like it was a dead baby rabbit. Then I hurled it at Carter's bed.

A couple of months before he took off, he started acting weird. Cagey and nasty. Some kind of secret pulsed through his veins. No riffs on his uke. He muttered and scribbled in his notebook. I'd looked inside it before—brain-eating amoebas, blue straggler stars, crap I didn't understand—but when I snuck into his room to peek inside the notebook again, I saw cramped dark words multiplying and spilling over the pages, sketches of disemboweled dogs, of monstrous creatures with jagged fangs. *They say terrible things will happen if I reveal anything*, he had written. *I've made a discovery though, about dendritic spines, about the connectivity of the interneurons. I thought it might help, but they say I can't tell, not ever. Not even to Ori. They tell me things about Ori that I don't want to believe, horrible things about what—*

Carter caught me. His eyes were grey and wild, filled with snarling wolves. He ripped the notebook from my hands.

"The proof is in here. About everything! Now they'll have to come and take me," he hissed vehemently.

"Who?" I asked.

His lips curled back to form the words. "You're not who you say you are. They said you would do this, that you would interfere!" My guts slithered and constricted into a tight coil. He dropped the notebook and turned his head sharply to the right. "Shut up. SHUT UP! GO AWAY!" I skittered out of his room. In the morning, he was gone.

Here's the thing. Carter and I look out for each other, because no one else ever has, not really. We spent most of our childhood bouncing around between our mom, our grandma, and foster care, which mostly sucked, except for Foster Home Three. Big funky farmhouse on the edge of Oshawa, lots of fruit smoothies, two wiry grey dogs, and a foster mom who was into drumming-circles and yoga. Stella. She bought Carter his first ukulele. I miss the dogs the most. Nancy and Grover. They both had those weird blue eyes that could pin you against a wall. She got sick though—Stella, I mean, not Nancy—so we moved on to Foster Home Four. Then back to our mom's for a couple of years before things fell apart again.

Foster Home Five was nothing like Three. No dogs, no smoothies, no yoga. Bunch of little kids with snotty noses, running around with dirty bare feet, wet diapers hanging down. Fish sticks and overcooked pasta with watery tomato sauce. Lots of beer-drinking and bad reality TV. Kathy was nonchalant about Carter's disappearance. Mr. Jepps didn't even notice Carter was gone.

So the vigil of waiting for Carter's return was mine alone. On the thirteenth day his postcard arrived. A touristy one, with a glossy Canadian beaver on the front, Toronto, written in large cursive script across the bottom. The back was crowded with the same dark cramped words from his notebook. My name, again and again. *Ori, Ori, Ori,* like he was calling out to me. *I'm at the edge of the universe,* THE FUCKIN' EDGE, *looking over. There's a pencil in my heart, right here, right here, and it hurts, you can't imagine how much it hurts me, but they can't take it out, they can't get to it, but every time I breathe I can feel it impaling me, the slivers of wood piercing, fiercely, fiery, fury, flurry, there's a flurry of words slipping out of my brain. Someone has tampered with it.* There were a few more sentences that I couldn't decipher, and then: *I can only eat tacos now. Ori!* I could hear his voice, pleading like he was being held hostage. There was a sketch, small and detailed, of some kind of pointy-nosed rodent. Like an earless mouse. But with rows of sharp teeth. And circling the outer edge, like a frame: *On earth we strive for earthly things and suffer sorrows daily. In heaven choirs of angels sing, while we play ukulele.*

I carried the postcard around in my back pocket for five days. Folding and unfolding that beaver's pelt into four. Re-reading all the craziness, until it was embedded into my mind. The beaver was magical; I thought it was an amulet that would bring Carter back. Until I realized that it wasn't bringing him back, it was calling me to him. A magnet, tugging at my marrow, pulling me to my twin.

Pulled on Carter's Blundstones, threw my clothes and my notebook into a bag, scrounged around for cash. I had a couple hundred stashed away. My life's savings. Carter had a Mason jar filled with change that I emptied out. Stole a couple of twenties from Mr. Jepps' beer fund. Hitched a ride with a neighbour to the city. Told him I was meeting Carter, like it was all planned. Big fat truck, driving fast along the 401, going west. On the drive he told me neighbourly stories. The bowling alley fire. Mr. Marshall's dog. (Twenty stitches. And that cone of shame.)

Graffiti on the war monument in the park. Eventually he turned on the radio. Soundtrack, his, not mine: "Sunglasses at Night," Corey Hart.

Here's the problem. I don't really know Toronto. So when Mr. Neighbour leaves the highway because there's construction, tells me we're in the city, I get all excited. Eager. Like Lana Briggs in math class, hand sky high, little tremor in the fingertips, lovin' her algebra. I'm not thinking right, just thinking Carter. He asks where I'm meeting up with my brother but I don't have an answer. I jump out at a random corner. Mr. Neighbour tells me to wait, that we're only in Scarborough, but I just wave bye. My first mistake.

Box of KFC gone, darkness falling. That's when I spot Nap-Away. Big old oak tree watching over it, ancient gnarled branches shadowed in green. The motel reminds me of something from a fairy tale. Something beautiful and loyal disguised in wretchedness. The old hag who beckons with a gnarled finger. Jesus the beggar. I'm guessing runaway teens don't rent motel rooms, but I slink into the office anyway. Nothing to lose. Skinny Santa guy at the desk talks to me through a hole in a thick wall of glass.

"How much for a room?" I ask. Trying to seem nonchalant. Like I don't really give a shit.

"Seventy for the night," he says. He coughs violently and horks into the garbage can at his feet. I pull out four twenties. He stares at me.

"You gotta have ID."

"No problem," I say. I push the money through the slot in the glass. He picks it up, counts it.

"You old enough?"

"Sure," I say.

"No visitors in the room allowed." He leans forward, shows his crooked yellow teeth. A Grinchy kind of smile. "Not between eleven and five." He gives me a form to fill out. I enter my grandma's address, even though she's been dead for two years. Show him my health card. It's fake, turns me into a nineteen-year-old. A seventeenth birthday present from Carter. He squints at it, copies down the number. Gives me a key to Room 11. As I leave I see a woman in stilettos staggering towards the motel office. When she passes by me I see that the back of her short skirt is hitched up, revealing the smooth curves of her butt cheeks.

SULEIMAN

Each morning of my exile in Room 6 at the Nap-Away Motel, I wake and think of my daughter, Amina. But thoughts of her weigh heavily on my heart, so instead I think of Khadija. *Insha'Allah,* God willing, today my wife will take me back. I stare at the spreading patch of orange mould on the ceiling above my bed. She has always been a head-strong woman. I admired that when I first met her, the way her eyes sparked with a fiery blackness, like a wild horse, the way she strode confidently down the streets of Saint-Laurent, insistent on meeting up with me, even though a blizzard had begun to rage through Montreal. She was as fierce as that icy winter storm.

I had admired other things about her too, not just her determination. She spoke several languages. Her hands gestured wildly when she talked, fluttering and soaring around her curves and shadows. She was working three part-time jobs trying to save for her studies. Her apartment had very little furniture, but was cluttered with things that overwhelmed the senses: scented candles, gauzy scarves, jewelry that sparkled and jingled, fringed cushions, bright flowers. She was devoted to God, yet she wore no hijab, and her black hair flowed freely around her laughing face. I often wonder how different my life would have been if I had not met her when I was twenty-two. Who would I have become without her? She opened me up to all the different possible versions of myself that might exist, allowed me to choose who I wanted to be, not who I thought I was supposed to be.

I scratch the thick black hair on my belly and rise out of the bed. The mattress springs squeak in protest under my weight. I pull on a stained white undershirt and a pair of red basketball shorts that feel a little tight at the waist, and slide my feet into worn leather sandals. As I urinate I stamp down with my left foot to crush a cockroach that scuttles out from beneath the toilet, and then go back into my room to pray.

I recite the *suras* from the Qur'an, after which I bow down and prostrate myself. I have no prayer mat, instead I kneel on the worn carpet of Nap-Away's floor. I should have a proper mat, but these last few weeks have been difficult. I have struggled to maintain an order to my days, to pray as I am obligated to, to find motivation to go forward.

I lower my head to the floor and a foul smell distracts me. The odour must be powerful, as my sense of smell is not that strong. Pungent and sour, perhaps stale vomit?

My distraction annoys me. I think of my grandfather, picture the darkened prayer callous on his forehead, the proof of his devotion, and I ask for forgiveness. I have always been faithful, but lately my prayers are irregular, and instead of bringing answers, I find my mind fogged with questions.

I finish praying, turning my head first right, and then left, as I address the unseen, wishing peace and the mercy of God upon them. For a moment I imagine I am wishing *salam* to Nap-Away, as if it too were in need of peace. I shake my head. I've been spending too much time alone, that's the problem.

I grunt as I pull myself up to standing. Carrying the crusts of last night's pizza, I step out into the bright summer sunshine, blinking, and take a seat in my green chair. So begins my morning ritual of feeding the pigeons. They recognize me now, and they flutter and flock towards me immediately, grey-bodied, their neck feathers shimmering with dusky purples and shimmering greens. Their heads turn sideways at me, their bright, honey eyes inquisitive.

The pigeons have been coming for several weeks now, greeting me each morning. They are faithful birds, I've decided. At first they all looked similar, but now I recognize individuals: the dark speckled wings of one, the yellow rings around the eyes of another, the shiny blue neck feathers on the shyest one, the mangled red foot of the small white pigeon. When I feed them, they bob their heads in thanks, murmuring and cooing. They seem to radiate things; I see their intelligence, their questions, their determination. As they leave, their wing tips beat together making sharp clapping sounds. I wish that I didn't, but every time they go, all of them moving as one, I feel foolish and alone, more alone than before they arrived.

I know it's my own fault that I'm alone, that Khadija wants nothing to do with me anymore. I sigh in disgust. "Be careful," I mutter, "for if you make a woman cry, *Allah* will count her tears."

As I turn to go back into my room, the door to Room 5 opens. A child peers out, her brown face framed by black wiry hair. She has wide green eyes that shine like spring leaves in the sun, and long eyelashes. She reminds me of my daughter.

"Hello Suleiman," she whispers. "Did the birds come already?"

I nod, pointing across the parking lot to the hydro lines in front of the mosque next door, where the birds have congregated. For a moment my gaze rests on the mosque, Masjid Umar Al-Farooq, a low red brick building that, like Nap-Away, is humble and unassuming. Tomorrow, Friday, I will be within its walls, at midday prayers, even though there is no *muezzin* to call out to me to come, to call out to the faithful five times a day. There is only a lone starling trilling from the branches of a tall blue spruce. Both the mosque and the spruce tree are enshrined behind a black wrought-iron fence.

"Come," I say, turning my attention back to the girl. "Let's bring them back for you." I retrieve another crust from my room, and scatter more crumbs for the birds. The girl creeps forward warily, like a small, scared animal. She crouches down and watches the birds, her thin fingers fluttering.

"They're so pretty. They look like rainbows." She reaches a hand forward then snatches it away quickly when one of the birds struts towards it. I'm about to show her how the bold one with golden-brown wings, the one I've named *Fajar Ayub*, will step onto my outstretched hand and clutch my index finger with her scaly red feet, when a shrill voice calls from the inside of Room 5.

"Tiffany, get your ass in here." The girl jumps up, startling the pigeons into flight.

"Thanks," she says, and she pats my arm before she scurries inside, her touch as soft as the wispy grey pigeon feather that floats down onto the asphalt.

I leave Nap-Away, heading west on Kingston Road to Sadie's Bar and Grill, three blocks away. I've come to this place for years now, each morning on my way to work at Five-Star Carpets. I order a large coffee, black. As I sit, staring out the window at the traffic, I decide to go to the house. I haven't done that in a week. I've tried other things: phoning Khadija, sometimes two, three times a day; leaving her gifts, a turquoise pendant on a silver chain, a pale blue silk scarf; calling our son, Ahmed, in Montreal, leaving messages asking him to speak to his mother, to make a case for my return.

I go back to Nap-Away to shower, but the water runs in a cold trickle, refusing to warm. I rub my hand across the coarse stubble on my chin, consider shaving. Normally I don't let my facial hair grow in for more than a day or two. Yes, the prophet had a beard, but I've come to believe that growing a beard is not a measure of my faith, not like prayer is, or fasting. Over the years I've become less rigid, less bound by rules and more bound by my own sense of what is right and what is wrong. Shaving is something I prefer to do after a shower though. At least a clean shirt then. But I find nothing except piles of dirty laundry. Ah well, maybe Khadija will pity me, when she sees the state I'm in.

When I knock on the door to our house, Khadija opens it instantaneously, as if she were waiting on the other side for my arrival. This cheers me, until I see she has her purse in her hand.

"Where are you going?" I ask. Her mouth tightens and her dark eyes burn. I regret having spoken.

"It's not your business where I go," she says in a clipped voice, her hand waving slightly into the distance. "Why are you here?"

"Of course it's my business!" I step towards her. She pushes against the door, but I slide my foot forward, stop it from closing. I pause. I'd come here in the hopes of making amends. This isn't the way to begin.

Khadija sighs. She lets go of the door, opens her hands towards me and gestures at my foot in the doorway. "You can't force your way back into our home. We've agreed to this time apart. You agreed. But you keep refusing to honour our agreement. We can't go on like this! I think it's best that you leave."

I glance down at my foot. I'll let it decide. Either my foot will step back and I will leave as she has asked, or it will choose to stay, holding my place in my old life. We both wait. My chest tightens. I reach my hand up, rub my thumb across the large mole that weighs down my left eyelid. It's an old boyhood habit, caressing its smooth surface when I feel agitated, but I've started doing it again these past few weeks. It's a sure sign of trouble. I've made everything worse by coming here, yet I can't seem to step back.

"Please," Khadija says, pleading. Her voice is soft, like the murmuring of the pigeons. "Do as we agreed. Stay away for a time. You have been so distant, you refuse to talk to me, you are angry all the time. It has become unbearable."

I slowly pull my sandaled foot from the doorway and turn away. I should resign myself to doing as Khadija says; it is what we agreed to. When she first suggested we spend some time apart I had felt so hopeful, had felt that it was the right course of action. But I'm not so sure anymore. I feel a growing desperation the longer I'm apart from her. And now, I feel a wave of anger surging up from deep in my belly. I spin back around and stumble forward, grabbing the door just before Khadija closes it.

TIFFANY

There's a new girl, in Room 11, across the parking lot from where I live, in Room 5 at the Nap-Away Motel. I used to live in an apartment building that was so tall it touched the sky, but I like Nap-Away better. At the apartment there was no place to play outside because I wasn't allowed on the balcony in case I fell off, but at Nap-Away there is a big parking lot with hardly any cars where I can jump rope and pick dandelions and play hopscotch. And I found a hiding place behind Nap-Away where no one else goes. There is a huge tree there and sometimes I see little yellow butterflies flying by.

The new girl at Nap-Away looks a lot like my big sister because she is tall and skinny and she has white skin. Except my mom told me to stay away from him, because his tight red pants spell trouble, so maybe she's a boy. I'm not sure. I don't get the part about pants spelling trouble because the letters aren't the same. I'm not going to ask though, because questions give my mom headaches and smacky hands. I'd like a pair of red pants. I think I would name them Margaret. I like M names the best, but I have a T name, Tiffany. We could be friends, the red pants and me, just like those Dr. Seuss pants, with nobody inside them. We had a Dr. Seuss party at school yesterday. The best part was the green eggs, which were the chocolate kind, wrapped up in shiny green foil. It was fun, except that I had to leave early because there was a test, and I did it wrong. The test was about lice in my hair. I wanted it to be a secret, but Jamal told Theo, and Theo told Angel, and then Angel told everybody.

I gave my mom the note from school about the lice. I did it because Mrs. Lynch said I had to or I couldn't come back to school. My mom didn't read it though. "I'm too strung-out for this, baby," she said, and then she let the note flutter away like a giant white butterfly. Her lips were all puffy. And her eyes were shiny, like the crying eyes of Jamal when Theo punched him in the tummy. I picked up the note and saved it for later. But the next time it wasn't a butterfly anymore, it was an angry crinkly bug that scurried under my bed.

This morning, when I ask my mom about buying the special shampoo, she says, "Come on, Tiffany, where am I gonna get the money for that?" I shrug and take a bite of my cereal. It's too crunchy, because there's no milk.

"But I can't go back to school."

"But I can't go back to school," she says back at me in a high whiny voice. "What kid wants to go there anyway?" She reaches for a cigarette, but the box is empty. She crumples it in her fist and throws it, just like she did last night with my note from school. "I need a fuckin' smoke."

I count to one hundred in my head. I made this rule up for when my mom is mad. I know she's mad when she says fuck. If I count to one hundred and she hasn't said it again, then I can talk. But if she says it again when I'm at twenty-seven, or fifty-nine, then I need to start over. This time I get all the way to one hundred. Then I count to one hundred and one for good luck.

"Maybe we could—" I start to say, but my mom's eyes go all flat, like her eyebrows are pushing them down too hard to keep them open. She has pretty eyes. They are blue, like birthday balloons, all shiny and light. But right now they are not so pretty. They are just two hard dark lines. So I stop talking. She gets up and stands behind me. I lean my head way back to look up at her, but she pushes my head back down and grabs a handful of hair.

"Ouch!"

"Jesus, what are you supposed to do with hair like this?" My hair makes my mom frus-ter-ated. She has the straightest hair, the kind that never tangles. She keeps pulling and tugging at my hair. "I don't see any bugs in here. I don't think the school knows what they're talking about! When's the last time you washed it?" I shrug. I don't know how to wash my hair. But if I say that it will only make her madder. She finally stops yanking at it. "I gotta go to work. You need to stay inside, you hear?" I nod my head. "Don't open the door for no one. And wash your hair!"

I pull the curtains open so I can watch her leave. She walks across the parking lot to the bus stop on the corner. She gets on the bus and I wait until the light turns green. Then I open the door and go outside.

ORI

I'm missing Carter like crazy. Best memory: the last time we played Wild Things together. *Let the wild rumpus begin!*

Carter brandished an enormous stick and stomped through the wooded ravine, his tongue lolling out of his mouth. I pelted him with pine cones, howled, swung from a low branch. We made crowns from leafy vines, climbed an enormous pine, had a spitting contest. Carter laughed his wicked hyena laugh. I cawed and flapped my wings. The sun beat down, the wind shimmered and stopped. Everything was stilled into perfection.

"We should stay eleven forever," Carter whispered.

Tree-bound, legs dangling, chewing Juicy Fruit. We talked about all things: the Chinese river dolphin, what yellow tasted like, *Harry Potter and the Deathly Hallows*, middle school, what it feels like to die.

Later, earth-bound, Carter pulled out the book that I had given him for his birthday. A field guide to mushrooms, dog-eared and weary. I'd found it in a bin at Value Village for a loonie. Filled with bizarre pictures—jellyfish moons on stalks, clusters of glistening black olives, dead fingers seeping out of the earth. I flipped through the book, quizzing him. Real or imagined: blue-staining slippery jack, hideous jack, dead man's fingers, dead man's tongue, rotten rooster.

Carter snatched the book back. "Listen to this," he said. "Mushrooms are sometimes discovered by finding a shrump. Once you start searching for shrumps you'll find them everywhere."

"What's a shrump?"

He stood, cleared his throat. "A shrump is a bump, a hump, a simple lump in the dirt or debris." He pointed dramatically to a small bulge in the pine needles underfoot. "Witness the shrump. It's the black hole of the mushroom world. You can't see the mushroom, just its effect on the surrounding matter."

"Carter, you're such a freak."

"Don't call me Carter, call me Shrump, Lord Shrump of the British Mycology Society." He named me Smut. Some fungal disease of corn.

"I do declare, Mr. Macpherson's ear hair is dreadfully cespitose, wouldn't you agree?" Carter twirled imaginary tufts in his left ear.

"Oh, Shrump, You're absolutely spot on!" We fell over, shrieking with laughter.

Carter jumped up, insisted we hunt for mushrooms. He rooted around like a snuffling pig, found some in a fairy ring, ID'ed them in his book. "Smut, you must try them. I insist." I nibbled; he smacked the mushroom from my hand.

"Dreadfully sorry chap, looks like I missed the skull and crossbones symbol." I feigned death in three acts. "Beastly. Absolutely beastly," Carter said. I finished dying, leapt up, raced off towards the creek. Carter passed me in the last ten metres. We kicked off our Converses, rock-hopped across the water. Settled under a giant willow, sheltered together in her long green hair.

"You know," Carter said, "sometimes you feel like a brother, and sometimes it feels like you're my sister." Our grey eyes met. The river water swizzled past, I couldn't move, afraid to shatter the moment. I felt strange, like I was suddenly real. Like Carter was the friggin' blue fairy. My heart chirped a sweet little song of love for him. He grinned, punched me in the stomach.

"Either way, I can still beat you up," he taunted, and we were suddenly tangled together, wrestling on the wet grass.

Later, back at home, we hung out on the garage roof, one of the places we went when we wanted to disappear. Foster Home Four was full of Our Lord and Saviour, Jesus Christ. Made me want to do bad shit to see if God really was watching me. I started shoplifting. Nothing big though. A dog leash, because I really wanted a dog like Nancy or Grover. A lighter for Carter, because I had the feeling that he was going to start smoking soon. A couple of bags of Doritos.

Our long legs dangled over the edge of the roof. Carter kicked the garage wall. A one-two thump, left foot, right foot, pause. The sun was starting to set and the clouds were streaked all pink and orange. Made you want to lick the sky, see if it tasted like rainbow sherbet. I kicked the wall too, joining in with the one-two beat. Carter nudged against me with his shoulder.

"Tell me one of your stories," he said.

"Ok. A twin one, just for you."

***

THE LEGEND OF POTO AND CABENGO
AS TOLD TO CARTER BY HIS TWIN

Once upon a time two girls were born, in a land far, far away. The two babies were alike in every way. They both had hair as black as midnight, shiny blue eyes, skinny arms and legs, and outsie belly buttons. They even had the same freckles on their cheeks—here, here, and here.

Soon after they were born a terrible curse befell them. The twins became sick, so sick that their shiny blue eyes rolled back into their heads and their bodies shook. They frothed and foamed at the mouth. The parents were terribly afraid and called a wise man, a wizard, to see if he could help. The wizard watched them shake, and he shook his head. "I'm sorry," he said, "there is no cure in all the land for this terrible sickness." After many long days and nights, the twins finally got better, but the wizard warned the parents that the babies would stay cursed. They will never speak, he said, or play, or learn to read. They will be dull and slow, like the cows that graze in the field.

The twins lived with their parents and their grandmother. Granny had beady brown eyes and black whiskers on her chin. It was her job to take care of the cursed twins when the parents were away. They spent long days and nights gone, trying to find money, here, there, and everywhere. Granny dressed and fed the babies, but she rarely spoke to them. She never played with them, or tickled their tummies with those cute outsie belly buttons, or kissed the freckles on their cheeks—here, here and here.

The babies started to grow and their skinny arms and legs got longer and soon they weren't babies any more, but little girls. They loved each other very much. They kissed each other's freckles and they laughed at their twin belly buttons. Their fingers fit together just right when they held each other's hands. And they chattered away like two little birds, talking to each other.

The wizard, you see, was wrong. He was an old wizard, and he had started to become forgetful as he aged. He sometimes said his spells backwards or upside down. He was so old that his eyes were clouded over, and he couldn't see what was right in front of him. When he said that the girls would be dull and slow like cows, he had made a mistake. Instead they were like hummingbirds, flitting around the house, fluttering their skinny hands and talking to each other in singsong voices. Since no one had tried to teach the girls to talk, they had invented their own language. A magical language, the language of twins. They made up words for everything. They even made up names for each other: Poto and Cabengo. No one knew what they were saying. The parents thought they were jabbering nonsense, so they kept them in the house, and didn't try to teach them to speak, or read stories to them, or send them out to play with the other children who lived nearby.

A year passed, and then another. The twins got older, and taller. They still loved each other more than anything in the land, more than the moon and the stars and the sun. They hooked their skinny arms together and skipped through the house, laughing. They whispered each other's names in the dark: Poto and Cabengo. They counted each other's freckles in the sun—here, here, and here.

One day the father heard of a new wizard in the land. The father had listened to the girls talking to each other, talking in their mysterious language, and he wondered if the wizard might be able to understand it. The wizard watched the girls for a long time. He listened to their singsong voices and he saw them playing clapping games together with their skinny hands and he heard them laughing with wide-open happy mouths. The wizard knew that they were not dull and slow like cows. "These children are no longer cursed," he told the father. "I can teach them to speak the language of our people. They can join the other children in their games."

The family rejoiced to hear the news, and they celebrated with a big party. With the wizard's help they began to teach the girls the language of the people. But the father was angry. He felt that the old wizard had lied to him, and that the girls had been tricking him. He forbade the girls from speaking their secret language, the language of twins, ever again.

Time passed. The girls' skinny arms and legs grew one last time, and they weren't big girls anymore, but young women. They learned to speak the language of the land. Over time they began to forget their magical words and their secret voices. But they never forgot their names for each other, Poto and Cabengo. And all through the land, and far beyond the land, they were remembered for speaking the secret language of twins.

The sun had almost set, the sky was painted purple. A mosquito whined near my head. Carter turned and looked at me, slapped his hand down on my cheek. He didn't say anything, just wiped a finger across my face, and then held it up to show me. Squashed mosquito body, legs like eyelashes. A smear of blood.

He started to kick the wall again with his one-two thump, and after a minute I joined in. We flopped back, bird-like shoulder blades pressed against the gritty shingles on the roof. A flock of starlings swirled above us, wheeling and darting, a feathered black cloud.

"Is it true?" he finally asked.

"Um-hum."

"Really? It's not one of your fairy tales?" He turned his head slightly, met my gaze. His grey eyes were wide and wild. Like living stones. Sometimes he scared me. But in a good way, like a wicked thunderstorm, the way the lightning can travel through your closed eyelids, right into your brain.

"Nah. 1970's in California. Or maybe Georgia."

"I can't decide whether it's a sad story or a happy one. I like the part about the names, how they named each other." We stopped kicking the roof simultaneously. "Do you think we spoke the language of twins?"

I nodded. Of course we did. How could we not have?

"I could name you," Carter said. He grabbed my hand roughly with his fretting hand. There were hard calluses on his fingertips from playing too much ukulele. "I would name you Orion. You're a constellation."

He pointed his other hand towards the dark sky, to the imagined stars above us that weren't visible yet. "Rigel, Bellatrix, Saiph. Here, here, and here." He was like that, a rememberer of stars. "Orion is a hunter. You hunt the truth."

SULEIMAN

Lately I've felt disconnected from myself, as if my body and its actions are not connected to me at all. Life at Nap-Away has taken on a dream-like quality. Sometimes I feel like I'm watching myself from afar, and I wonder, Who is this man? This is not who I know myself to be. What has happened to the Suleiman I once was? What has become of Suleiman and Khadija? What has become of our life together?

There is a certain day that I revisit often in my mind. A day that held complete happiness, not just the fragments and shards of happiness that make up a lifetime, interspersed with all the sorrows and hardships. On that day happiness did not come in pieces, it cascaded over me in its entirety. We had only recently arrived in Toronto from Montreal. Ahmed was a baby, tiny and mysterious, a little brown nut, still hidden in his shell. We were living in a high-rise, in St. Jamestown, on the twenty-third floor. I spent the first few days at the apartment on the balcony, marvelling at the view of St. James cemetery, watching the traffic stop and flow through the intersection of Parliament and Wellesley, staring at the city lights that never went out, following the journeys of the delivery men zipping in and out the back door of the Pizza Pizza, laden with their flat boxes. I felt like a small cog in a giant piece of city machinery, but what my role was I couldn't quite say.

A few weeks after we moved in, there was a blackout in our building. A neighbour, a stooped and elderly woman with a single front tooth, knocked at our door, offering us a box of candles. Khadija lit them, one after another, placing them along the ledge of the long windowsill that overlooked the balcony. Our apartment was sparsely furnished—a bed and dresser, two hard plastic chairs and a low table, a wooden box that was

Ahmed's crib. The living room was empty, except for an enormous indigo carpet that spread like the sea across the floor, golden threads rippling across its expanse. The carpet was a gift from Khadija's cousin, who lived in Toronto. He had offered me a job at his business, Five-Star Carpets on Danforth Avenue. It was why we were here, why we had moved from Montreal. It was a beginning, a promise of a new life.

We ate a light meal, spicy chicken and rice, and then Khadija sat on one of our two chairs, Ahmed nestled on a stack of cushions in her lap, suckling on her breast. He took his task seriously; he latched on and drank, looking up at his mother with unblinking eyes. Khadija murmured to him, admiring his long toes, the whorl of black hair on his soft head, his little fist flailing in the air. He had not cried, not really, not the way I had heard other babies crying, since being born. He cried if something was not right, and once it was made right, he stopped. I admired this trait in one so young. My son had a practical nature and a reasonable disposition.

When Ahmed fell asleep Khadija placed him in his wooden box. We laughed together at how little we had and at how happy we were. Then we sat together on our blue ocean carpet, floating above the city, listening to Ahmed breathe, marveling at what we had created together. Since the birth, Khadija had been less restless, serene almost. She was rounder and softer, her body like warm doughy bread. Her skin glistened from the olive oil she rubbed on it. Her eyes were bright, but hooded with soft lids that blinked heavily, as if each time, they might not rise up again. My attraction to her almost felt like a betrayal to the old Khadija, the one who was all motion and fire, whose body was firmer and sharper and slimmer. I had not dared touch her since the birth, even though she no longer had *nifas*, the blood after childbirth, and weeks had passed. She was split into two—the fiery sexual Khadija that belonged to me, and this new soft and milky mother who belonged to Ahmed. They needed to become one, the old Khadija and the new, this is what I thought.

I caressed her bare feet, touched her hair, kissed her lips. And then I dared to place my mouth on her breast, the breasts that belonged to Ahmed. Warm milk spurted into my mouth, watery and sweet. I sucked harder, swallowed, reached a hand down between her thighs. She moaned softly. And so. Afterwards, Khadija fell asleep quickly, the carpet enough of a bed for her.

I carry this moment with me always. The candles flickering in the darkness, dancing circles of light on the ceiling, Ahmed, our child, small and helpless in his precarious raft, his lips pursed and suckling, even in his sleep. Khadija stretched out naked on the plush carpet, the golden threads glittering in the candlelight. The beautiful name of *Allah, Al-Muhyi*, The Bestower of Life, fully in my heart, without any doubts. My life circles around this moment, the axis of my world. All of my happiness is held there, breathes from there, swells from there.

And Amina? What about my daughter? She too brought great happiness with her arrival, twelve years after Ahmed; the long wait between children due to the miscarriages Khadija had suffered. But tangled in with the joy was the trouble Khadija had giving birth—the c-section and her recovery, Ahmed's jealous rages, after being a single child for so long, my own long days of working that prevented me from being there to help Khadija. Then of course, there is what happened last fall, with Amina.

No, life was never as simple, as pure, as utterly whole as that moment on the blue carpet.

TIFFANY

Sometimes when I am alone in my secret place I tell stories to Nap-Away. I tell it about my sister Nikki who I wished lived with me so that we could play together. My sister is older than me, and she lives with her dad, who is not the same person as my dad. We don't really look like sisters because I'm black like my dad and Nikki is white, like her dad and our mom. Except that doesn't make any sense, because her skin isn't white, it's like the inside of a seashell, all smooth and creamy and pale pink. And mine isn't black at all, it's soft brown, like gingerbread cookies, which I love. Mrs. Lynch's puppy, who is called Luna, has fur that is like gingerbread too, with some tufts of black hair around her face and also some black whiskers. Mrs. Lynch said Luna is called a wheat terrier.

Mrs. Lynch brought Luna to school one day so we could meet her. She was very wild, even wilder than Theo! But Mrs. Lynch could make Luna calm down, just like she does with Theo. She said if we wanted to, we could line up and feed Luna a doggy biscuit. I wanted to, but I didn't, I just watched instead. Maybe Mrs. Lynch will bring her back again, because next time I think I will be brave enough to hold out my hand and give Luna her biscuit. I am brave enough to play with Theo, even though he bit me once when we were in junior kindergarten.

Last week at school Mrs. Lynch asked us to make a picture of our best day ever. I thought for a little while about what to draw. I remembered the day that my sister Nikki took me to a fair in the parking lot at the mall. There was a huge wheel with seats that went up into the sky and cotton candy and a merry-go-round and some huge horses called Clydesdales. I wasn't brave enough to go on the big wheel, and I was too scared to go close to the horses because they were stomping their hairy hooves and curling their big lips to show their teeth, but I wasn't scared of the cotton candy, which was very yummy, and I wasn't scared of the merry-go-round. I drew a picture of Nikki and me on the merry-go-round, with horses that flew up and down on swirly gold sticks.

That night after school I asked my mom to tell me about her best day ever. She told me a story about her best friend Tiffany, the person I am named after. I have never met Tiffany but I have seen lots of pictures of her. She has big pink lips and lots and lots of blond hair that falls far down her back and she wears shiny clothes and very tall shoes. My mom and Tiffany went to high school together.

The best-day-ever story that my mom told me was about Halloween. She said that they dressed up like twins in matching blue dresses with lace and big white belts that my mom called sashes around their tummies. She said they were the shiny twins. It doesn't sound scary, but my mom said that they were really spooky, because they didn't smile or laugh, they just walked around asking everyone to play with them. Maybe they were like zombie twins. After the Halloween party they climbed out her bedroom window and sat on the roof in their blue dresses. They stayed up all night long laughing and watching for shooting stars and telling each other secrets and singing. And eating salt and vinegar chips and mint chocolate chip ice cream straight from the tub, and drinking beer from bottles that they clinked together every time that they took a sip. My mom said that when they finished their beers they let the empty bottles roll down the roof. I asked her if they checked to see if anyone was walking past, but she said nah. Then I asked if they went down to pick up the broken glass and she told me to give it a fucking rest, so I didn't ask any more questions. But I wanted to ask if they got to see the stars shooting across the black sky and if they made a wish. My favourite part of her story is when they climbed out the window together.

I wish I had a best friend.

ORI

Day Two of the Carter Quest. It's only June and early in the day, but
already sweltering, hot like the core of a Supernova. That's a Carterism.
Can't get the door to my room at Nap-Away closed when I leave. Like
the door and the doorframe aren't made for each other. I yank and curse,
until it finally surrenders. When I turn to go, I see a little kid, alone in
the parking lot. Skinny arms and cinnamon skin and solemn green eyes.
She's scratching her hair, kicking little stones, talking to herself. Looks
a little like Nap-Away: thin grey t-shirt that maybe once was white, the
same colour as Nap-Away's worn shingles, dirty yellow shorts that match
the walls, eyes shining green like the broken wine bottle glittering in the
sun at my feet.

"Hey kid," I say. She doesn't move, but her eyes widen. Soundtrack
"Rabbit Heart," Florence + the Machine. I can almost hear her little heart
thumping wildly. If I stamp my boots she'll skitter away, disappear into
a crack in the concrete. Like a little gecko. I tell her a couple of stupid
jokes, work hard to get a little laugh to choke out. She smiles, lopsided.
Her upper lip is swollen on one side, split.

"What's your name?"

She whispers her answer to my boots. "Tiffany," falling from her mouth
like a discarded trinket. I pick up a small grey stone that glitters in the
sun, place it in her hand, close her skinny fingers around it.

"Not everybody knows when they've got something special," I tell
her. "Tiffany, huh? I think I'll call you Tiff instead. No, Iff!" Her green
eyes widen, deeper waters.

"Oh!" uttered with such sweet surprise. I make a move to tousle her
whirl of black hair, but she's head-shy, like a timid dog. "I got bugs," she

whispers. I offer out a high-five instead. She mumbles something about my pants, but I don't catch it.

"See ya later," I say.

I look back before crossing Kingston. She's watching me leave. The motel shines golden in the sun behind her. The whole building slumps forward, like an old granny, embracing the parking lot between its two rows of rooms. Embracing the kid too.

I wander for a bit, get the lay of the land. The sun beats down. Ruthless. Little beads of sweat gather on my forehead. I stop and buy a Slurpee, grape, and some Doritos for breakfast, using a handful of my Carter-change. Hang out in the AC of the 7-11 until the cashier kicks me out. Find the public library in a strip mall, wedged between a mani-pedi shop and a sub shop. Weird. Nothing like the libraries I've been in before in Oshawa.

I hook into the wifi, cruise around social media for a bit, even though Carter hates it all—Snapchat, Instagram, tumblr, whatever. Don't even bother with Twitter or Facebook. Find out that Suzy Zammit busted her arm playing ultimate Frisbee day before yesterday. My phone creeps down to sixteen-percent battery. Which is shitty because my charger forgot to come with me. It's sitting in Oshawa, being useless. So I get half-an-hour on a computer instead. Discover a blog that Carter started over a year ago, but he hasn't posted anything since January. The last entry is about purple sea cucumbers in Marianas Trench. The ocean, not the band.

I change tactics, check out places for runaway teens in Toronto. Jot down the address for Covenant House on Gerrard. Maybe Carter's there, but if not, I might end up checking it out, once my cash runs out. I start to feel weird. A bit homesick, but not for my foster home. A bit nauseous. Probably from the Slurpee and Doritos. A bit freaked out, looking at the beat up face of a kid on the website, tangled up in sex trafficking. Her big brown eyes are lost in the shadows, like chocolate donuts in the dark.

I unfold the postcard, place it down on the desk beside the computer. I whisper his name, "Carter, Carter," and again, a third time. Type WHERE ARE YOU CARTER into the search box and click on the first hit, song lyrics to Lil' Wayne's "Mr. Carter," asking where he's at, 'cause they've been looking for him. Yo. The tiny hairs on the back of my neck stand up, my primitive hackles. A cold shiver runs down my spine. I am back in Carter's room, his fierce eyes, so grey they're almost black, clawing at me. *They're coming to get me!* The notebook fluttering to the floor. Carter screaming at the demons in his brain. I shake my head, send the fear scurrying.

I glance back down at the postcard, my doorway to Carter. I Google TACOS TORONTO, find the best-of list. *Grand Electric, Playa Cabana Cantina, La Carnita, Frida, Tacos El Asador.* But what about all the Taco Bells? The crappy taco places that'll never make a best-of list? Shit, what about Carter bingeing on a couple of packs of store-bought *Old El Paso Stand 'N Stuff* in some back alleyway? Tacos to nowhere. Instead I type in: PENCIL IN HIS HEART. There's some twelve-year-old kid in Montana whose heart was pierced by a pencil after he lunged onto his bed to catch a football. It went all the way into the right chamber of his heart, the tip embedded in the back wall. It was his birthday. How does it feel, to have a pencil piercing your heart?

What the fuck am I doing? Carter's no Montana miracle. There's no pencil in his heart, I know that, even if Carter doesn't. Maybe what I need to know is how to take the damn pencil out. To save him. Pull him back from the edge, the fucking edge of the universe. Sing to him, like a choir of angels with ukuleles. Feed him some raspberry pie instead of tacos. Find him.

I type: IN HEAVEN CHOIRS OF ANGELS SING, WHILE WE PLAY UKULELE. I discover the words are a ukulele benediction by a dude named David Newland. That sounds about right, Carter worshipping his ukulele. Corktown Uke Jam, every Wednesday night at the Dominion, downtown Toronto. I scrawl the address on my palm, 500 Queen St. East. Tomorrow's Wednesday. So, Covenant House today, Ukulele Jam tomorrow.

My half-hour's up. I track a science geek through the shelves to Dewey Decimal 520. Astronomy and Allied Sciences. Find the edge of the universe there. Not the real edge, just a couple of books about the edge. One's about peering over the edge of emptiness and finding everything. I flip through another, trying to decipher it. Lots of darkness—dark matter, dark energy, black holes. My brain runs away a little, thinking about Darth Vader and the dark side of the force. Then runs some more, thinking about Carter's favourite books, the trilogy *His Dark Materials*. Lyra and her ever-present daemon, Pan, the animal embodiment of her inner self.

Sometimes that's how I think of myself. Ori and her daemons, Orion and Orianthi. Sometimes they flutter around me, all soft-winged and dreamy, other times they skitter and claw and fight. They love each other. They wish each other dead. They take turns hiding, one behind the other. They refuse to be one daemon. Or maybe it's me; maybe I refuse to choose one over the other. I love them both, love being a boy, love being a girl, love what lies in-between.

I read on, find a section about the multiverse. Who knew? The universe is no longer single. Supposedly new universes are constantly and eternally springing up. Some weird warping of time and space. I thought this was just the stuff of stories, like in *His Dark Materials*. But it seems to be real. In the multiverse, anything that can happen will happen. I know, right at that moment, that I'll find Carter. Anything that *can* happen *will* happen.

Right then a guy appears, talking to himself. Takes me a minute to realize he's talking to me. I'm trying to understand the discovery of an absolute epic emptiness, a supervoid in the constellation Erdanus, but also daydreaming about hooking myself up with some of those fine tacos at *Fridas*.

"Hey, is that your ferret?" That's what I hear. But that's just wrong. So I make him repeat it. He does, enunciating each syllable carefully. And at the same time, he points to the ferret, perched atop the 500's. Random.

"Dude," I say, "the beady-eyed weasel's not with me." He laughs then, offers a fist for props. He's taller than me, messy black hair, lots of happy teeth, shiny white against brown skin, eyes like obsidian. Inked. Cute, if you like boys. Which I don't, not like that.

"I'm Moffit," he says. We both stand in silence, consider the misplaced library ferret. I wish a lot of adjectives upon it. Glossy-pelted. Fierce. Mischievous. Sly. But it's just sad, in a yellow, greasy, baldish kind of way.

"It smells kinda skunkish," I say, wrinkling up my nose.

"Anal glands," Moffit says. He tells me that the secretions are used to make perfumes. Civets, beavers, animals like that, he says, but not ferrets. He reminds me of Carter when he talks. We study the ferret for a bit longer. Discuss possible protocols. The ferret watches us, red eyes, nose twitching. Waits. When Moffit reaches a hand out, the ferret weaves up onto hind legs, and offers a narrow, clawed paw towards him. Moffit glances at me, arches a single eyebrow up, high fives the ferret.

"Insane!" he exclaims.

We try to turn the ferret over to the librarian, as if it's a Lost & Found item. She squeaks when Moffit dangles the ferret out towards her. A librarian's version of a scream. She suggests we 'take it elsewhere.'

We leave the library together, the three of us, the lost ferret curled around Moffit's shoulders. We get pizza. Moffit gets his without cheese, which I think is weird, but I don't say anything. He does the talking; the ferret and I listen. Sometimes I get what he's saying. But mostly not. He says shit like *anti-oppression framework* and *speciesism* and *non-binary discrimination*. I thought I knew binary, but I guess there's more than one. Carter spent a weekend teaching me to count up to thirty-one in binary on just one hand. I still don't get it, how one-zero-one is five instead of a hundred and one, but I know middle finger up is four, peace sign is six, pinkie up is sixteen, all five up is thirty-one.

Moffit is talking about non-binary as if I should know all about it. I just nod, take another bite. Whatever. He's a believer in the truth of ideas. Carter was a believer in the truth of science. Me? I guess I'm a believer in words. Words are full of magic and deceit. They're trickster gods. They tell truths. And lies. They break the rules. They conjure up demons. They're lovers. They open locked doors, tumble down walls. Words are power.

I mumble through my pizza-crust-filled mouth, "Words are power." Moffit grins back at me. I feel a bubbling happiness. My stomach is full of cheesy goodness. I'm going to find Carter. I've met a friend and a ferret. I tell Moffit that I'm looking for my brother. He nods like he knew already. He offers to help me look.

"Tomorrow," I say, "we'll find him tomorrow at the ukulele benediction." I say it with a weird conviction, like I know already that he'll be there.

SULEIMAN

The framed photo of my daughter, Amina, hanging in the hallway, stops me in my tracks. She is five years old in the picture, as old as she will ever get. She smiles down at me, with a closed mouth that seems to be holding a secret in. Her brown eyes follow me as I step forward. She has long eyelashes, like a camel. I used to joke with her: *I have a camel for a daughter, not a girl. No child ever had lashes so long!* Amina sees me now, sees my anger. My jaw is hard and tight, my hands are clenched into fists, my breath is coming out forcefully, my nostrils widening like a stallion's. I stop and stare back at her.

"Ah," I say, "ah, ah, ah." Perhaps I'm trying to say Amina's name, but I don't think so. Or perhaps it is the name of *Allah* I'm trying to invoke, *Al-Wasi*, The All-Comprehending, who has the insight to see all things clearly, to help me understand what is driving me forward. But no, it is simply an utterance of pain, a pain deep in the marrow of my bones. I fall to my knees heavily and lay my forehead against the floor. I'm unsure what is happening, unsure what I should do with my limbs, with my mouth. Perhaps Khadija can help me, save me from myself. Absurdly I start to laugh.

I hear Khadija's footsteps; she leaves and returns a moment later with a glass of water for me. She places it down beside me, wordlessly. I sit up, finished with the laughter. The human body, I marvel, has the capacity to do things of its own accord. None of this—the foot forced in to the doorway, the surge of anger, the fall to my knees, my harrowing laughter—seems to be of my own doing. The last thing I remember choosing to do was to leave Nap-Away, to come and speak to Khadija, to see her beautiful sad smile and her fierce eyes, to make amends for how I have treated her, neglected her. I sit up, reach my hand towards the mole, wanting to caress its smooth comforting surface, but stop myself. Instead I reach for the glass, gulp a mouthful of water. I sigh heavily.

"I'll go now. I made a mistake coming here."

"Yes. You've come again to me with anger," Khadija says. I wince. When I stand I see the unshed tears in her eyes. We face each other. Amina watches from the framed picture on the wall. She has a scar on her upper lip, from a surgery to repair a cleft lip. The surgery took longer than expected. We were trapped in the waiting room, trapped in imagining what might be going wrong. I remember when that was the worst thing possible, the not knowing of that moment, before the surgeon came to say she was in recovery. I wish for that day again, when hope was possible.

I look at Amina's picture, look back at her mother. "I know that it was Amina's time to go, that she belongs to *Allah*, not to you, not to me. Of course I know this. I know that everything happens for a reason. But sometimes my heart wishes for it to be otherwise."

"At times my heart wishes for it to be otherwise as well. But your anger will not make it so." Khadija doesn't meet my gaze, looks down at the floor between us.

"I know it seems that I am angry," I say. Someone inside my head laughs. I don't seem angry, I am angry. I am so angry at times that it seems to be a force of nature, bubbling and flowing like lava inside my blood. "I have sought forgiveness for my anger. I have prayed, trying to make peace with the accident, to understand why this has happened to us."

My mind flashes back to that day. Khadija, always fast, always rushing, on her way out to the grocery store, to buy some spice she was missing for the evening meal. Amina, crouched on the driveway, studying something, a woolly caterpillar perhaps, or a shiny green beetle. She had always loved animals, been curious of even the smallest of spiders crawling across the basement floor. Khadija had not seen Amina there in the driveway. She had put the car in reverse, run over our daughter in a single, distracted moment.

In the months that followed, Khadija and I had prayed together many times and found comfort in God. We reminded ourselves, again and again, *Truly to Allah we belong, and truly to Him shall we return.* But we were unable to speak of our feelings about the accident. No, that is not true. Khadija was able to speak about what happened, speak of her grief and remorse; I could not. And the more I refused to speak of it, the more the anger grew. I wished to reach out to Khadija, to share in her suffering. But instead I became cold. I became angry. Angry at Khadija for her distracted driving, angry at Amina for foolishly playing in the driveway, angry at my wife for pestering me to speak about how I was feeling, angry at myself for my inability to console my wife in her time of need. And perhaps more than anything, angry at my lingering grief, for I can't help but see it as a failure of my faith in God.

Oh I've struggled with anger before, many times. And I've been angry with Khadija before, and she with me. We have exchanged hurtful words, I have yelled at her, and she at me. I've slammed doors, shaken my fist; she once threw a teapot at the wall while we were fighting. But this new anger of mine is something more fearsome.

I remember what I said to Khadija once, when I was overcome by the anger. It had started with a simple comment: she had complained about her ride home on the TTC, about the bus driver being distracted. I no longer remember what she said the driver did, I only remember the way my mind had drawn back, like the water tugging back just before the tsunami, and the way the rage had started streaming in, a rippling curl of incoming water.

Distracted! I had begun to tremble, and the full force of the anger had rushed in, swept over me. Was that not what had caused the accident, her distraction? I tumbled in the wave, struggled to surface, gasped for air. There was nothing but the surging fury, and my helplessness in the face of it.

Amina was gone, but my grief was not, and now it clutched on to my rage, like long-lost twins, finding one another. My fists constricted, squeezing the blood from my hands. Everything constricted, my chest, my beating heart, the cords of muscles running down my back. Amina was dead and yes, I knew that if it hadn't been the accident, it would have been something else, because it was her time to return to God. I knew this to be true, and it brought relief. But at that moment, I lost sight of it.

"You," I had thundered, "you are responsible for this! You were distracted. You!" My fist had slammed down on the table, shattering a small blue plate. For months I had been unable to speak about the accident, and then suddenly these words had come tumbling out, full of blame. I had scared Khadija, scared myself. Worse, I had betrayed her with my accusation. That was clear to me when I looked at her stricken face. Khadija was never one to keep her thoughts to herself, but she was painfully silent after my outburst. Shortly afterwards we agreed to a separation, agreed that perhaps some time apart could mend the unbearable tension between us.

I bend down to pick up the glass of water, accidentally knocking it over instead. The water pools around Khadija's delicate feet, her golden sandals. She steps aside, and gestures at the door.

"I think it is time for you to go," Khadija says.

As I open the front door to leave a wave of heat hits me. I take a few steps down the walkway then look back at Khadija, who is standing in the doorway.

"I will not be here tomorrow," she calls out to me. "Please stay away, Suleiman. Please do not come to me again in anger." She slams the door and leaves me standing there alone in the oppressive sun. I glance to my left, to the driveway where my wife accidentally killed our daughter. My breath catches in my throat, the air is too hot to bring into my lungs. I feel like I am suffocating, like I am dying. I raise a single fist to the sky, to the great ball of fire that burns there, and shake it. Angry even at the sun.

I hurry back to the motel, thinking about crawling into my bed, about the coolness of the sheets against my hot skin. This morning Nap-Away had seemed like a place of disgrace and exile; now I think of it as my haven, a place to retreat to. But when I arrive, I see a slight woman, overdressed in a long brown jacket, peering into the window of Room 5. If Khadija is a raven, this woman is a sparrow, pecking at the glass.

"Oh, hello," she chirps when she spots me. "A quick word? I won't take much of your time."

TIFFANY

The new girl's name is Orianthi. I had to try it three times before I got it right. I asked her if she was a boy or a girl. She said I could choose, so I picked girl, because of the purple tips on her shaggy brown hair. It looks like grape Kool-Aid. She told me a joke about a duck stamping out a fire. I didn't really get the joke, because why would a duck step on fire? It could just fly away. But then she started waddling and quacking and flapping and stamping all around the parking lot. So I guess it was a funny joke after all.

She has a weird laugh, like a witch's cackle, but I didn't tell her that, I just thought it in my brain. I told her I liked her red pants. She smiled, mostly with her eyes though. They're super big and grey. They're spooky, but maybe magical too.

"I think I'll call you Iff," she said, and then she gave me a shiny grey rock that glittered like my mom's silver nail polish. It felt hot from the sunshine that it was holding inside.

After Orianthi leaves, I go back to my room to see if I have any chalk for drawing on the parking lot. I look under my bunk bed and under my mom's bed and other places too, but I can't find any. But that's good, because I remember just in time that I am s'posed to stay inside, so I shouldn't leave chalk clues outside. I stay inside for a little bit. I eat spoonfuls of peanut butter and watch a big black bug scurry up the wall. My mom would've squished it flat. It walks all the way up the wall and then across the ceiling. It can walk upside down!

When I go back outside no one is around. I go across the parking lot to Room 11, where Orianthi lives. I kick the rock she gave me and it zips across the parking lot. I chase after it, trying to catch it. Most of the time I miss and the rock gets away again, all skittery and bouncy, but sometimes I pounce on it. Nap-Away watches me with all its windows. When I catch the rock, Nap-Away cheers for me, fluttering all of its curtains like flags in the wind. When I get hot and tired of that game I use the rock to write words on the ground. This is something you can do when you don't have chalk. You have to push really hard and it only makes thin lines, but it works. First I write my name and then I draw a pigeon. I try to draw the toes on its feet, but it's too hard to do with just a rock. I write 'Orianthi' under the picture. Here is something I discover: OR, I, ANT, HI. I wish my name was like that, with lots of little words all put together. Here is another word like that: HEART. I draw one and then write HE, EAR, ART. It's like the little words are hiding inside the big word. Inside of the heart I write my new secret name, Iff. It's tiny and perfect. I draw hopscotch, and I throw my special rock in the boxes, and every time I jump I say *Iff.* I keep saying it, over and over. *Iff… if… if,…*

When I get bored of hopscotch I sneak around to the back of Nap-Away to my secret place that's between the rooms and a fence. On the ground there are green weeds and lots of old leaves, all brown and crunchy, and some garbage, like empty bags that used to be filled with chips, and coffee cups from Tim Horton's, and plastic bags for groceries.

"Do you want to play a clapping game?" I ask Nap-Away. I know it can't say yes or no, but if it could, it would say yes. I hold my hands up and start clapping them together and then against the wall.

"I'm a nut, in a hut, I stole my mamma's credit card, so what? Whatcha gonna do, kick my butt? I'm craaaazy, I'm foooooolish, I'm craaaaazy, I'm foooolish, I'm C-O-O-L," I chant, spelling out the letters with my hands at the end. I cross my arms and stare at Nap-Away, trying to look tough, because that's how the game goes. Whoever looks away or moves first loses. I lose because Nap-Away can't ever look away. I look away because I hear a squirrel running down the trunk of the big tree on the other side of the fence. I can stretch and reach over the fence and touch the bark, which is rough and scratchy.

Sometimes when I come here I tell stories that I make up to Nap-Away and Tree. Today I find a stick on the ground that reminds me of antlers.

So I tell them a story about a baby reindeer. She has short antlers that are all bent and branchy and she is brown with white rings of fur around her eyes. I saw a dog like that yesterday.

The baby reindeer's name is Ant because she's so small, way smaller than all the other reindeer. Even though she's small, she's super brave, braver than the biggest boy reindeers even. One day a pack of husky dogs comes and they are all drooling and growling and trying to eat the reindeers. But Ant isn't scared at all. She runs straight at them with her head down, so her little antlers poke at them. And the dogs all run away, squealing.

When I go back to the parking lot I can see my neighbour, Suleiman, standing outside of Room 6, talking with a stranger. She is wearing a long brown coat even though it is hot outside. I try to duck back behind Nap-Away, but before I do she looks up and spots me with her sharp eyes. She waves. Suleiman gestures with his arm—come!—and so I go.

"You must be Tiffany! It's nice to meet you." She holds out her hand, like grownups do, for shaking. But I don't hold out my hand because it's dirty from playing with the sticks and leaves and garbage. "My name's Miranda. I'm a social worker, a person who helps children and families." She smiles. She has pretty teeth. They are tiny and shiny white. She also has very curly hair, which makes me happy. And she has an 'M' name!

"Shouldn't you be in school today? Are you sick?"

I don't like it when adults ask two questions at the same time. It's too tricky. I scratch my head and look at Suleiman's big toes, sticking out from his sandals. He has gigantic toenails. Like they belong on a hippopotamus. I pop my shoulders up and down.

"I came to talk to your mom today." Everyone is very quiet for a long time. Then Miranda asks, "Is she inside?" I glance at our door. Maybe she is, maybe she came home and she's sleeping. I look back at Suleiman's feet. But she would have yelled for me if she had come home. I look towards the road where the bus stops. Maybe she's on the bus right now, on her way back. I look up at Miranda's smiley teeth. I shake my head no.

Miranda crouches down in front of me. She has tiny freckles on her cheeks, like she splattered brown paint at the art centre. "What happened to your lip?" She points towards my face. I have a puffy lip and a cut on it. It doesn't hurt too much anymore, just a bit if I stretch my mouth wide open, like for a big smile, or a yawn.

"I fell down on it." This is true.

"You fell down? How did that happen?"

"Theo pushed me." This is sort of true. Theo did push me and I did fall down. But I didn't hurt my lip when that happened.

"Who's Theo?"

"A boy at my school."

Miranda makes a little huffing sound and nods. "Ok, well, where's your mom now? Did she leave you alone?" When my mom comes back, I know I'm going to be in trouble. I was s'posed to stay inside. I was s'posed to lock the door. I was s'posed to not answer the door. I was s'posed to wait for her to come back. I was s'posed to wash my hair.

"She went to get the shampoo," I whisper.

"But who's looking after you?" My heart is making little pitter-patter sounds. Like a tiny mouse running away. Maybe I should run away, back behind the Nap-Away to my secret spot with Tree. I take a step back.

Suleiman has been listening the whole time, leaning back against his door. Suddenly he stands up tall and straight, like maybe Nap-Away gave him a little push forward. At school Angel sometimes does this to Theo if he is not standing up right for 'O Canada'. She pushes him. But sometimes he pushes her back.

Suleiman looks right at me. "I am looking after her," he says. "She is like my daughter." I look around because I didn't know he had a daughter.

"Well." Miranda says. "Hmmmm. But..."

I move a little closer to Suleiman and slide my hand into his. His hand is big, just like his feet. It swallows my hand up. His hand is very hot and sweaty too. His hand is brown, just like mine. It feels safe.

"We feed the birds together," I tell Miranda.

"Oh, that's nice," she says, but she crunches up her nose, which I think is a clue that she doesn't like birds.

Miranda looks down at me and then up at Suleiman. I smile back, but I don't smile too big, because I don't want my lip to hurt again. I look up in the sky and I see a seagull flying without flapping her wings, just floating on the wind, and I can hear the sound she makes, *kyow-kyow-kyow*. The sound is far, far away but I hear it as if that bird is right here on my shoulder, whispering in my ear. I sniff the air and I think I can smell the wet smell of the lake where that bird lives.

Then I see my mom coming across the parking lot towards us and I stop smiling.

ORI

When I get back to Nap-Away after checking out Covenant House, shit's happening. A couple of bearded guys, clad in leather, sit on lawn chairs outside of Room 9 with their Harleys beside them, leaning in like faithful black dogs. There's a big brown bear of a man, shuffling around the parking lot in sandals. Muttering to himself. He's got dark eyes, black hair trimmed close to his scalp, a hooked nose. Swarthy, in need of a shave. Big hands cradling a bottle of 7-Up.

The kid, Iff, is sitting on the ground, scratching her hair and looking up at Nap-Away's roof. Maybe she's praying too. Or looking for fairies. Or watching the pigeons, perched on the edge. There's two women, one blond and screechy, the other whispery and timid, talking. The blond is jabbing her finger at everything. The kid, the man, Nap-Away, the other woman, Kingston Road traffic, the Harleys. Jabbing with her long painted nails, screeching like a cat with its tail on fire. Reminds me of Janet, foster mom number two.

"Hey," I say, as the bear-man in sandals shuffles my way.

He looks at me, then back at the women. "We all have troubles, neh?"

"Sure."

He shifts the bottle of pop to one arm, starts to extend a hand. I think he's about to shake mine, but instead he reaches up, slides his thumb across his upper eyelid.

"We have to be strong in our beliefs that our troubles are necessary, that *Allah* has a plan for us. There must be a good reason he creates so much distress."

Sounds a bit like a question to me.

"I don't know about that," I say. Up close his dark eyes are brown, softer than I expected. Cow-like. Long lashes. "A lot of the crap that happens seems pretty pointless to me."

"Yes, it does seem that way sometimes." He looks over at Iff, shakes his head. "I am Suleiman. Room 6. "

"Ori. Room 11."

"Yori. You're what, eighteen, nineteen? You look to be about the same age as my son. He is studying political science at university in Montreal."

"Yeah."

"What brings you here?" He gestures widely at the parking lot, the two rows of rooms, meeting together, the oak tree that towers over the sad grey roof of Nap-Away.

"My brother."

"Ahhh." He glances around. "Where is your brother?"

"Lost."

"Are you your brother's keeper?"

My brother's keeper. I always thought Carter was mine. The tight grip on my wrist, dragging me away from the house when he knew what was brewing inside. Something snorted, something injected, something swallowed. His small furious fists flying in the playground as I watched, my face already busted up and bleeding. An ode to my grey kitten on his ukulele, after our mom kicked her down the basement stairs.

I nod. "Yeah, I'm his keeper. He's in some kind of trouble."

"We have circled back, like the pigeons above us, back to our troubles." He raises his chin towards the blonde screecher. "Shelley, the mother, is like a child herself. I know. I hear what is going on in there, in the next room." He shrugs. "But they're my neighbours. And I believe in helping my neighbours. It is part of my religion, a way of showing faith in *Allah*."

I don't know much about *Allah*. Or Muslims. Crap from the news mostly—terrorists, 9-11, al-Qaeda, ISIS. Suleiman's *Allah* sounds a lot like Jesus. That love your neighbour stuff. I heard a lot about J.C. when we were in Foster Home Four. Super religious house—naked and nailed Jesus above my bed, Bibles for all the foster kids. Except that they had a big hate-on for their neighbours, because of the barking Rottweiler chained in the backyard and the rusty, busted-up car in the front.

"Well, rock on Suleiman." He looks at me like a dog, head tipped sideways. Perplexed. I look over at Iff, who is inching away from her mother, towards the Harleys. Maybe that's how she'll make her escape.

"She," he continues, pointing at the quiet woman, who has backed away from Iff's mother until she is trapped, pressed against the dirty yellow wall of Nap-Away, "is a social worker. Maybe she's not the best person to speak to the mother. She's like a sparrow, neh?" He points again, this time at Shelley, who has grabbed Iff by the arm and pulled her back towards their room. "And she is a like a sparrow hawk."

"Don't you tell me how to raise my kid." The words shriek across the parking lot. The hawk, plunging for its prey. The Harley guys clap and whistle. Nap-Away's walls are the only thing keeping the social worker standing.

Suleiman turns back to me. "So this is the trouble. Tiffany has lice in her hair. She needs shampoo, but her mother hasn't bought it for her, so she can't go back to school. Do you know it?"

"Sure. I'm down with the lice protocol." Carter used to pick lice out of my hair sometimes and then study them under a magnifying glass. Suleiman frowns at me.

"Nix. She needs Nix," I say.

He puts down his bottle of pop and pulls out a wad of bills. Crisp fifties. He peels one off and extends it out to me. "Can you go up Kingston Road to the drugstore and get the shampoo for her?"

Is this for real? I look back and forth between Iff, her black curls filled with nits, and this Muslim man offering me a sweet fifty. I hesitate. Then I remember the nights of endless scratching that one winter when Carter and I were infested.

"It doesn't cost that much," I say, refusing the bill.

"Take it. Take it. Take what you need. You could buy some shawarma for us as well. The shop beside the drug store. It's the best shawarma in the city."

I shrug. Pocket the bill. "Sure."

He claps a hand against my back. "God will thank you." I'm not sure about that part, but Iff will, that's for sure. And me and my hungry belly. I turn and stride up the street, for Nix and shawarma.

SULEIMAN

I'm weary. Weary of troubles, my own, my neighbours', the city's. The headline in today's paper tells the story of another shooting in the city, this one in a Scarborough highschool. One teenager is dead, another in critical condition. Gangs, they say, and drugs. I think of my son, Ahmed, only one year out of high school. *Insha' Allah*, he will be safe in Montreal.

There is a sharp rap on my door. I rub my hands over my eyes, heave myself up from the bed. The boy, Yori, is at the door. I notice for the first time the purple tips on his hair. I've lived in Toronto most of my life; I've come to accept these things, but it has not been easy. Yesterday I saw a young mother on the bus, just a girl really, with her hair in dreadlocks, like a Jamaican man, her story written all over her body in tattoos, her breasts barely covered, free for all to see. I've come to see it as a way of speaking, the way each person shows themselves to the world. Sometimes I even imagine bubbles of speech above the people I see, like the ones in the books Ahmed was so fond of, saying things like *I am here. I need you to see me. Look at me.*

This teenager, Yori, is like a colt, not fully grown into a man, not sure of who he is. He is girlish, but that is not new to me. I've seen boys with long hair and curling lashes like Amina, girls with bald heads wearing men's boots. It is the way of this city that I call home. Each can choose their own way of living, their own rules. I've struggled with this way of being, but admire it at the same time. Khadija and I wanted this for ourselves, for our children, this freedom. The girl with dreadlocks and tattoos, the woman curtained in a burqa sitting beside her on the bus, this boy with his tight red pants and shaggy hair, each free to be as they wish. I try not to sit in judgement; I know that it is not my role.

"Come. Come." I gesture him in but Yori stays at the threshold of the door.

"Hey. Here's your change." Yori holds out the money.

"No, no, you can keep that." I wave the money away. Everyone has a need of money, I know this. The last time I tried to give Ahmed money he had refused, as if he no longer needed a father, as if he were an independent man. He is at university on a full scholarship, and working for the summer with the government. But this boy, Yori, I can see his need. The boy's eyes widen, looking at the money in his hand. I expect nothing but Yori looks me in the eye and then bows his head in a graceful gesture of gratitude.

"Sweet. Thanks a lot. I mean, I really appreciate it. The shawarma and the money and everything."

"We will eat the shawarma together," I say. I sweep the discarded newspaper and dirty clothing from the chair in the room, gesture for him to come in, to sit. He shrugs. I know this gesture well from Ahmed. It does not mean 'I don't care' but rather, 'sure, sounds good.' I sit on the edge of the bed; Yori sits on the chair. He takes a first bite of his wrap, then smiles.

"It's good," he mumbles, with food in his mouth. "Never had shawarma before. Looks like a burrito. But tastes way better."

"Yes, my son Ahmed loves it too. My daughter not so much. She loved to eat sweet things, but not meat. When she was little she would spit it out. Phhttt. Sometimes I wondered if she did this because she knew it was the meat of an animal. She loved them all, cats, dogs, squirrels, spiders. She had so many books filled with animal pictures. She wouldn't even let me squish a bug. *No Baba* she would say, *you must not hurt any animal, not even a bug. Just because you are big, you can't squash the things that are smaller than you.*" I sigh, put down my wrap and wipe my mouth.

"She was like Tiffany. Very much like her. So gentle, so kind. Sometimes in the morning when I am still foggy from sleep, I think she is Amina." Yori has stopped eating. He leans in towards me.

"Where is she? Amina, I mean?"

I shake my head, look down at my hands. This thing that has happened to Amina, I cannot speak of it today. I have had to tell the story many times, and each time the ending remains the same. Each retelling has become harder, because the ending clings tighter and tighter, refusing to vary. I clench and unclench my fists. If it is God's will, why am I still struggling to accept it?

"Her brother, Ahmed, he has started his studies at university. Will you be going?"

"Nah. I suck at school. Except sometimes in English."

"And your brother?" Yori shrugs again. This time I'm not so sure what it means. It is not a shrug of indifference, nor is it a shrug of ignorance. I decide it is doubt.

"Something's wrong with him." Yori puts down his shawarma and reaches into his back pocket, hands a folded postcard to me. I study it carefully, flip it over in my hands. The words are like black ants scurrying madly across the page, too many ants for this small space.

"He sent this to you?" Yori nods. "He's thinking too much, neh? Is he an artist then? Or perhaps a scientist, with too many ideas spilling out of him?" Yori does not answer. He seems to be looking elsewhere, at a distant horizon, at something far away from Nap-Away. "What about your parents? Aren't they helping you find your brother?" Another shrug. I think that this shrug is a white flag, filled with helplessness, but teenagers do not say they are helpless. Instead they fly off a bridge after school one day, their knapsack of homework still hanging from their backs, or they open their parent's medicine cabinet and pour all the pills into their empty, needy hands. Khadija, who works at the hospital, has told me many stories of the teenage suicides.

"Where are your parents, Yori?" I expect silence, another shrug, but no, this time he speaks.

"Not really part of the picture. They didn't seem to notice that Carter left. Or care."

"That's not right."

Yori laughs. I startle, unsure for a moment if it is laughter, or a sound of distress. "You find that funny?"

"You're funny. I like you, man. Sul-ei-man. Thanks for the shawarma."

"Yes, the shawarma. Food, I think, is sometimes the best gift we can give one another, neh? We all have to eat." I pause, look more closely at the boy. "You must need other things as well. Is this true?"

Yori shrugs and looks down at the floor.

"Do you have money?" I ask. "To pay for your room? To buy your food? To ride the bus when you go to look for your brother? Did your parents give you money to come searching?"

"They're not my real parents," Yori says.

"Ahh," I say, although this does not answer the questions, but simply creates more. I clap my hands on my thighs and stand, wipe bits of food off my chest. "Nap-Away is no palace, but it's good enough, neh? If you let me, I can pay for your room, so that you may be safe. A roof, a bed, a door to lock at night."

Yori stands too but doesn't speak. I worry for a moment that I have offended him, that my intention has been misconstrued.

"I didn't know people really did stuff like this," he says. He shrugs again, but then smiles at me.

"I will go to the office tonight to pay for your room," I say. I crumple up the wrapper from my shawarma. "Yori, I hope we can share another meal together soon. Maybe next time it will be with your brother. Now I will take the shampoo to Tiffany." I say it resolutely, though this is not how I truly feel. Shelley has not spoken to me, refuses to look in my direction when our paths cross. She said nothing to me when she arrived back at the motel earlier, even though her daughter's hand was tight in mine, like it belonged there.

I knock on her door. She swings it wide open, narrows her bright blue eyes at me. A billow of cigarette smoke shrouds her.

"For your daughter," I say, offering out the box of Nix.

She takes a drag on her cigarette, stares at me without blinking. "I don't need your fuckin' charity," she says. She draws back and starts to swing the door shut in my face. That same treacherous foot takes action, and I find my sandal blocking the door from closing. We both look down at my foot. I wiggle my big toe self-consciously.

"Your daughter is in need of the shampoo." I toss the shampoo into the room, where it lands with a slight bounce on the unmade bed.

I would like to stamp my foot for emphasis, but it is impossible to do so without throwing myself off balance. I wait for my anger to rise up, but it does not. I feel frustration, pity, but no rage. I pull my foot back, and she slams the door shut.

TIFFANY

I still can't go to school because of the lice that are itching my head. Suleiman threw a box of shampoo on to my mom's bed last night but it made my mom the worst kind of mad, the kind where she doesn't say anything at all. I hid the shampoo under the bed to make her forget about it. Sometimes she gives herself time-outs in the bathroom when she is super mad, like the time-outs Mrs. Lynch gives to Theo at school when he is punching and biting.

After her time-out my mom didn't remember about the shampoo at all. Her eyes were not angry blue lines anymore. They were big black buttons. And she was laughing and talking and skittering around like a squirrel. She said "Let's dance!" and so we jumped on the bed together but we kept falling down so we pretended we were in a bouncy castle instead. After that we ate some cold pizza together sitting on the floor, like it was a picnic.

But then she started scratching and saying the damn lice were crawling all over her skin. I guess the bugs made her sad because she started crying and saying her life was shit. I held her hand the way Mrs. Lynch sometimes holds mine after I fall down in the playground. My mom's hand was shaking like popcorn popping in the microwave. She had lots of tears and snot on her face and she cried so much that some blood came out of her nose. She fell asleep on the floor, right between her bed and my bed, so I pulled a blanket down from my bed and tucked her in like she was my doll. I used some of the pizza napkins to wipe up her face. When I kissed her goodnight she smelled like pepperonis that were all burned up.

In the morning my mom is still sleeping so I go outside to push my doll stroller around. My doll, who I named Marvelous, a word that my teacher, Mrs. Lynch, says a lot, is not in the stroller though. She got left behind at the apartment where I used to live. The stroller is a little tricky to push because one of the wheels fell off. I have to tip it backwards a little bit to make it go forwards. Marvelous used to like going for tippy fast rides, so I tip the stroller back and I start to run and I can hear Marvelous laughing. That is when I see Orianthi.

She looks different. Her purple hair is gone, hiding under a black hat that fits tight against her head, but hangs loose at the back. It's the kind of hat that the older boys at school wear. She is also wearing a thick black bracelet on her wrist. It looks like a mean dog's collar, with silver spiky things all over it. And she is wearing a shirt like Mr. Whitman the principal wears, except she has all the buttons open and a black undershirt underneath. I tell her that she looks like a boy today.

"You can call me Orion then," she says. "Sometimes I'm a girl and sometimes I'm a boy and sometimes I'm both."

"Is that allowed?" I ask. Orianthi nods. "But how will I know who you are?"

"I'm always just me," she says. Or I guess he says.

"Ok," I say.

Orion picks up the towel that I stuffed into the stroller. "Where's your doll?" he asks.

I shrug. "She got left behind," I say.

"That sucks," he says. "I got left behind too." He tells me his brother went away and forgot to take him. Orion shows me a secret postcard from his brother, Carter.

"He's my twin," he says. There are twins in my class named Mithura and Mathura. My mom doesn't believe me when I tell her their names. She just laughs. They look exactly the same, and they dress exactly the same, but I can tell them apart because of Mithura's nose.

"Are you the same?" I ask. Orion nods his head yes.

"People mix us up all the time."

Orion lets me hold the postcard. Usually postcards are hard and shiny, but this one is all warm and soft, like the baby blanket Angel showed us at sharing time in school. The picture on it is a beaver, but it doesn't look very good anymore because of all the folding and unfolding. He doesn't show me the words, but he reads the message to me. It is a poem: *On earth we strive for earthly things and suffer sorrows daily. In heaven choirs of angels sing, while we play ukulele.*

He says that his heart is hurting because he misses Carter so much, but he knows Carter's heart is hurting too, because Carter wrote it down on the postcard. Orion bends down on his knees so that we are the same height, and then he looks at me without saying anything. I can hear the breathing coming in and out of his nose. And I can see his grey eyes up close—they have little black dots scattered in them, like freckles. When he finally says something, it comes out in a scratchy kind of whisper. He tells me that he is going on a quest to find his brother. I touch the beaver, with all those scrunchy lines through his furry body.

"How will you find him?" I ask.

"The postcard will show me the way," he says.

Orion is special. Not just because he is a secret that my mom doesn't know about. But for other reasons I don't know the words for. Maybe I just haven't learned the words yet. I could ask my teacher Mrs. Lynch. Maybe she knows the word for a person who can be a boy and a girl at the same time. Or a word for someone who can change something plain into something magical, the way Orianthi changed a little grey rock that was nothing into something that holds sunshine hidden inside of it. Or the way he changed an old crumpled postcard into a fairy tale.

After Orion leaves I go to my secret place behind Nap-Away. I pick up my reindeer stick and sit down in the leaves and think about secrets. I like secrets. When you have a secret it feels all tickly inside, like when you drink fizzy pop and you can feel all those little burps wanting to come out. I bet Nap-Away has a lot of secrets that it's keeping.

I want to tell somebody about Orion because he's a fizzy secret that's bubbling up inside of my tummy, so I whisper it to Tree. But I am pretty sure that Nap-Away is listening too. First I tell it about how Orianthi can be Orion if she wants to, and about the red pants, and about how her name is hiding all of those little words in it. Then I tell Tree about the beaver postcard that Orion carries around in his back pocket, and about the QUEST!

While I am sitting there, I see something moving in the leaves. I jump right up. I am pretty sure it is a rat because I have seen rats come visiting before. I am part way excited and part way scared. I creep a little closer when I feel excited and creep a little back when I feel scared. I can see the rat's grey fur moving around under a paper bag from McDonald's. The bag is making a sound like it does when I reach inside to pull out my French fries. I wonder if I could make friends with the rat. Maybe I could feed him, like how Suleiman feeds the pigeons.

I am scared of a lot of things. I wish I were braver, like all the kids at school who were brave enough to give Mrs. Lynch's puppy, Luna, a biscuit. Or like my mom when she was brave enough to tell Miranda to go away because she was bugging her.

I creep two baby steps closer to the grey rat. I wish I had some pizza crusts with me. Maybe I could run back to my room and get some. But what if my mom is awake and she doesn't let me come back? Or what if when I come back the rat is gone? I check my pockets in case there is something to feed the rat in them. In my left pocket I have the spar-kly grey rock that Orianthi gave me, and two pennies that I am saving because they are extinct now, just like the dinosaurs. In my right pocket I have a yucky pizza napkin covered with my mom's snot and blood. But under that I find a jellybean, all covered with pocket fuzz. Angel says that pocket fuzz can grow in your belly button. I have the jellybean left over because it is the black kind that tastes yucky. Orange jellybeans are the best. They taste like chewing on sunshine. I wonder if rats eat jellybeans.

I can't decide if I should throw it to the rat, or hold it out in my hand for the rat. I take another baby step towards the moving leaves and sud-denly its little head pops up. I squeal. A kitten, not a rat! I love kittens! I scoop it right up in my hands. The kitten is fluffy and grey, with blue eyes like my mom's. I stroke his fluffiness and whisper to him how happy I am that he is not a rat. Then the best part of all happens. The sound of the leaves moving happens again, and another kitten pops up, and then another, and another! There is a parade of kittens happening right there in my secret place behind Nap-Away. I decide that maybe this is the best day ever, instead of the day I went riding on the merry-go-round with Nikki and we ate cotton candy.

There are four kittens all together: the grey one, a tiny black one and two that look the same as each other, orange and black and white, like a handful of Halloween candy. Twins! My hands are too little to scoop up all of the kittens, so I lift up the edge of my t-shirt to make a pocket, like we do at school when we collect pinecones in the playground, and I put all four kittens in it. Then I make my own little parade, me and my kittens, back to the parking lot.

ORI

Moffit shows up at six, with the ferret wrapped around his neck. His dark skin and the ferret's white fur make a kind of yin-yang thing, same as the tattoo on his bicep. He grins when I open the door for him. Teeth like Chiclets, all white and square and even. I feel awkward. Like I remember who he was yesterday, but not who he is today.

"Hey," he says. "Quite the place you're living at."

"I'm growing fond of Nap-Away," I say. "It's not pretending to be something other than what it is."

Moffit quirks up a single eyebrow. "What is it then?"

"Refuge."

"Refuge," he repeats slowly. "Sounds like there's a whole poem in that single word." I stop feeling awkward, remember that I like how he talks.

"Yeah, the poetry of Nap-Away," I say. Wild-haired Iff running through the parking lot with her empty broken stroller, laughing.

Moffit holds up a paper bag, take-out Chinese. No chicken balls with sweet and sour sauce though.

"I'm vegan," he says.

"What's that exactly?"

"It's like extreme vegetarianism. No meat. But also no eggs, no milk, no cheese." He offers a piece of tofu to the ferret perched on his shoulder. The ferret holds it delicately between her paws, nibbles at it with sharp predatory teeth. "You want to know more?"

I shake my head. Suzy Zammit, closest thing to a friend that I had in middle school, used to try to make me watch the videos. All those chickens crammed in wire cages, trying to peck each other's eyes out. Cows hanging upside down in slaughterhouses. Diseased pigs being buried alive in a pit. She liked to make herself cry, watching them over and over. I'd already seen enough shit to make me cry, I didn't need more.

"So, your brother," he says, staring me down with his dark eyes. "What's the story?"

I give him the basics: the notebook and the run from home, the postcard, my journey to Nap-Away, the ukulele jam discovery, the trip to Covenant House. I realize I might sound a little crazy. Using a postcard and a ukulele benediction to find a missing person is kind of like using a pet psychic to find a lost dog. Or one of those Y-shaped sticks to find water. If I were Carter looking for me I'd have charts and data. I'd have one of those detective walls with strings connecting all the clues. Maps with pushpins in it. Yellow sticky notes. But it's the other way round. It's me looking for Carter. Listening to the story on the postcard.

Moffit eats a spring roll in two quick bites, picks up another. "But you two are tight, right? Why'd he leave in the first place?"

My chest hurts, like the ferret is gnawing at my heart with those little razor teeth. I take a deep breath. "I think he was hearing voices. He kept screaming at me to shut up, but I don't think he was talking to me at all."

"That's serious shit. What's your plan then, when you find him?"

I stare at Moffit. Leave my mouthful of rice unswallowed. The plan? There is no plan. I just need to find him. I want Carter back. I swallow the rice in a single gulp. Choke some back up, swallow again.

"I just need to find him. We'll be ok. We've been through a lot of stuff together."

"But if he's got voices in his head, you need to get him to a doctor, find out what's wrong, get him some support, get him on medication maybe. It could be schizophrenia, something like that."

"He's not schizo!"

Moffit puts his hands up, palms out. Surrenders. "Chill," he says. "I was just saying maybe something's wrong, you know?" He offers me a fortune cookie. I crack it open, pull out the slip of paper, crumple it without reading it, toss it at Moffit's head. Eat the cookie. The ferret weasels down from Moffit's shoulder and sniffs at the crumpled fortune.

"Really? You don't do fortunes?"

"Naw." I don't tell him I'm scared that it will tell me something about Carter.

"So, no plan?"

"Yeah, there's a plan. The plan is to go to the Corktown Ukulele Jam on Queen Street and find out if anyone there has seen Carter. See if there's a place that sells tacos nearby. Check out the hangouts that are nearby." I pick up another fortune cookie and crack it open. Nibble on one half of it. "The plan is to pull the pencil out of his heart."

Moffit quirks that single eyebrow up again. The right one. He laughs. "She's got a plan." He claps a hand to his mouth. "Oh sorry. Is it he? What pronoun do you use?"

I love words, but not grammar. Takes me a sec to remember what a pronoun is. Nobody's ever asked me this before. They've called me lots of nouns though: faggot, dyke, sissy, tomboy, freak, he-she.

"Thanks for asking," I say. "Either's good. I don't really care. They're just labels."

"Are you bi-gendered then? Gender-fluid?"

"I don't really know," I say. Shrug. "For a while it was a struggle. Like I was being pulled one way and then another. When I was little I didn't really think of myself as a girl or a boy. It didn't really matter. Carter and I were the same, you know? We dressed the same; we had matching green sweaters with rabbits on them. If he pulled off his t-shirt when we played soccer, I did too. People thought we were identical twins."

I slide the fortune out of the other half of the cookie. Catch a glimpse of the word magic before I crumple and toss it at Moffit. "When I got older, started thinking about things, I realized that I was different. Not just different than Carter, different than everybody. I knew I was a boy and I knew I was a girl. Sometimes I'm one, sometimes the other. Maybe someday I won't be either. I'll find myself somewhere between the two." I look at Moffit and then avert my glance. Find my awkward again.

"Cool," says Moffit. He opens the fortune. Reads it and laughs. But doesn't tell me what it says.

"Your turn," I say.

"To do what?"

"Tell me a story."

He runs his fingers through his messy black curls.

"Promise not to laugh," he says.

I laugh. Then promise.

"My dad is from India. He works in marketing. But in India he was a prince."

"Seriously?"

"Yup. I'm royal."

"What else?"

"My family really wanted me to marry the daughter of their best friends, so they sort of set us up. Like arranged marriage, but it was just arranged dating. The weird thing was I really liked her. But then I met her brother, and I really liked him too."

I stop chewing my fortune cookie. "What happened then?"

"My dad found out. Walked in on me and the brother together. He kicked me out."

"Shit," I say.

Moffit jumps up. "Enough family crap." He reaches inside one of the takeout bags and pulls out the ferret, who has curled up in a ball and is asleep. "We need to name this beast." He lifts his tattooed arms into the air, holds the ferret aloft. The ferret unfurls, like a white ribbon, and chatters something in ferretese. Moffit translates: "She suggests Zelda."

I feel like we've travelled through time zones getting to the Ukulele Jam, across the city first on a bus, then a subway, then a streetcar. Same as the trip to Covenant House. Nap-Away's supposedly in Toronto, but it's as far from the action as it could get. The city is kind of like the slime mold Carter grew for a science fair in grade eight, stretching and oozing outwards.

Moffit leaves me on Queen Street standing outside the Dominion Bar to go to the bank machine. I'm feeling jittery. Like that jerky ride up the first hill on a roller coaster. Chewing my bottom lip, jiggling my Blundstoned foot. All I'm thinking is Carter. Carter and me. I'm missing his laugh, which sounds just like mine. I'm looking out at the world with the same big grey eyes he has, filled with flecks, like black stars in the twilight. I'm wearing his boots. I don't know how to be me, without him.

We both love raspberry pie, both hate the sound of a whinnying horse, adore the band Florence + the Machine, loathe the bumper cars. We kept each other's secrets. I knew his: the notebook, filled with traversable wormholes and red-eyed vampire squid; the tequila incident; the crush on Suzy Zammit; cheating on the grade 9 French exam. Just like he knew about mine: the shoplifting, the poems, the orphaned grey kitten, the barbed wire bracelet from Mark Curtis-Meehan. Trying to keep a secret from him was like trying to keep it from myself.

Here's the thing about secrets: they hide in different places in your body. Laughing at the back of your throat, effervescent like New Year's Eve. Burrowed into bone marrow. Thumping through your ventricles, *sec-ret sec-ret sec-ret*. But they're all on the same trajectory, all looking for the path out. How did Carter keep that last secret in, keep it hidden from me? People whispering in his head. The eviscerated dogs, snarling. Black words spilling out. Carter on the fuckin' edge and I'm in the kitchen eating buttered toast and jam. His name is screaming in my head, louder and louder. *Carter!*

"Carter!"

Someone is actually saying his name. Coming along Queen Street towards me.

"Carter? What the fuck are you doing here?" He's a big guy, all in black. Black jeans, black hoodie, black Converse. "You really think it's a good idea to show your face around here, after what you did?" He's coming at me. At me, not just towards me. I should maybe run. But I don't.

"Wait! I'm not Carter. I'm his twin."

He closes the gap between us with six long black strides.

"Don't give me that twin bullshit," he says. His pupils are black too, big black Frisbees. I take a single step back, hit a wall. His fist pulls back and slams into my face. My head smacks against the wall and I stumble but Carter's boots keep me standing. My face feels scorched. There's blood in my mouth.

"Stop!" I say. "I'm not Carter! I'm looking for him." I extend my palms, unclenched. "I just want—"

His fist comes at me again, but I duck and swivel, fall down to my hands and knees. I'm praying to his black high tops.

"It's not me. I'm not him!"

"You're messing with me!" I can see his foot moving, slow motion, just like in the movies. He's going to kick me. Kick me and leave me here. I look up at him. I hear my name, *Ori*, but his lips don't move.

"Ori!" There is the sound of footsteps coming closer. Moffit.

The sneaker connects with my ribs. A crackling rocket flares through my chest. My arms give out and I collapse on the ground.

PART TWO

SULEIMAN

I wake up, thinking of the kittens in my bathroom. Two weeks have passed since Tiffany came marching across the parking lot with the squirming, mewling bundle clutched against her. I had no plans to take them in, but with Shelley threatening to throw them in Nap-Away's dumpster and Tiffany's tears streaming down her cheeks, I didn't feel like I had a choice. I wanted them to live, to be cared for.

Khadija and I never had pets. But I remember long ago, when I was a young boy in Cairo, caring for a stray cat in the alleyway behind my home, a skinny brown tabby I named Nada. I had smuggled stringy bits of meat to her, offered her platters of milk, stolen a hairbrush from my sister so that I could brush the cat's matted fur.

So many years ago! I give my head a quick shake, bring myself back to the present. I have many things to do today. The little black kitten is sneezing and her eyes are watering, so I need to take her to a veterinarian. The kittens are growing quickly and always hungry. There is only one tin of food left, and the kitty litter tray is dirty. Khadija would not tolerate such a smell. She would not tolerate the mess in this room either. I sit up and survey the room, the dirty clothes on the floor and chair, the take-out containers, the old newspapers. A clean-up is needed, and a trip to the laundromat. Then I need to get to a bank machine and get some cash to pay for another week at Nap-Away, both for myself and for Yori. I was right about Yori needing money and if Ahmed has no need for my money right now, well then, Yori does.

"I have things to do, neh?" I murmur to myself, as I get up and stretch. Before I begin the tasks, I pray. I will not go to the mosque today, but I've been there often in the last two weeks, for *salat al-jama'ah*, to find comfort in praying with others. And I have left Khadija in peace, as we agreed. I have begun to feel more hopeful about our future together. Perhaps our difficulties are coming to an end.

When I am finished praying, I swing open my front door, inhale the cool morning air, and settle down on my chair. The metallic legs of the chair are spotted with rust, and the green vinyl seat has a rip in it that exposes the white stuffing. There is a slight wobble when I sit. I found the chair abandoned beside the dumpster the day after I arrived. Despite my embarrassment at picking up someone's trash, I had been drawn to the chair, had felt that it was meant for me. A gift from Nap-Away, a gift from *As-Samad*, The Satisfier of All Needs. It is not a chair anyone would covet. But I'm fond of it. The chair reminds me of the past, when Khadija and I had so little, and yet were so happy.

I tear the pizza crust into small pieces, tossing the crumbs onto the pavement. My pigeons flock down with a whoosh and flutter. I imagine I can hear all of their hearts, little blood-filled acorns, beating together, a pulsating prayer to the morning, giving thanks to God. *Fajar Ayub*, the bold pigeon with golden-brown wings, struts forward, pecks a piece of crust that lies near my foot. I survey the flock like a proud shepherd, filled with a sense of satisfaction. They are plump and pretty, their feathers are bejewelled, dusted with emeralds and amethysts. Amina is right, they are like rainbows.

There is a sudden terrible pressure in my chest, a clutching pain. My throat closes, cuts the air from flowing. Both of my arms hang lifeless from the shoulder sockets, crumbs trickle from my left hand. It is like having a heart attack, this assault of grief.

Tiffany told me the birds were like rainbows, not Amina. Amina is gone. I can't share the beauty of the birds with her. Immense black wings of sorrow beat against my face and chest, suffocating me. The blackness chills my heart, turns it dark, fills it with rage.

I pause. I breathe deeply, once, twice, three times. The pigeons stir and coo at my feet. I watch my thoughts spin down dark paths and I bring them back to the light. *Truly to Allah we belong, and truly to him shall we return.* I repeat the words in my mind, again and again. My breathing returns to normal, my heart settles, my fist unclench. I don't hear the door to Room 5 open, but Tiffany suddenly appears at my side.

"Suleiman? Can I see my kittens?"

Amina's presence is still with me, but it is Tiffany I see now, her green eyes shining in the bright morning light. Tiffany, who is so like my daughter, who I wish was my daughter, now that I've lost Amina.

Could Tiffany *be* Amina? I know this is a foolish question; *Allah* is *Al-Ba'ith*, The Resurrector, not the Reincarnator. I don't believe in reincarnation; but the question catches my attention.

"Suleiman?"

I feel her small cold fingers touching my arm. No, of course Tiffany is not Amina come back to me. But the workings of God are mysterious. Perhaps there is a reason that I've chosen Nap-Away instead of the home of a relative, a reason that I was placed in Room 6, next door to Tiffany. Is it possible that there is a deeper meaning to my presence here? The thought plants a seed of hope.

I fling the last bit of pizza crust far across the parking lot. The crumbs arc into the air, sending the pigeons into a frantic flutter.

"My friend," I say, turning my attention to Tiffany. I stand up and pat her head. The lice are gone now. How strange, that it was the teenager, Yori, who washed the child's hair and then sat for hours, pulling through the strands with a tiny metal comb. Tiffany had sat still the entire time, with two of the kittens asleep on her lap.

And where was the mother, Shelley? Gone. She leaves the child alone for hours at a time; sometimes she returns with a bag full of groceries, sometimes she returns with a young man who lights her cigarettes and calls her 'babe', sometimes she returns with a case of beer and a bucket of fried chicken. Sometimes she returns with nothing.

"Come. We will feed the kittens, and then you can play with them while I clean their litter box. Little Mini is sick. I will take her to see the doctor today. You must give her extra care."

Tiffany slides her hand into mine and we step into my room together.

TIFFANY

If I had a dad, I would wish for him to be like Suleiman. His skin is brown just like mine, and he is a good hand-holder, and he likes kittens as much as I do. I don't have a dad. Well, I guess I do somewhere because you have to have a dad to make a baby, everybody knows that, but the place where he is has never been the place where I am.

Suleiman has a daughter. He showed me a picture of her on his phone. He doesn't talk about her very much, but when I named the tiny black kitten Mini, because she is so small, he told me that he used to call his daughter, Amina, that some times. Mini Mina, he said and then his eyes got all shiny and wet, like little brown puddles.

Mini is our favourite kitten, but I still love the twins a lot. They are so many different colours at the same time, black and white and two kinds of orange and also grey. One is named Rainbow and the other is named Massarat, which is the name that Suleiman picked when I said to pick an M name. It means joy. They are very troublesome together, Suleiman says. They are always chasing each others' tails and biting each others' ears with their tiny teeth and using their feet like little bunny rabbits to kick each other. Ori says that is what it's like to be a twin. She has the other kitten, the fluffy grey one with blue eyes. She told me she used to have a kitten that looked like the grey kitten, but he died. I wanted to keep the grey one, but when she told me about the kitten dying, I said she should have him. She hasn't given him a name yet so we just call him The Grey One. Rainbow, Mini, Massarat and The Grey One. Those are the four kittens.

I pick up Mini first because she is sick and needs taking care of, but my mom bangs on Suleiman's door and pushes it wide open.

"Tiffany, are you in here?" I pop my head out from the bathroom, where I am using some toilet paper to wipe Mini's nose, which is very runny.

"Hi!" I say. I dash over to show her Mini.

"What're you doing? I thought I told you not to come in here anymore."

"But I have to see my kittens."

"I don't like finding you in here. This guy could be a friggin' terrorist, or some kind of pervert!" She has her hands on her hips and she is wiggling her foot up and down. She gives Suleiman her flat-eyed look. Sometimes my mom says mean things. I look at Suleiman to see if he is mad because she is calling him names, but he is ignoring her. He steps around us and leaves, taking the bag of dirty litter and kitten poop with him. Their little poops make a great big stink.

Rainbow and Massarat come tearing out of the bathroom, chasing each other like fast cars on Kingston Road. They nearly crash into my mom's feet, and then they start playing some kind of peek-a-boo game around her legs. She bends down and picks up Rainbow. Then her eyes stop being so flat, and they go back to being big and shiny blue.

"She is pretty sweet," she says. She rolls Rainbow over in her hand and tickles her belly. "But I still don't want you spending so much time in here with *him*." She uses her chin to point at the open door. My mom has a very cute chin. It looks like someone pushed their finger in it and left a little hole.

"But I like Suleiman," I say. "He's like my dad." My mom turns into a statue. She stares at me without blinking and her blues eyes turn to ice. All the colour disappears from them. She stops breathing. She drops Rainbow, and the kitten falls to the ground with a little kitten thump. Then my mom cracks, like a frozen puddle when you jump on it, and she comes towards me, super fast. I squeak and run towards the open door, but I trip on Mini and my mom catches me. She grabs my arm and twists me around.

"What the fuck is wrong with you? Why would you say something like that?" She says the words like a snake, all scary and hissy. "He's not your family! He's nothing like us!" She is holding my arm so tight that I can feel all her sharp nails digging in.

"It hurts," I say, but she doesn't stop. Instead, she grabs my other arm and she starts to shake me. My teeth hit together, like when I'm outside on the playground at recess in the freezing cold.

"I didn't mean it," I whisper.

"Don't you dare come back in here again." She stops shaking me and pulls me towards the door.

"Wait!" I say, because I can see all the kittens going towards the open door.

"WAIT!" I scream.

But she keeps her icy hand on my arm and drags me out of the room. I wish for her to be so mad that she slams the door closed, but she doesn't. It stays open and I see Mini's little black face peering out and smelling summer.

ORI

Two weeks of searching. No Carter. I've been back to the ukulele jam. I've been to the places where the homeless kids go: Covenant House, Turning Point, Second Base. I would have ended up there myself, except that Suleiman started paying for my room and buying me all kinds of shit. Shawarma. Toothpaste. Flip-flops. Peanut butter. Take-out coffee every morning. I stopped freaking out about running away, about my dwindling cash supply, about being sex-trafficked.

But I know enough now about the shelters that I feel like I could hang at the bus station, greet the new kids, send them off in the right direction. I've been to the places where the homeless guys go too, the Gateway, the Good Shepherd, the Salvation Army. Old-man faces on skinny young guys with missing teeth and dirty clothes. Old-man faces on skinny old guys too. I've been prowling around Queen Street, east and west, making wider and wider circles away from the Corktown Ukulele Jam. I've been looking for places that serve tacos. Sometimes I hang out on the steps of the museum, eating hotdogs, waiting for Carter to come by and see the fossilized bones of the giant ground sloth. And I've been looking for Mr. Black.

"It's racist to call him that," Moffit says. We're sitting on my sagging motel bed, eating falafels from the shawarma place. Falafels are vegan-friendly, Moffit tells me. He's feeding the ferret Zelda nibbles of pita bread, but I'm guessing she'd rather have the carnivore-friendly shawarma. The Grey One is clawing his way up my leg. I was kind of worried about Zelda at first, worried that a ferret might think The Grey One was carnivore-friendly. Snack-size. But Zelda's cool with him. Moffit thinks maybe Zelda lived with cats in her previous life. Makes it sounds like she's reincarnated.

"It's not racist," I say. "He's not even black. He's one of those men-in-black. One of those ominous men working for some mysterious organization. Why is he out there, hunting down Carters?"

"Don't know. But at least we know Carter's out there." Moffit and I have said this to each other a gazillion times since he found me on the sidewalk with a big grin on my smashed up face.

"Oh, I've got the bruise to show that Carter exists," I say. Moffit laughs. Then he does something unexpected, at least by me. He touches my bruised cheek, which has morphed in ripeness from eggplant to zucchini, and is now the colour of a banana. Slides his thumb down my cheek just below my left eye and runs it across my bottom lip. It catches on my lip, pulls my mouth open a little.

I do a shitty thing. Which is nothing. I should tell him he's the first real friend I've ever had, aside from Carter. I should tell him he's awesomeness, with all his cool tattoos and his chocolaty skin, but not my kind of awesomeness. I should tell him it's never going to happen, not the way that thumb wants it to. But I don't. Because if I do, I'm sure he'll leave.

"The falafels are great," I say. Which is lame.

"Yeah," he says. "Orion—" he starts to say, but a rapping at the door interrupts him. It's Suleiman.

"The kitten, Mini. She's gone!" He gestures towards the parking lot.

I jump up and the Grey One skitters down my leg. "What happened?"

"Tiffany was in my room with the kittens this morning. Her mother must have made her leave, all of a sudden, without closing the door. I've searched already but can't find her anywhere."

"Maybe Tiffany has the kitten with her."

"I knocked, but they didn't answer. Maybe they are there, maybe not. You can check with them first."

"Come on," I say to Moffit. "A kitten hunt has got to be a lot easier than a Carter hunt." He slides Zelda the ferret around his neck, like he's putting on a scarf for the outing, and trots after me across the parking lot. I send him to scout around for the missing kitten while I check in with Room 5.

Shelley peers through the crack between the curtains, then answers the door. She's got a pretty face. Pert little nose, dimpled chin, cornflower blue eyes with lashes that you can picture opening and closing with a little click, like a doll's.

"Whaddya want?" she says.

"Just checking for the black kitten, from next door. Have you seen her?" Shelley's shoulders pull up and down, a couple of times. Jittery. Her nose twitches like a little rabbit. Swipes her hand under it a few times. Big black pupils staring at me. Cracked lips. Looks just like my mom did when she was using. Shit.

I glance behind her to see Iff standing there, freaky quiet, sucking her thumb, watching me with those solemn green eyes. She's holding on to the doll that I got her last week at Value Village. I was looking for one with brown skin and black hair. But every doll there was white. The one I picked had matted blonde hair, sticking-up in every direction. Cute yellow sleeper though, with little dogs jumping on it. At least it's better than the dirty towel she was wheeling around in her stroller.

"What the hell happened to your face?" Shelley says, as if we know each other. Which I guess we sort of do.

"Case of mistaken identity," I answer, with a shrug. "The kitten?"

"Nah. It's not here." She starts to swing the door closed.

"Hey, do you need a babysitter?" I blurt it out. "I'm good with kids. I was always looking out for my little brother." Carter was always looking out for me, but he is my little brother. Seventeen minutes younger.

She narrows her blue eyes at me. "I can't pay you."

I shrug. "No big deal. I just thought, you know, that maybe you needed a break. That's what my mom always said."

She jiggles her foot, chews on her chapped lip for a second, considering. Then she smiles, and I can see how the boys must have swarmed around her when she was in high school. How she could've made one of them think they loved her just by blinking those eyes a couple of times.

"Yeah," she says. "I could use a break." She looks back at her daughter. "Ok. Sure. What's your name again?"

"Ori."

"That's a weird name," she says. "No offence."

"I can look after her for the rest of the afternoon, if you want."

"Yeah, that'd be good. But keep her away from the guy next door.

I think he might be some kind of perv, you know, the kind that likes little girls."

"Sure. No problem. Come on, kid," I say. Iff looks at me as if I'm Christmas morning. I give her a wink.

SULEIMAN

I sit down heavily, sigh with satisfaction. My room is tidied, my clothes are laundered and folded neatly, the kittens have a clean litter box, and a stack of tinned cat food towers on the TV shelf. There has been no trip to the veterinarian for the black kitten yet, but I will do that when Yori and Tiffany find her. How far can a small animal like that wander?

I reach for my cell phone and call Ahmed, but there is no answer, just Ahmed's polite voice requesting a message, the same as last week and the week before.

"I'd like to visit you," I say into the phone. "Perhaps you could show me the new place where you are living. And your workplace. Call me back, neh?" I end the call, scroll through some of the photos on my phone. There is a series of pictures, taken by Tiffany, of each kitten. I pause on Mini's photo, shake my head in dismay. It shouldn't have happened, the little kitten getting lost. The world is too dangerous for such a small creature on its own. I've heard the expression, 'curiosity killed the cat,' but only now do I really understand it. Perhaps Mini heard the chirp of a cricket, or smelled a chicken bone tossed carelessly on the pavement, or saw the flutter of the pigeons, coming down to land by my door. The kitten was curious, and now look what has happened. I stand and look out the window for Yori, hoping to see the rescued kitten in his arms, but the parking lot is empty.

The next pictures are older ones. There is one of Ahmed, on the day he left for Montreal, his normally reserved smile replaced by an open grin, and then a photo of Amina, standing outside of the mosque next door to Nap-Away, touching the unfolding scales of a reddish pine cone on the blue spruce. Over the years I have watched the blue spruce grow. I've always loved the tree, the beautiful symmetry of it, the way the branches circle the trunk, curving upwards, each one slightly shorter than the one below, until, at the very top, the last few branches point directly up to the sky. In the sun the waxy grey-green needles shine with a hint of silver, and in the winter the snow clings to the layered branches, like clean sheets hugging on to a bed.

Amina is looking down at the cone, those long black lashes curling against her cheek. Then there is a photo of Khadija's face, her laughing eyes, her thin arching eyebrows raised, a half-smile teasing her closed lips. I touch the screen gently. May *Allah*, known as *As-Samee'*, The Hearer of All Things, listen to my prayer for forgiveness.

How has everything gone so far astray? I caress the screen, as if I might feel her flesh, then swipe the picture away with a quick jerk of my finger.

The next picture is one of Amina, covering her mouth with her hand. It was a habit she had developed, covering the thin scar on her upper lip with her fingertips when she was feeling shy or self-conscious. I stare at the picture, willing her to life, imagining I can hear her voice. She liked to show me pictures from her books in the evening, when her schoolwork was done.

"This is a manatee," she might say. "They are very gentle, like cows. They only eat grass that grows in the sea. People must be more careful, because their fast boats are hurting them. I'd like to go swimming with them one day. Would you like to go too, Baba?" I smile at the idea, imagine myself as a buoyant brown sea-cow, floating down the river.

As a baby Amina had been difficult for me to love. She had trouble feeding because of her cleft lip. Khadija pumped breast milk, but Amina refused to take a bottle from me. She preferred Khadija's comforting arms to mine, as of course, any baby would. She was colicky. She cried for hours sometimes, for unfathomable reasons, so unlike Ahmed. Khadija and I were often anxious that first year, worrying about her feeding and her growth, about her excessive crying, about her upcoming surgery, at five months of age. By the time Amina turned one, she was headstrong and stubborn, refusing to cooperate with the simplest of tasks. How she made me miss Ahmed's easy babyhood years! But then she learned to talk. It could not have happened overnight, but that is how I remember it, the way she changed into a happy, chattering little girl, left her difficultness behind. And then, oh, how my love for her grew. She was like a flower, blooming before my eyes. Beautiful and kind and funny, and so gentle.

She is lost to me now, just like the tiny and sickly black kitten. They are all gone, not just Amina: Ahmed, who is far away and so independent now, who has stopped needing me years ago; Khadija, my only love, who I've betrayed with my coldness and anger. I feel bowed down by grief.

I stand, stumble to the bathroom, splash cold water on my face. I must not think too long about these hardships, for surely, soon, will come some ease. The kittens, Rainbow and Massarat, curled up asleep on the bathroom mat, yawn and stretch. I pick them up in my hands, cradle them both.

"Come," I say to them, carrying them out to my bed. "You must be lonely in there, neh?"

TIFFANY

Orianthi has a new friend that I have seen a few times now. I think he is her boyfriend. But maybe he's not, because he doesn't kiss her on the lips, or squeeze her bum, or call her names like 'baby.' He looks like Abishek, a boy in grade two who is a bully. Except Abishek doesn't have a giant white rat that he carries around on his shoulder, and he doesn't have any tattoos. And Abishek doesn't have messy hair. His hair is so short you can see his bald head underneath it. Here is a list of the tattoos that I've seen on Orianthi's maybe-boyfriend:

    —a baby dragon that might be a lizard with wings (look at all the hiding words: drag, rag, a, ago, go, on)
    —a poem written in tiny letters that are too hard to read
    —a cow wearing a flower headband (this one is my favourite)
    —two little fish all snuggled up together, one white fish and one black fish.
    —the words: ALL GOOD THINGS ARE WILD AND FREE
    —the letters V-E-G-A-N. I don't know if this is a word or not. I wrote it down so I could ask Mrs. Lynch when I go back to school except school is finished now for the summer so I will have to remember the word until September.
    —a black tree with no leaves. It might be scary or it might be pretty.
    —one letter on each finger of each hand, but the only letter I know for sure is an 'R' because he moves his hands around a lot when he talks. I think it might say SATURDAY. I am guessing there are more tattoos hiding on other parts of him.

He is helping us look for Mini. He has a big smile and he runs his fingers through his messy black hair a lot. Sometimes my mom's boyfriends ignore me, but Orianthi's maybe-boyfriend, Moffit, is nice to me. He said I could pet the rat Zelda, but I shook my head no. So instead he showed me how Zelda can high-five, and roll over and dance.

We start our search for Mini in the parking lot and near Kingston Road. I take them to my secret place behind Nap-Away to show them where I found the kittens, because maybe that will give us a clue about where she went. But there are no kittens there, only dead leaves and garbage, and my antler stick. I tell Orianthi the story about Ant, and I tell her that Tree listens to my stories.

"Maybe she scooched under the fence," Orianthi says, pointing at a gap at the bottom. Moffit grabs the fence and hops over it in one big sideways leap. Orianthi tries to do the same thing, but her pants get stuck on the top of the fence, and they rip.

"Dang," she says and she spins around trying to see if her bum is showing and starts to laugh. Then Moffit starts to laugh. I look at their laughing faces and it makes me laugh, even though ripping my pants would not be a funny thing for me because it would make my mom mad.

"Come on, Iff," she says, and she boosts me right over the fence and I feel like I am flying. The big tree is on this side of the fence, and there are some smaller trees and lots of messy bushes that look like they need their branches combed straight. There is also a lot of garbage, even an old fridge and a big dirty chair. There are some broken cars too, because we are in the backyard of a place that sells old cars. We all go on a big hunt, looking inside of things and under things and all around. I call Mini's name in a quiet voice so that she will not be scared. We see some big cats hiding in different places. I find a quarter and Moffit finds an old shoe that he says is cool and Orianthi finds a comic book that she stuffs in her back pocket to read later. But none of us finds Mini.

"Maybe if we stop looking for her, she'll come and find us," Moffit says. Orianthi says it's a good idea.

"'Let's play Wild Things while we wait for her," Orianthi says and she makes a cross-eyed face at me with her big grey eyes.

"How do you play?" I ask.

"You get to be Max," she says, "king of the wild things. So you need a crown." She looks around and then pulls some branches from a not-spiky bush and somehow ties them up into a perfect circle of pretty green leaves that she puts on my head. "And you need a big stick."

"Oh! I have one over there," I say, pointing to the other side of the fence, where my reindeer antler is. Moffit hops back over and grabs it and hops back again. He is like a kangaroo.

"For the king," he says, and he bows to me and holds the stick out. I should say thank you but I feel too shy to talk to him. I whisper to Orianthi and ask her what kind of rat he is wearing, and she tells me it is called a ferret. I think the ferret should probably be the king of the wild things, but I don't say so.

"Ok, now we'll be the wild things and we'll roar our terrible roars and gnash our terrible teeth and show our terrible claws and roll our terrible eyes. But you can tame us, because you are the most wildest thing of all!"

"I am?"

"You are," Orianthi says. "All you need to do is say 'Be Still' and the wild things will always listen to you." Then she leans down to me and whispers that I have to say the magic words: *Let the wild rumpus begin* to start the game.

"What's a rumpus?" I ask.

"It's what the wild things do," she says. So I wave my stick and I say the words and the wild things go wild. There is a lot of screaming and roaring and running and laughing. There is chasing and tickling and giggling. Then Orianthi tries to knock Moffit over, and he wrestles her down to the ground and I shout 'Be Still' and they have to stop. They are both grinning and panting like dogs and there are leaves and sticks in their hair. Orianthi says I am the best Max she has ever seen. Orianthi and Moffit jump back up and leap back over the fence and I climb over after them and then I chase them to Nap-Away's parking lot and we find Suleiman there.

"We're wild things," I tell him and I give a big roar. He looks around at all of us and smiles and then he makes the biggest roar of all. I'm pretty sure he is a better wild thing than me.

If we had found Mini it would have been the best day ever.

ORI

Tonight I discovered a Mexican place called Milagro Cantina Mexicana. It's not really close to the ukulele jam, but still. I'm pretty excited. I glance at the menu out front and discover some octopus appetizer from Tijuana for fifteen bucks, and I'm not so hyped up anymore. Moffit makes a move to go inside.

"Carter would never eat here," I tell him, pulling him back out onto the street. We grab some takeout Thai food and ride the 501 back to Queen East and the Corktown Ukulele Jam at the Dominion. It's another Wednesday; maybe this time Carter and his ukulele will show. We are across the street at the Sweet Marie Variety Store, buying Juicy Fruit when I see him.

"There he is!" I grab the gum, grab Moffit, race out onto the street. The light is red and the 501 streetcar rattles past, blocking my view. "Come on, come on," I say, swerving around the streetcar and dashing into traffic.

"Hey," I yell. "Hey." A couple of pedestrians glance my way. A cyclist blows a whistle at me. Orange and green taxis blare their horns. "Hey!" I yell one more time and he turns and looks at me. Moffit, who has stayed at my side, brakes to a stop.

"That's not Carter!" he hisses, grabbing a hold of my arm. He starts to back away slowly, the way those survival manuals tell you to when confronted by a grizzly. Mr. Black is standing outside of the Dominion, carrying a ukulele case. It's an old-fashioned one, made from tweed cloth, the edges lined with strips of deep brown leather. It makes him look not so men-in-black after all. In fact, he doesn't look anything like I remember him. Just a regular dude. Not wearing any black.

"Hey," I yell again, "Remember me? I'm looking for Carter."

He lifts his ukulele case, and Moffit gasps. I'm guessing he thinks there's a machine gun hidden in it. Like Mr. Black is some kind of gangster. But he lifts his other hand as well. White flag disguised as a ukulele.

"The twin," he says.

We eye each other. I'm wary, keep my distance.

"Yeah," I say. "The twin. Not Carter." He's wearing an orange t-shirt, jeans. Flip-flops. "I remembered you scarier," I blurt out.

"I remember me scarier too," he says. "Shit, I can really be an asshole. He looks me up and down. "But you really do look just like Carter."

"We cool?" he asks.

"Sure," I say. We're not cool at all, but I need Carter more than I need for us to be cool.

"What can you tell me about Carter? I need to know where he's at."
He sighs, shakes his head.

"I doubt you'll see him around here anymore," he says.

"Why? What happened? I mean, why were you so pissed at us?"

"You know how he's a little off, right?" I nod my head, wonder what Carter's been doing. "That's fine, I'm down with that. We played together a couple of times here," he says, gesturing with a thumb behind him, at the Dominion. "That kid is a wicked uker." I grin. Feel proud of my little bro.

"But the last time he was here, he set my ukulele on fire. Started saying that he needed to destroy the evidence, that I should let it burn, so they wouldn't be able to track him. Said the song I was playing was calling them. Crazy shit like that. I tried to put it out, but he went nuts, started clawing at my face, screaming at me."

He takes a step towards me. I take a step back. Moffit takes a step between us.

"But where is Carter now? Do you know where he's staying at? Or where he's hanging out?" I step towards him and grab his arm. I want to shake information out of him. Except his arm feels all bulgy with muscles, so I let it go. Take a step back.

"I dunno," he says. "He said something once about his roommate touching his stuff at the place where he was staying, trying to steal his documents or whatever."

"Did you ever meet the roommate? Or get the address of the place?" I bounce up and down on my toes. "Do you think it's near here?"

He shrugs.

"If you see him," Moffit says, "can you give him my number, say that Ori is looking for him?" I can't give him my number. My phone is long dead. RIP iphone 4S.

"Which one of you is Ori?"

"I am," I say. "This is Moffit."

"I'm Joel," he says. No more Mr. Black. He pulls out his phone, types in Moffit's number. "You guys want to come to the jam?" he asks. Moffit quirks his eyebrow at me. I want to. I miss Carter's riffs, the happy sounds that come from a ukulele.

"You in?" I ask Moffit. He nods his head, and we follow Joel into the Dominion to the Ukulele Jam.

It's like a cult in there, a ukulele cult. Lots of oldsters, with beards and glasses, some hipsters with fedoras and pinstripe pants, a smattering of gals, some librarian-type, some funky-hippie type. Joel looks even less like Mr. Black now, tapping his flip-flopped foot, strumming his little ukulele. I flash back to his fist in my face. Picture Carter, lighting his ukulele on fire.

It's an open stage with lots of sing-a-longs. Moffit seems to know the words to lots of old-timey songs. There's cheering and whistling, ukulele thwacking. Then a young woman takes the stage. Her black hair is pulled back into an untidy ponytail, but most of it falls loose over her face, hiding her. She never looks up to the audience. Eyes for her ukulele only. She starts with a quiet plucking, sings the most beautiful song, about surviving the rains of November. She's like the choir of angels, all by herself. Her fingernails drum against the wood of the uke, pattering the rain down into the room. Then she strums and the skies do open.

Behind her, in the darkened windows, there are sudden streaks of red and white, as the traffic streams past. I'm picturing Carter out on the street somewhere. My chest feels tight, like the E string of a ukulele, wound too taut. Tuned to the wrong octave. Like if I keep listening to this song, the peg will turn one more time and the string will break. I'm thinking I'm not sure if we're going to survive this storm.

It's 2 AM at the Nap-Away. I'm stoned. Weed from Joel. A fist-in-the-face apology. It feels so achingly delicious that I can't stop laughing. Moffit keeps saying 'shush' which sounds so hilarious that I simply shriek more.

"You are collallasly funny. Collallosally funny. Whatever. Bigly funny. Like a platypus," I say to him. I am so funny I am making myself laugh. We are lying down and my head is on his stomach and it bounces a little with each shush he gives me. It's like being on the double air mattress Carter and I slept on the year we were seven. Moffit's fingers are wrapped up in my hair. The Grey One is pouncing and chewing on my bare toes with little pinprick teeth, which should hurt, but doesn't.

"I've never been so stoned before," I whisper to Moffit. This sets me off again, because I don't know why I'm whispering.

"Shush," he says again, "you're shrieking like a banshee." My head bounces again. I hold my breath, try to stop from laughing.

"Bansheeeee," I say. Start giggling. "It's like floating in space, isn't it? Nothing can touch me." I reach my hand out and grab the air. "Everything's so perfect."

"Shush," he says again, even though I am quiet now. "Shush."

"I wish Carter were here." And just like that it's not quite as perfect anymore.

"What's he like anyway, this brother of yours?"

"A lot like you. But not. He's really smart and really funny. Fun and funny. And tough. But not brown. And no tattoos." I roll over and study Moffit's inked arms. "If he had one, it would probably be a trilobite. Or pi."

"Apple? Or raspberry?"

I startle. "Yeah. Pie. Raspberry pie." I dance a fingertip across his knuckle tattoo from one pinkie all the way to the other "Yours are mostly not his style, except for this one." A single letter on each finger spells out 'stardust'.

"That's what we are," Moffit says. He grabs my hand. "The atoms in us, in everything, came from stars, exploding supernovas, scattering their elements across the universe, snowing them down into space where they got packed back up together again into planets, like giant snowballs. Gravity, playing out there in the cosmos, making snowballs from the stardust." He gestures wildly, bringing my hand along. "Everything.

You. Me. Zelda. This bed. We're all the stuff of stars." He lets go of my hand and touches my chest. "Maybe the atoms in your heart are from a different star than the atoms in your eyes."

"Wow," I say. This must be what it's like for Carter, looking out over the edge of the universe. "Wow," I say again. I am at a colossal loss for words. Thoughts are spinning around in my head. Some of them are exhilarating. Some terrifying. Some so simple that I start to laugh again. I feel infinitesimally small. I miss Carter.

Everything is made up of stardust. The library ferret, my chewed-upon toes, all those strumming ukuleles, my missing twin. All made up of the stuff of stars.

"Shush," Moffit says again. He tries to kiss me on the lips, but I can't stop my mouth from laughing.

"It's just so amazing," I say. "I'm just so hungry." I launch myself off the bed, tug Moffit up. "Come on. We've gotta go get some food."

Out in the parking lot there's a guy leaving Room 5, Iff's room. He looks shifty, but that could be because it's 2 AM. He glances from side to side, the way shifty guys do, and then trots over to Kingston Road and hails a cab. We stay in the parking lot. The clouds are scudding across the night sky, making room for the moon shine. Now that the shady guy is gone, Nap-Away looks sweet and innocent, its yellow walls glowing white in the light from the moon. I picture little Mini sheltered somewhere behind the motel, Nap-Away's shadow covering her with a soft blanket of darkness, keeping her safe from harm.

I look up at the moon, see a couple of stars beaming down. When my eyes travel back down I notice for the first time how Nap-Away's roof slopes down in a single direction, making it look like a hobbit-house, tucked into the hillside behind it. Fallen stardust, that's what Nap-Away is.

I grab Moffit's hand and I spin him around. Then I keep going, twirling like I'm a snowball planet on my orbit around Nap-Away. Moffit catches me mid-twirl and pulls me against his chest, and we start to kiss. Part of it feels great, because of the high I'm on, because of the darkness and the spinning and the stardust and the shadows hiding from the moon. Part of me though feels like it's all wrong. I want to tell him, but the words stay tangled up in my stoned and stardusted brain.

SULEIMAN

I am up before sunrise. I move with intention: dressing, feeding the kittens, making my bed, performing my ablutions, rolling out my prayer mat, bowing and prostrating myself in morning prayer. As I recite the words, *Allah-hoo Akbar*, God is great, their familiarity brings calmness to my mind, clarity. I have made a plan. Later this morning I will go to the house to see Khadija, not to ask for anything, not for her forgiveness, not to return to the house, not to speak with her. I've seen clearly that I must not ask anything of her. If I ask, I am requesting an answer. But if there is no asking, there can be no refusal. I will simply tell her that I am ready to end the separation, ready to talk about whatever needs to be spoken of, ready to take the steps needed to fix our marriage. Most importantly, I will be restrained. I must show absolute ownership over my anger. There is an underlying movement that I can see, now that my mind is clear. Each time grief arises, I turn away from it, clutch onto anger instead. Like a pigeon's wing in flight, folding and unfolding, I have been moving between grief and rage. Now that I see this clearly, I will sever it.

I pray for a long time. Then I spend an hour with Rainbow and Massarat, making playthings for them from take-out bags and toilet paper, allowing them to pounce on my wiggling fingers, petting them until they purr with delight. Why did I never allow Amina to have a kitten? They are so filled with spirit, always ready to play, so easy to love. They bring me little sparks of happiness. An idea starts to shape in my head, takes form. I will not ask anything of Khadija. No, instead of asking, I will give. I will bring a kitten to her. This has more meaning than a trinket, a piece of clothing, sweets. The things I have been giving her have been trivial, but the kitten will not be. It will be like a little piece of Amina's heart, running free and wild.

I have been waiting outside of the house for an hour. Perhaps Khadija is inside, refusing to answer the door, but I don't think so. The drapes are drawn closed; Khadija likes the sun to pour in to the room when she is at home. I glance around. The lawn is freshly mowed and the flower garden weeded. I take this as a good sign, that she is taking care of these simple tasks.

A car approaches, circles the crescent, pulls in to the drive. But it is Ahmed, not Khadija, who steps out.

"Ahmed! But I thought you were in Montreal. I left you a message."

"No, I'm here." Despite this obvious fact, I stare at him, disbelieving.

"But you should be at your job, not here at the house. Is something wrong?"

Ahmed tilts his head to the side, as if considering. He shrugs and sighs. "Dad," he says, "I took a couple of days off. It's not a big deal. I wanted to spend some time with Mom." I try to digest the 'Dad.' It holds none of the intimacy the title Baba used to have; instead it has the faint odour of disrespect.

"Where is she?" I ask. I look in the car, and back towards the house.

"She's at the hospital."

"What's happened?"

"Nothing," Ahmed says with a shrug. "She's taking care of some work stuff, signing papers or something."

There is a pause. Ahmed does not say any more. I wait, shifting from one foot to the other. Finally I nod my head at my son.

"Ahmed, it's good to see you. It's been too long, neh? Look at you. So like a man now, I can hardly believe you are my boy." Last time I saw Ahmed he was clean-shaven; now he has a neatly trimmed mustache and beard. He is not any taller, but he seems wider, his shoulders and arms more muscular. I step forward, hug my son to my chest. Ahmed stiffens in the embrace, does not return it.

"I'll take you out for some dinner then," I say, releasing him. Ahmed looks down at the ground, rubs his hands together. When he meets my gaze, he pulls his shoulders back, stands taller.

"I don't think so," Ahmed says.

"But, you're here. I was planning to come to Montreal to visit, to see you."

"Dad," he says, "things are different. I need to be with Mom. I need to give her my support."

"You are a good son to her." Ahmed lets a small smile slip out. "But you're still a son to me."

"I am your son," he replies. "But that's not what matters right now. I don't want to go to dinner, to talk. I'm here for Mom, not for you."

"I am here for her as well," I say. Ahmed laughs, a sharp bitter sound, and shakes his head.

"You! You managed to take the most awful thing that has ever happened to her, to us, and you made it worse. You've pardoned her for what happened, but you've never truly forgiven her. You've been giving her the silent treatment for months, instead of just talking to her. You've shut her out of your heart."

I say nothing. A great pulse of anger beats through my chest. I wait for it to subside, watch to see what hides underneath. I begin to feel like I am shrinking in front of Ahmed, that my son is towering over me, and I am becoming smaller and smaller: the size of Amina; the size of Massarat, cowering in the carrier at my feet; the size of a cockroach scuttling into a crack in the floor at Nap-Away.

"We all need to heal," Ahmed says. Even as a child he would say such things, mature beyond his years. I remember exchanging glances with Khadija when Ahmed would speak like this, wise words that seemed far beyond his age.

"She's coming back to Montreal with me for the summer. My roommate is going out to B.C., and Mom's going to move in. We're leaving tomorrow."

My breath stops. I've lost my balance, Ahmed's words have pushed me forward off a steep edge.

"No," I say. "No."

"Yeah, Dad. That's what's happening."

"But—"

Ahmed expels a large breath through clenched teeth. "There's no buts. She needs to get away from here. And she wants to spend time away from you."

"You shouldn't be telling me this. She and I should decide these things!" I take a single step towards my son, my fists tight. Ahmed reaches out his hand, places his palm against my chest, commanding me to stop. And I do. I feel my anger and my thoughts folding and unfolding, like the pigeon's wings, inviting me down treacherous pathways, but I don't follow them. I am aware that we have reversed roles, that Ahmed has become the man, caring for Khadija. I have become the little boy, protesting what I seem to have no say in. I am the one who needs guidance, not Ahmed.

"She's already made the decision," Ahmed says. "It's already done."

I nod my head. I step back and pick up the cat carrier.

"What is that, anyway?" Ahmed asks.

"A kitten. I brought a kitten for your mother." Ahmed peers briefly through the wire door of the crate. A look of disgust crosses his face.

"You thought giving her a kitten would make up for how you've been treating her? Really?"

I want to explain, want to tell Ahmed how I have been feeling, reveal my intent. I consider how to begin, but no words come. Everything is damaged. Words will not repair any of it. I turn and walk away from my son.

TIFFANY

My sister Nikki is here. This makes today, the day after Mini ran away, a better day. I feel sad about losing Mini, and nobody has found her yet, even though Suleiman and Ori have been looking. To make me feel better, Nikki is taking me out to McDonalds for lunch, not the one I usually go to, but the one that is farther away and has a big playground on the inside. She is walking too fast for me though. She is wearing the kind of short shorts that the older girls at school are not allowed to wear. They make her legs super long, which maybe is why I can't keep up with her. Last year she was like the big kids at school, but now she's different.

She looks more like a mom than like a kid. She is wearing make-up on her eyes that reminds me of the black fur around Massarat's eyes. Massarat's face is mostly orange and white but she has thin black circles around her eyes. They make the green of her eyes jump out at you like the jack-in-the-box at the puppet centre.

I am following behind her, looking at her long hair hanging down her back. Her hair is blond like my mom's, but with more white in it, not white like the lunch lady's hair, but white like the moon.

"Wait up," I yell. She looks back at me and stops.

"Sorry," she says. She waits and grabs a hold of my hand so that we can walk together. Mostly she is nice to me. Someday, she said, I can come for a sleep over at her house where she lives with her dad and her stepmom and some other sisters that are not me. But I know she can be mean too, because I've seen her fighting with my mom. Nikki can do that same thing with her eyes that my mom does, make them change shape from round to flat. She told me once that she beat up a kid at school too, a girl who called her a ho.

"So what's been going on, Tiff?" she asks. I talk the whole way to McDonalds about how I was going to be friends with a rat that turned into four kittens and about how The Grey One lives in Room 11 with Orianthi, who is the same person as Orion, and how the troublesome twins live in Room 6 with Suleiman and how Mini has a cold and has run away and is missing.

"Wow," she says. "Cool. Except for the part about Mini running away."

While we eat our Big Macs and French fries with ketchup I ask her if she's ever played Wild Things.

"What's that?"

I explain about Max, the king, and about the wild things that do the rumpusing, and the magic words.

"I remember that book," she says. "Did they read it to you in kindergarten?"

"It's a book too?"

"Sure. It's about this naughty kid in a wolf suit. There's some kind of minotaur on the cover."

"What's a minotaur?"

"Must be one of the wild things. You want to read it? We could go to the library, see if they have it." I'm so excited I practically fall off of my chair. Our class went on a trip to the library, but I've never been back there again. Mrs. Lynch said that they let you take books home for free, just like we do at the library at school. But the real library is way bigger than our school library.

The library is a long way away from McDonalds, but I don't mind walking so far. Nikki holds my hand the whole way and tries to teach me how to whistle. She also tells me two secrets: she has a boyfriend now and she has a tattoo.

"Me and Mike got them together," she says. "Dad said I could. But don't tell Mom. She'll say I'm too young. I'll show you later, 'k?"

Waiting for the red light to change she looks down at me and asks, "Is Mom using again?"

"Using what?"

She frowns at me. "You know that I used to live with Mom, when I was a little kid, but that Dad took me away because—"

"Because Mom was too sick to look after you."

"She wasn't *sick*, she was using. I guess you could say she was sick *because* she was using."

"Using what?" I ask again. Nikki is making me frus-ter-ated.

"Drugs. She was such a crack-head. Strung out all the time. Dad came one time, found me alone in the apartment, took me home. When mom got there she was too wrecked to even notice I was gone." I am not sure about the words that Nikki is saying, about mom being cracked and wrecked. It sounds like she's a broken car, like the ones I see behind Nap-Away. Nikki pulls me forward when the light turns green.

"When someone takes drugs it can make them do crazy stuff, stupid stuff. And they act different, mean or sad or whatever. Sometimes they forget important things, like that they need to buy groceries for their kid," Nikki says.

"Do you think she's using?" I ask.

"I thought she looked pretty rough this morning. Made me wonder." She stops walking and looks at me with a serious face. "Don't ask her though." I shake my head no. How would I know if she is using drugs or not? Everyone can be mean or sad or do stupid stuff. Mrs. Lynch says we are at school to learn not to do mean things, like being a bully, and not to do stupid stuff, like pushing on the stairs or running in the hallway. Except she doesn't call them stupid, she says making bad choices. But what if my mom leaves me alone at Nap-Away and forgets about me? What if she doesn't notice I am lost, like Mini is?

When we get to the library, the librarian takes us to the shelf where the book is. *Where the Wild Things Are*, by Maurice Sendak. Maybe Nikki doesn't know that I can read, because she reads the book out loud to me. But I like listening to stories. It's sad when Max sails away and leaves the wild things behind, because they love him so much. But I guess it's good too because if he stayed with his wild things then he wouldn't go back to his mom. I'm excited to take the book back to Nap-Away and show it to Orianthi, but I can't. I don't have a library card.

The librarian says I can get one, I just need to bring my mom with me and she can give them the address and everything. Nikki says she has a card, but it's at home with her school stuff.

I read the book a few more times to myself before we go, so that I will remember it. I look at the pictures and I practice rolling my eyes and gnashing my teeth, so that I will be an even better wild thing next time. When we leave, Nikki decides to get her nails painted at the place beside the library. She picks a blue colour that is the same as her eyes. I sit in a big red chair and look at myself in a mirror and make wild thing faces. They make me feel scary and brave.

ORI

So my little Iff has a sister. Who knew? She's beautiful. Not beautiful like Iff though. The sister's all pale, bloodless like a vampire. See-through skin, with a watershed of blue veins leading to her heart. White blond hair like a million icicles shimmering. Eyes like their mom. The faded blue of a flower pressed in a book. You can see right through to the words behind. I can't look into them for long.

"This is Nikki," Iff says. They're holding hands. Iff is grinning.

"Hey," I say. "Ori."

"You could call her Orianthi if she's a girl and Orion if she's a boy," Iff says. "She can be both." She stands on her toes. Bounces. "But I don't think at the same time." Bounces again. Grins.

Nikki stares at me with her pale see-through eyes. I shiver. It feels great. And terrible. Like the hot flush when you pee your pants.

"What the—?" she says. "Don't mess with me. Whose junk do you got?" She juts her chin at my crotch. She's like a spitting cat, hackles raised. I try on Iff's grin, but lopsided. Then I try to quirk an eyebrow, like Moffit does. Haven't got that down yet though.

"Nikki has a tattoo," Iff blurts out. "Like your boyfriend does. But it's a secret."

"I don't have a boyfriend," I say. "Or a girlfriend."

"You're gonna show me. Right?" Iff tugs Nikki's arm and looks up at her, green eyes shining like fireworks. Damn, I miss my brother, miss his grey eyes looking at me like that. Miss their wildness, like storm clouds over the water.

"Sure, kiddo," she says, "I'll show you my tat." But she's looking right at me. My breath gets tangled up somewhere inside my lungs, refuses to come out. I keep looking into the blue.

"Can I show her The Grey One?" Iff asks. I nod and lead the way back to Room 11.

"Do you like kittens?" I ask Nikki. Give myself an imaginary kick. Lame.

"Duh," she says. "Only psychopaths don't like kittens." I try to redeem myself by shutting up. Iff fills in all the silence. Tells the story about finding the rat that turned into four kittens. Describes all the wild things that were in the library. Lists Moffit's tattoos.

"So what's your tattoo of?" I ask Nikki. She stares at me without blinking. I look down at my boots. She laughs.

"Guess," she says. So Iff and I try. Iff guesses a unicorn, a heart and a kitten. I guess Miley Cyrus's tongue, a wild thing, and a Dorito chip. A cheesy orange triangle on her shoulder blade.

"A butterfly?" Iff asks. Nikki shakes her head.

"I give up," Iff wails. Nikki leans down and whispers in her ear. Iff nods and smiles, looks satisfied.

"Hey, what about me?"

"I guess you'll just have to wait and see," Nikki says. I blush. She laughs again. I think the last time I blushed was in Grade 3, when I fell out of the school bus.

"So, I gotta go soon, Tiff," she says. "I better go check in with mom."

"Wait," I say. Iff and Nikki both look at me. I don't want her pale skin, inked with some mystery tattoo, to leave yet. I don't say anything else. Nikki shrugs.

"See ya," she says, and they turn to leave.

"Wait," I say again, grabbing her thin wrist. She looks at my hand, raises her eyebrows. They're the same pale moonlight colour as her hair. But I've got nothing that'll make her stay.

They go, and I'm left behind. Gripping loneliness tight against my own beating heart. I go back to my room and flop down on my bed. The Grey One curls up tight in the corner at my neck and collarbone, like it's made for him, and starts to purr. I'm yearning for things that aren't here: Carter's wolfish grey eyes, Nikki's pale skin, Moffit's laugh chasing away the bleakness. I reach a hand up, cup it around the small ball of fur pressed against me.

SULEIMAN

I wake with a start. It is still light outside, but it must be evening. Massarat is crying out from the locked carrier; her littermate answers from the bathroom, a muffled and thin meow. I reunite them. They touch noses, such a simple act of affection. They have no need of a home because they have each other. Perhaps this is why Yori is so in need of his brother.

I wonder, not for the first time, how Amina's death has affected Ahmed. Does he feel like a piece of himself is missing? I picture Ahmed, standing tall like a man, defying me earlier today. Despite everything, a part of me feels pride in my son. What was it he said? *We all need to heal.* There is truth in this wisdom. But, I think, why must we all be apart to heal? Perhaps what we need is not a separation, but a fresh start.

Of course Khadija needs to get away from our home. Every day she must look out the window to the driveway and re-live the moment she put the car into reverse, the moment that altered everything. She knows the accident was God's will and Amina has returned to God. This brings relief. But still, the driveway serves as a reminder each day of the tragedy. It is the same for me, I realize. Each time I walk towards our house, I must avert my glance from the driveway; but still, I hear each brick calling out Amina's name. By the time I arrive at the door, anger is already knocking inside my chest. But it does not need to continue in this way.

I pace back and forth along the threadbare carpet between the door of my room and the bathroom. I can't let Khadija go to Montreal with Ahmed. I will go with them. I feel a surge of resolve in my step, as I open the door and leave Nap-Away.

Our car is in the driveway and the curtains are drawn back, letting in the evening light. For the first time since leaving the motel, I falter.

Haven't I already done this today? I had such a clear sense of purpose this morning, and everything has already gone astray. But if I do nothing, tomorrow Khadija will be gone. I must at least tell her how I feel, tell her that I am ready to talk, ready to end the separation. And I can tell her that I can come to Montreal with her.

I have a key but I rap on the door instead. The door opens immediately and I am caught with my hand to my face, my thumb stroking the smooth surface of the mole over my left eye.

"Ahmed," I say, stepping forward without hesitation. "I must speak to your mother." Ahmed is forced to step aside as I walk forward.

"Dad, stop."

"I know you have good intentions, that you are protecting your mother. But if she is truly thinking of going to Montreal with you tomorrow, I must talk to her before she does. This decision affects me as well."

Ahmed sighs, nods his head. "She's in the kitchen."

I gather my breath, inflating my lungs so that my chest expands, and then exhaling swiftly. *Insha'Allah*, she will hear my plea.

"Khadija," I say, stepping across the threshold. She is seated at the small kitchen table, her hands cradled around a cup of tea. She startles when she sees me. Her face looks thinner, almost gaunt; her black eyes no longer remind me of a wild horse, but of a sorrowful dog, caged and alone.

"Did Ahmed not tell you?"

"Yes, yes. He said that you are going to Montreal. I think it's a good idea. It will be good for you to be away from this house."

Khadija nods her head, looks back down at her tea.

"You've always loved Montreal," I say. I pull out a chair, and sit near her. I reach my hand forward to touch a lock of her black hair, so shiny that the lights overhead cast a halo around the crown of her downturned head. She flinches, ever so slightly, and I stop. But I don't withdraw my hand; it stays there, suspended in the air, unable to touch her, unable to pull away.

"Khadija," I say, "I know that there is a problem between us. You were right that we needed to be apart. It has helped me to see more clearly how I have turned away from you. How I have blamed you. I have handled my anger poorly." I wish to take hold of her hand but I restrain myself, lay my hand down, palm open, on the table between us.

She turns her black gaze on me, and it is my turn to flinch. Her sorrowful eyes are burning through me. "I feel like I have lost you. You have become a different man. My Suleiman is gone. I don't know you any longer; don't recognize this anger in you, this coldness." She takes a shaky inhale. "You have always tried so hard, tried so hard to do what is right, tried to be a better man. But now, it is like you are being swallowed up by this anger. You have stopped trying." She shakes her head slightly. "We are changed," she says, the words punctuated by a small gulping hiccup.

"I am…" I begin. My thoughts falter. I wish to protest what Khadija has said, but it all sounds true. "I am changed," I say, "but I am also trying to find my way back to you, back to us. I am still the same man inside. You have not lost me. I will show you, prove it to you. Let me come to Montreal with you. It will be a fresh start for both of us."

Khadija's dark eyes widen, she opens her mouth to speak, then closes it again. She places her tea down, and stands. She takes a single step back, and another.

"No. No, you will not come with me. Not now."

"But…"

"NO!" She launches the word at me; I feel it like a blow. I wait for more words, want to revel in them, feel the sting of each lashing syllable. Perhaps if we can yell at one another, say all the unsaid things, purge our feelings, then we can rise up again, weak at the knees, but free from the blame.

But instead of speaking, she starts to scream. It starts low, deep in her belly, rippling through the kitchen, then rises in intensity, in pitch, turning into a piercing cry that seems unstoppable. It perforates my internal organs; I can feel the bleeding start, deep within my belly.

Ahmed is suddenly there, standing beside me.

"You need to leave," Ahmed says. "Now."

I don't argue. I step out of the kitchen and into the hall. Amina smiles down at me from the portrait in the hallway, her expression knowing. I wrench the frame down, turn it away, so that it faces the wall. I leave. I don't know how long the scream lasts for, but I am still hearing it when I reach Nap-Away.

TIFFANY

I dream that I am lost in the woods. I am walking and there are crunchy leaves under my feet. I'm not alone though, because my wild things are there too. Some of them are mean, and some of them are sad, and some of them are doing bad stuff.

There are five of them. One of them has shiny blue claws and round black eyes. One of them has enormous wings that are covered in feathers, all different colours, like a rainbow. One of them has a unicorn horn and black tattoos on his arms. One of them has a rat-face that is long and grey and whiskery. The littlest one of them is lost. In the dream my mom is looking for me, but she can't find me.

When I wake up my bed is wet. I haven't peed my bed in a long time. I whisper my mom awake. I think she will be mad, but she's not, not really. She sighs and she says shit and she huffs around pulling the sheets off my bed and throwing them in the bathtub, but when I tell her I had a bad dream she stops.

"Me too," she says, and she hugs me tight. I feel squished and I can't breathe right but I don't mind. Then she lights a cigarette and has a smoke.

"Come sleep in my bed," she says. When we snuggle up she sings to me, one song about ponies and one about New York and one about stars.

"My dad use to sing to me about the little ponies going 'round and 'round," she says, "when I had bad dreams." She sighs, and I can feel her warm smoky breath on my cheek. "But other than that he was a real asshole." I almost fall asleep but wake up again. She is still sitting beside me, smoking a cigarette, stroking my head. All the wild things that I dreamed about have gone away and I don't hear their sniffing noses or growling sounds anymore.

"Go to sleep," she whispers. Then she snuggles down beside me and I press against her and burrow into her armpit. I sniff in the smell of her hair, which smells like pink flowers and raspberries, mixed up with the smell of cigarette smoke.

"No more bad dreams," she says and she kisses me on the forehead. I don't think she's using.

ORI

I find Mini. She is under a low rambling bush, on the next lot over, at the used car dealership. Moffit and I had looked there yesterday, and the day before, and the day before that, with Iff. We'd looked everywhere: under the toppled fridge, in the secret spaces of an abandoned armchair, inside a milk crate and an overturned garbage bin, through the leaf mold and litter, in a decrepit shed with a rotted wood door hanging loose on its hinges. In and under the broken-down cars. Other cats haunt the place. Someone's been trying to look after them. There are traps scattered around, bowls of food. A gnarled white cat bared yellowed fangs at Moffit. A matted black cat with green eyes like Iff's raised her hackles at me but stayed frozen in place. A thin grey tabby hesitated between bolting and coming near, finally rubbing a figure-eight around my boots. But no kittens until today.

Mini's dead. Her black fur is sticking up in sharp little clumps. Death has flattened her, sucked away her kittenness. She's a shrump, a kitten shrump, just a small rise in the earth that marks where a kitten once was. There are a few flies buzzing around her, scouting for rot. I scrounge around, find a KFC bag to cover her up with, tuck it around her body. The tip of her tail sticks out. Dead kittens suck.

Back at Nap-Away, I find Suleiman in the parking lot, sitting on his green chair, feeding his pigeons. He stands when he sees me, steps forward in anticipation, and the pigeons rise up around him in a flurry of beating wings.

"I found the kitten," I say. I shrug. Shake my head. Bite down on my bottom lip. Squeeze my eyes to keep the tears in. Stupid.

"Ah," says Suleiman. He looks over at the mosque, then up at the sky and nods his head a couple of times. "*Al-Mumit*, the taker of life," he murmurs under his breath. "Just as *Allah* gives life to us, so too is he the bringer of death, neh?"

He gives me an awkward pat on my arm. I don't mean to, don't want to, but I stumble forward against his chest all the same. He smells like the shawarma place and man-sweat. The cry is a quick one, for a dead black kitten under a bush. Mostly for that, but for some other things too. I pull away just as fast, wipe a hand across my eyes.

"I'm going to the dollar store to buy a shovel. I'm going to bury her," I say.

He looks to his left, to the door of Room 5.

"No," I say. "Don't. I'll tell her later. I'll tell her…"

"It's a hard story to tell," he says. "You must be brave and kind." He looks back to the sky now, where the flock of pigeons is circling up and away from Nap-Away. He hasn't told me the story of his daughter yet, but I know. I know his story is a hard one to tell.

***

THE TALE OF THE LITTLE BLACK KITTEN
AS TOLD TO IFF BY ORIANTHI

Once upon a time four kittens were born in a land not so far away. The kittens were all the same, and they were all different. They all had stubby tails that pointed up to the sky, fat little bellies and round blue eyes, pink pads like jelly beans on their feet. There was a grey kitten that was fluffier than all the others. There was a black one, who was tinier than the others. And there were calico twins—black and white and orange—who were very much alike, except one had black rings around her eyes and the other didn't.

The kittens lived in the wilderness with lots of other cats. Their home was under a giant oak tree that marked the border between a castle and the woods. Each day the kittens scampered about with their mother, learning how to be cats. They crept up on each other on their pink-padded feet and leapt on each other with ferocious kitten pounces so that they could learn to catch mice. They washed each others' ears and muzzles and stubby tails so that they could learn to be clean cats. They took catnaps in the sunshine, all curled up together. They learned to purr when they were happy and to hiss when they were scared. They learned to use their whiskers to feel where they were going in the night, and they learned to scratch at the earth to hide their stinky poops. They were good little kittens.

One day hunters came to the wilderness. They set traps for the wild cats. There was food in the traps, but the kittens were not interested in it. They were still babies, and they liked to press their little paws, with all the pink jelly-bean pads and the tiny sharp nails, into their mother's belly, kneading it until sweet warm milk squirted out. But the mother was hungry, hungry from making all that milk for her kittens, hungry from eating only tiny mouthfuls of mice, still hungry after a long harsh winter. She went into the trap to eat the food, and the hunters came and took her away.

The kittens yowled for their mother to come back, but she didn't, and by nightfall they knew that they were alone in the big, big world. They slept together in a tangled kitten pile, dreaming about their mother and the big metal trap that stole her away. In the morning the kittens set out to explore the world. Perhaps they could find their mother, because they missed her so much. Perhaps they could find some milk, because they were so hungry. They didn't find their mother and they didn't find their milk, but they found something else—a little girl!

The girl lived in the castle by the oak tree, a castle called Near-and-Far-Away. The girl was human, but there was talk in the kingdom that her father was an oak-tree fairy. If you looked at her closely, you would see that she had leafy green eyes, brown acorn skin, and wild hair like the rough black bark of the oak tree. She was as still and quiet as the oak. She wore an acorn around her neck, and carried an oak stick that some said was a wand and others said was a weapon. She could speak with the oak trees, and she listened to the whispers from their leaves.

This little girl was brave and kind, and when she saw the kittens, alone without their mother, she brought them back to the castle, back to Near-and-Far-Away, so that she could care for them. The kittens loved their new home, and they loved the little girl. But kittens are curious, everyone knows that. One day the little black kitten found an open doorway in the castle. The kitten saw a little blue butterfly fluttering near the ground. She should have known better, but she was just a kitten, and so she left the castle, all alone, to chase after the butterfly. And when she did she got lost, so very, very lost. Everyone searched for the kitten, the little girl, all the knights and squires and ladies of the castle, but none could find her. And though they searched for many long days and long nights, they would never find her. I will tell you why.

In another land, far, far away, so far away that you could never find it, even if you travelled through the spring blossoms until the snow fell, there lived another little girl. Even though she was still a child, she had been told to go on a long and perilous journey without her mother or father or brother. She travelled for many long days and long nights, through dark woods and over treacherous mountains, until she came to a magical place.

There were golden apples and sweet honey to eat, a river to dip her bare toes into, a willow tree for her to climb, and a small cottage with a cozy bed for her to sleep in. There was even a horse there, a beautiful white horse that she named Winter. In this magical place it never grew cold or snowed, but she remembered long ago, playing in the snow with her brother, and it made her happy to think of winter sometimes. Winter the Horse was a good friend. Together they rode through the meadows and explored alongside the river and ate the golden apples. At night the little girl would brush Winter's mane and feed him carrots and kiss him goodnight before leaving him in his stable.

She would curl up in her bed and look for the moon through her tiny window. Sometimes she would listen to the wolves from afar begin to howl, and she would grow lonely. One night she became so lonely that she began to sing a song. Though beautiful, it was not a happy song; it was filled with longing and loneliness. Anyone who heard this beautiful song yearned to be near to the little girl, to take away her loneliness. Winter begin to whinny in his stable, and the wolves padded down the mountainside, howling their own mournful songs in reply. A swift red fox crept into her room and brushed against her with his white-tipped tail. The girl stopped singing and began to pet the fox, but he soon grew restless and began to pace in quick circles around the room, for he was too wild to stay indoors for long. The girl began her song again, and a trio of squirrels climbed in her window, chattering in distress. They were silly animals and they made her laugh with their busy paws and their bushy tails, but they soon got distracted by nuts and seeds and other squirrel-things, and disappeared back out the window.

Once more, she began her song. A great white bird swooped down and landed on the roof of her little cottage. The bird began to sing with the girl, because it was as lonely as her. The great white bird was the only one left of its kind in the kingdom and it wished for a mate, to fly high over the mountains with, back to the sea. The girl and the bird sang their lonely songs together, but they were lonely for different things, and the bird soon flew away again.

In the silence that followed the bird's departure, the girl heard, far far away, another song just like hers. A sad and lonely song that drew the girl out of her bed. Though it was very dark outside and she felt afraid, she set out to see who was so lonely and what she could do to help.

She stepped outside the cottage and strained her ears. Yes, she could still hear the song, faint and far away. She crept out into the darkness. The moon saw her and came out from behind its clouds so that she could better see her way. She followed a little path away from her cottage towards the wilderness. On the edge of the wilderness stood a majestic oak tree. At the base of the tree she stopped, for it seemed like the song was coming from inside the tree! She placed her hands against the bark and pressed her ear against it. Yes, she could hear the song more clearly now, and it sounded like a little kitten, crying for its mother, lonely little mewls that hurt her heart. As she moved around the oak tree, hands to the bark, she came across a small door in the tree that she had never noticed before. If there is a door, she thought, I should go through, even though I do not know what I will find. And because she was brave and kind, she did go through.

The door in the oak tree was a door between two worlds. The little girl stepped out of the oak tree into a world that she felt she knew, once, long ago. She thought she saw, in the distance, a man who looked just like her father. She called out to him, but he turned away. No, it couldn't be her father. And she thought she saw, over a little hill, the place where she used to say her prayers. She took a few steps towards it, but each time she did, it seemed to get a little farther away. No, it couldn't be the place that she remembered. Just then she heard the sad little song, and she knelt down and found a little black kitten, all alone. The kitten was tiny and sick, so she tucked her close to her heart and began to sing to her. But this time, she sang a warm song, a lullaby, to the kitten.

Carrying the kitten, she turned and stepped back towards the tree. She thought she saw, just on the other side of the tree, a little girl who looked like her. Maybe she was looking for this kitten too; maybe she had come here because of the pitiful, lonely meows. She held the little black kitten out to her, but the girl did not take her, even though she had been searching for the kitten for days.

This girl, standing on the other side of the tree, wanted to take the kitten, because she had been missing her, and because she loved her, so very, very much. But she did not, because she had heard the song of the lonely girl from far, far, away, all the way through the door in the oak tree between the worlds. She had heard the song, even though no one else in her world had, because she had a little bit of fairy magic in her, oak-tree fairy magic.

"You should keep the kitten, because you have been so lonely. Please keep her safe and warm," the little girl said, and the leaves of the oak tree sang a happy little song filled with the whispering sound of the wind.

"I will. I promise," the lonely girl from far, far away replied. The two girls reached out and hugged each other goodbye, with the little black kitten between them, and then the little girl opened the door in the oak tree and stepped back through into her own world.

And that is why, though they searched for many long days and nights, the knights and squires and ladies never did find the kitten. For she is far, far away, curled up on the bed of a little girl just like you.

"Mini's gone forever?" Iff asks. I nod my head yes.

"Is the story true?" she asks.

"Um-hum."

"But I don't have an acorn necklace."

"Yes, you do," I reach into my pocket and pull out a golden chain with an acorn hanging from it. Moffit helped me make it earlier, after we buried the kitten. Iff's eyes widen.

"It's like from a fairy tale," she whispers, touching it with a fingertip. She hesitates and then pulls her hand away. Looks down at her feet.

"But I never heard the sad song. I'm not special," she says.

"I know an oak-tree fairy when I see one." I slide the chain over her black curls, plant a kiss on her forehead. "Sorry your kitten's gone."

 PART THREE

SULEIMAN

I am lying in my bed. The light through the shades tells me that it is afternoon. I can smell cat urine, last night's shawarma, which I had lost my appetite for and left tossed on the floor, and my own body odour, sharp and stale, all at the same time. I pull myself up, struggling against a great inertia that has trapped me here in my room for days. I try to count the days since I saw Khadija. Six, maybe seven? I don't even know the date today.

I sit on the edge of my bed, studying my feet. They are much larger than most men's, wider too. I remember how they grew before I did, gave me an awkward heavy-footed gait when I was young, stranding me in pre-puberty with flipper-like feet that I had to lift high and flip over with each step. They have carried me from my boyhood in Egypt all the way to another continent; carried me to Khadija, striding down the street towards me in a Montreal blizzard, and now have carried me away from her.

Where should they carry me to now? They are not rooted to one place, not like my father's feet, and his father's before him. Should they chase after Khadija and Ahmed, go to Montreal, just to be in their proximity? Should they walk down the street, away from Nap-Away, turn the corner and carry me back to our house? It is sitting empty now, awaiting my return. For so many weeks I've dreamed about returning to my home, but it wasn't supposed to be like this.

There is no point to leaving Nap-Away, no point in trying to end my exile. The exile will await me at my bungalow on the quiet crescent, it will await me if I leave Toronto, and it will await me if I return to Montreal, or to my childhood home in Egypt.

I am displaced. There is no longer a home for me to return to. My life with Khadija, with Ahmed and Amina, has shaped my identity. I remember the same feeling, when my family first came to Canada when I was a boy, struggling with a feeling of wanting to go back to a home that no longer existed. But I no longer feel displaced in that way. My parents are no longer alive, my children have both been born in Canada, and I know this city better than I remember the streets of Cairo.

Was it only last summer that we went, all four of us, driving east along Kingston Road, on our way to Sandbanks Provincial Park for a day of picnicking at the lake together? I consider the possibility of leaving the city now, of driving nowhere, anywhere but here. But the inertia weighs me down. What is the point of leaving? There seems to be no point to anything at all. At least I have the kittens to care for if I stay.

I watch them chase each other, tumble into a wrestle. Massarat locks Rainbow's head in an embrace with her front paws, proceeds to kick her twin in the belly with her hind legs. They are wild things indeed. I smile, thinking of Tiffany, eyes ablaze, a circle of green leaves crowning her curls, charging at me across the parking lot. No, I will not leave Nap-Away yet. I slide my giant feet into my sandals, head outside to look for Tiffany.

I find her in the parking lot, jumping over a pink skipping rope, singing a quiet rhyme to herself. She smiles and waves when she sees me, skips towards me.

"Can I come see Rainbow and Massarat?"

"Of course," I reply, leading her back to my room. She follows me in and stops.

"Phew. It's stinky in here." I nod my head in agreement; I can smell the odours even more strongly now, after breathing in the summer air.

"I must clean up. I have been lazy. Perhaps we can take the kittens outside to play." Tiffany bites her lower lip, her green eyes lowered.

"What if they get lost? Like Mini?"

Ahh, Mini. The death of the kitten has been troubling me for many days. All that happens, both creation and destruction, is by God's command. I believe this. There is no point in believing in good fortune or bad, lucky charms or dire omens, for all events are in the hands of God.

But since Amina's death I have felt a need to ask questions. Why did God choose this time for Mini to die? I wish to understand. A series of events led to the moment Yori found her, and I have been trying to follow them back to their origin. I think that perhaps if I can understand this, I will have greater insight into the order, the structure to my own unravelling. I wish to untangle each act, each decision, each thought, each word that led to the moment that Khadija unleashed her scream. Somewhere there is a thread that I need to follow, that will allow me to weave a different ending. But no, God has been guiding me, God is the master weaver. These thoughts are leading me astray. I shake my head swiftly, chase the questions away.

What if the kittens get lost, Tiffany has asked. What, indeed?

"I saw a woman at the pet store who had her cat in a harness, with a leash. Perhaps we could do the same for our kittens, neh?"

"I thought a leash was only for a dog!"

"I always thought that too, but I guess it's not true."

"I've never been to a pet store."

"I will take you," I say.

I knock on the door to Room 5, but Tiffany shakes her head at me.

"She's not there," she says.

"Who's looking after you today?"

Tiffany shrugs. "Lots of times Ori does now, but he's not here today." I consider this information. At one time it would have been unthinkable for me to take a child that is not my own away without permission. But now, many unthinkable things have happened. What is one more? Where is her mother anyway? She shouldn't leave Tiffany alone like she does for hours on end, playing in the parking lot of a motel. It's no way for a child to be cared for.

We leave the motel together, hand in hand. As we walk, Tiffany tells me a story about Mini. It is a very complicated one. There are the four kittens, fairies in an oak tree, a horse in winter, a castle, and two little girls.

"They are both brave and kind," Tiffany says. The words echo in my head. Brave. Kind. These are my own words to Yori. But who am I to say these words? In the face of Amina's death, and Khadija's grief and guilt, I was neither. My thumb slides across my mole, once, twice, a third time.

"She had to go away, somewhere so far away that no one can go there, even if they climbed a mountain for a year! And she had to leave her mom and her dad and her brother, so she was all alone without her family. That's why Mini had to go and live with her," Tiffany says. I stop walking abruptly, yanking Tiffany to a stop at the curb. How can it be that Tiffany is telling me the story of Amina?

"What?" she asks. "The light is green, Suleiman."

"Please, can you tell me the whole story again, from the beginning?"

TIFFANY

When my mom comes home she has a new boyfriend with her. His name is Tim. He is wearing a red baseball cap and his face is covered in tiny whiskers. He has white skin like my mom, brown eyes, and a crooked nose. He is carrying a box of beer and a pizza. I want to show my mom how Rainbow likes to walk on her new leash and roll in the sunshine, but she says maybe later, so we eat the pizza instead.

Tim likes my mom. He makes her sit on his lap and he holds on tight to her stomach and he kisses her neck. He pretends I am not there. Or maybe I have become invisible, like a super-hero. But right after I think that he says, "I thought we were gonna party. Can you get rid of the kid for a while?" My mom looks at me. Maybe she wants to get rid of me and maybe she doesn't.

I can't tell.

"Do you want to go see if Ori is home?" she says. I nod yes. She walks me over to Room 11 and knocks on the door. Ori says that I can hang out and my mom leaves.

"Are you a boy or a girl today?" I ask.

"Whatever," he says, with a shrug. "Mostly a boy." He is eating a bag of Doritos that he shares with me. Then I play with The Grey One. He is getting bigger and fluffier and wilder. He likes to use his little nails for climbing up things, and he likes to hide and then pounce when you are not looking.

Orion asks me about Nikki, so I tell him she is sixteen years old, so she is old enough to wear makeup and shorty shorts and to have a tattoo and a boyfriend named Mike.

"She has a boyfriend?" Orion asks.

"They got matching tattoos."

"So what's her tattoo, anyway?" But I don't tell the secret, which makes Orion laugh. Then I tell him that Nikki can whistle between her teeth and play the trumpet and that she beat up a girl at school who called her a ho. This makes Orion laugh too. I'm not sure which part was funny though.

I ask him to tell me the fairy tale about Mini, so we snuggle on the bed and he tells it again. The story has all the same parts but this time there is also a big adventure for Winter the horse because he gets lost in the mountains. Later we decide to go outside and look for stars. I think I see a shooting star, but Orion says that it might just be an airplane. We see the moon peeking out from behind some clouds so we do some howling together, like we are the wolves in the mountains where Winter lives.

While we are out in the parking lot we see Tim leaving my room. So I wave bye to Orion and go home.

"I'm not feeling so good, baby," my mom says when I come in. "Tim wouldn't even stay. Said I was bringing him down. Wrecking his high." She stumbles a little and bangs her knee against the bed. Then she runs really fast to the bathroom and throws up. I don't see it but I hear the sounds. She is sick two more times before she comes back.

"I just wanna feel good, you know?" she says. She is walking kind of funny. She reminds me of the Pinocchio puppet at school that is on strings. It always jitters around when you try to make it walk or dance. It has funny red shoes with pointy toes. Someone tried to bite them once, because there are teeth marks in the paint.

"But I feel like shit." She sits down on the edge of her bed, then stands up again. "Those damn lice are all over me again," she says. She sits down again and bounces right back up.

"I think they only go in your hair," I say. "That's what Orion said."

"Well, something's biting at my skin," she says and then she scratches at her arm and at her face. "Damn bugs are everywhere." Her nails leave red lines on her cheek. "I think I'm gonna be sick again," she says. She sits back down on the bed though, instead of going to the bathroom. Then she stands up and takes a step towards the tiny sink hiding in our little kitchen that my mom says used to be a closet. But she doesn't get all the way there and she throws up all over the floor. It smells bad, worse even then when Massarat and Rainbow had poops that were all wet and splooshy. The smell makes me feel kind of sick too. I can feel all my pizza and Doritos moving around in my tummy trying to decide where to go.

After she throws up my mom holds on to the wall. She is changing colours like that lizard that Mrs. Lynch read us a story about. I can't remember what it is called, but it can be green or pink or yellow or grey if it wants to. If it is green it could hide in the leaves and if it was pink it could hide in something like cotton candy, I guess, if there was some in the jungle. It has weird eyes that can look all over the place. One eye could look at the moon in the sky and the other might be looking at a bug on the ground.

My mom was green before the throw up, but now she is so white that she looks like the sheet on the bed. She is holding on to the wall and being white and then a bit of blood starts to drip from her nose. She wipes it away with the back of her hand, but more drips out. I am wishing that Tim had stayed, even though he wanted to get rid of me and he didn't like my mom's party, because I think maybe he could have taken care of her and made her better.

My mom starts to say something, but it comes out without any words, just a sound that is all gurgly and choky at the same time. Then the worst thing happens. She falls down on the floor. Some of her pretty hair lands in the throw-up. She doesn't say 'gross' or try to get up or anything. She just stays there.

"Mom, get up," I say. I don't want her to be sick anymore. She starts to shake all over her whole body. Every bit of her is shivering. I make a little scream. It sounds just like Massarat when Suleiman stepped on her tail.

I run right out of our room into the parking lot. There's nobody there but the dark. I go to Suleiman's door and I bang on it with my fists. Bang, bang, bang. I want the sound to be a bigger sound, but my hands are too small.

"Suleiman," I yell. "My mom fell down." I bang some more. "My mom is sick." A hiccup sound comes out of my mouth. I want Suleiman to open his door, but he doesn't. "Help," I say. "Help."

I try to decide what I would do if I was brave. Maybe I would be brave enough to run to the phone booth on the other side of the parking lot near the road and see if the phone is fixed so that I could call the number nine-one-one. Maybe I would be brave enough to roll my mom over and get her out of the throw up, even if some got on my hands. Or maybe I would be brave enough to go to the bus stop on Kingston Road, because I can see a man waiting there for the bus. He is wearing big headphones and he is dancing and the streetlights are shining down on him. But I'm not supposed to talk to strangers because of stranger-danger.

I start to run through the dark across the parking lot towards Room 11 where Orion is but before I get there I trip and I fall forward onto my hands and knees because I am running faster than my feet can go. I do a little slide on the ground. I can feel the skin on my knees rubbing off onto the pavement. It stings like how I think it stings if bees were biting me. I start to cry.

I want my mom to get up and come to the door of Room 5 and yell at me. 'Tiffany, get your ass back in here,' she might say, or 'sorry, baby, I gotta go to the doctor. I'm feeling like crap.' I look back at our room. The door is open and the light is spilling out. It looks happy, like Nap-Away wants you to go in. It doesn't look like anything bad is happening at all.

ORI

I'm feeling kind of bummed out. After Iff leaves, I wander along Kingston Road. The neighbourhood has started to seem like home. Places that I recognize radiate out from Nap-Away. Suleiman's mosque, Zak's A-plus Auto, the ugly apartments across the street, the KFC, the 7-11, the library, The Best Shawarma Place.

It's dark, but not really. Street lights, headlights, flashing signs, lit up windows. Big city, bigger lights. I see red-baseball-cap guy, the one who just left Room 5, strutting his stuff on the other side of Kingston. He's talking nasty to a couple of teenage girls, leering, trying to put his hands where he shouldn't. Thinking he can do what he wants, to who he wants. I'm mostly not scared of guys and the shit they give, but tonight I am. Tonight I feel little inside. I feel no bigger than Iff. And I'm just like her, wishing for white horses and howling wolves, getting dead kittens instead. Wishing for shooting stars, getting airplanes blinking in the night sky.

I walk on. I feel like I'm lugging my insides around, my guts, my lungs, my sodden heart.

I'm thinking about Carter, wondering where he is, right this minute. I just want him back. The quest is tiring me out. They don't talk about this part in the epics. There are dragons, ogres with spears, fisted men-in-black, desperate moments when all seems lost. But when does the hero ever just curl up on the sidewalk, too tired to go on?

Once, Moffit asked me what the plan was. Carter and I never needed one. The plan was always unspoken: stick together and survive. What is the damn plan? Why did Carter have to go and mess things up by leaving? I've never been Carter-less for this long. I can't imagine limping on through life without him. I'm crippled by twinlessness.

I stop at the shawarma place on the way back, pick up something for me and Suleiman. He's been up at night lately, pacing the parking lot at midnight. I leave the shop, trot down the street, paper take-out bag in hand. An ambulance soars past, wailing. A Husky, up ahead of me, stops in his tracks, throws back his grey muzzle. Howls. A long, low lament. The sounds mingle, rising and falling in unison. Crazy dog. I'm laughing, until I see the ambulance swerve across three lanes and turn in to Nap-Away's parking lot. I can see a police car there already, lights blinking out danger in stark colours. A flashing chant: red for fire, white for death, blue for distress, red for fire, white for death, blue for distress.

I sprint the rest of the way back, shawarma bouncing against my thigh. Everything's probably fine. But maybe not. I want everything to be fine. The dead kitten, no Carter, Suleiman pacing like a caged animal, Iff's mother all strung out. That's enough trouble already, isn't it?

Nap-Away's yellow walls are reflecting the flashing lights of the police car and the ambulance. The colours are too loud for the night; they scream trouble. I skid to a halt beside the ambulance. It's parked outside of the first row of rooms, where Suleiman and Iff live. Iff's door is wide open and the ambulance attendants are wheeling a stretcher into the room. Suleiman stands outside of his room, with Iff in his arms, holding on to him like he's a life raft.

I race over to Suleiman. "What's going on?"

"Something woke me. I was dreaming about Amina. She was riding on a white horse, and the hooves were pattering against the ground, *thunk-thunk-thunk*. She looked so happy, waving at me." He sighs, rubs his thumb across his eyelid. "I woke up and thought I should look for her. But that doesn't make any sense, I know." I try to peer into Iff's room, see what's going on. Wait for Suleiman to finish his story.

"But I looked, as if I might see a white horse galloping across the parking lot." He laughs sharply. "That's when I saw Tiffany, on her hands and knees, alone. And when I went to look I found her mother lying unconscious on the floor in their room." Suleiman shakes his head. "She looks bad, very bad. I couldn't help her. I called 911."

"Hey," I say, touching Iff. "Hey, Iff." Her back is to me. All I see is a scraped and bloody knee, the curve of her skinny back, her little back bones pushing through the thin cotton of her t-shirt like a row of tiny pebbles, a tangle of curls hiding her face.

"What about Iff? Tiffany? Where will she go? Are the police taking her?" My belly feels tight, ready for the blow of a fist. I want to grab her and run for it. "Will Children's Aid take her?"

Suleiman frowns at me. Shakes his head sharply.

"She will stay with me."

"But—"

"There is no but," he hisses. "What do you want me to do? Send her alone in a police car? Where would she spend the night? Who would take care of her? Strangers? No! Besides, these police are fools. They think she is my daughter. They think we are the neighbours. I'm not going to tell them otherwise."

The police officers are standing to the side, talking. The bigger one has a bald head that shines red, blue, white, red, blue, white. He is laughing. His partner is leaning back on the car, arms crossed, nodding his head. Nothing's wrong, that's what they seem to be saying.

"She'll be furious when she finds out you've got her."

"What would she prefer? That I tell the police I found her daughter crawling on her hands and knees in the parking lot? How she leaves her alone for hours at a time? That I call the Children's Aid, tell them what I see, what I hear? That she buys her drugs from a teenage boy like you?"

He shakes his head vehemently. "Then they will both be lost. Each alone, without the other."

The ambulance attendants emerge, wheeling Iff's mother out of the room. She looks like she might be dead.

"Is she…?" I ask, making a slicing gesture across my neck.

"I don't know," Suleiman answers. "*Insha'Allah*, she will live."

I walk over to the paramedic as she closes the doors to the back of the ambulance.

"Will she be ok?" I ask.

"Who are you?"

"I babysit her kid." I start to glance over at Iff. Stop myself.

The paramedic looks at me sharply. "There's no kid in there."

I shrug. "She's got a couple of daughters. I look after the youngest sometimes, when she's around. They live with their dad." I scuff my boots on the ground. "I'll try and get a hold of her older daughter. What should I tell her? Where will her mom be at?"

"We're taking her to Scarborough General."

"Is she ok?"

"Can't say yet." She turns to leave.

"Wait. What happened?"

"What do you think?" she says. Mocking. Like the red, white and blue lights are flashing DRUGS KILL YOU on to the walls of Nap-Away. Like I'm too stupid to read the words. She hops into the ambulance and it pulls away.

I look back at Iff. She has turned her head to look at the ambulance leaving. Her glance slides over to my face. Her eyes are twin planets in the darkness, huge and remote. I walk back over to her. I try to smile.

"They told me she's gonna be ok." She says nothing. Just turns her head away and burrows it into Suleiman's shoulder.

SULEIMAN

Tiffany sleeps. I sit in the chair, which I have placed at the bedside, and watch her. The kittens sleep with her, compact balls of fur tucked in beside her tiny body. Usually she is so still, but in her sleep she moves about, flinging her arms, curling and uncurling, rolling over. The kittens squirm when she moves, stretch and readjust, but settle back into sleep.

I feel the same restlessness as Tiffany. My mind is tossing and turning, flinging thoughts that should not be into existence. I'm thinking of a new life for myself, and for Tiffany. I'm thinking of keeping Tiffany, of taking her away from Nap-Away, from her mother.

"It can't be," I whisper to myself. But still I continue to consider it. Amina's bedroom has remained unchanged—there are clothes, books, toys. Tiffany wears t-shirts that show her belly button, dirty shorts, broken sandals. Amina's clothes would fit her. She is skinnier than Amina, perhaps a little taller. I'm not sure. I try to remember Amina, but all that I see in my mind's eye is the portrait in the hallway, smiling down at me. Amina shakes her head at me. *Baba*, she scolds, *she is not yours to take.* I run my thumb across the mole. A shudder travels through my body. I shake my head, try to clear my thoughts.

Tiffany has no books but I know she can read. At the pet store she read aloud to me, a book about caring for your kitten. "Provide your kitten with a scratching post and reward her with toys, praise or treats when she uses it," she had read, and so we had asked the store clerk to show us the scratching posts and brought one home for Rainbow and Massarat. She would like Amina's storybooks, filled with pictures of animals, Ahmed's hand-me-down graphic novels.

She has no toys either. Amina's room has many toys that no one plays with any more. I see Tiffany sometimes, playing with a stick, a rock, a broken stroller. At least now she has the kittens to play with.

No toys, no books, and now she has no mother, at least not tonight. What if Shelley does not live? No one would come for Tiffany. There is no father, no family that I've ever seen. Perhaps the social worker, Miranda, would come in the fall, looking for her. But who else? And if they came, they would not find her. I could take Tiffany away from Toronto, move to another city. I think of Montreal fondly, but no, I can't go there, not with Khadija and Ahmed living there. Ottawa maybe, or Quebec City, or even Kingston. I shake my head sharply. These thoughts are ridiculous.

But my mind spins, and I start to wonder about my car. It is no longer in the driveway: Ahmed and Khadija would have driven it to Montreal. But I can lease a used one at Zak's A-plus Auto in the morning. *Stop!* I scold myself. I need to stop imagining that this is a good idea. I don't need God to help me decide this. I can bring judgement myself. What kind of man steals another's child?

I look back down at Tiffany's sleeping face and then I lean forward and kiss her forehead, carefully, as if she is a newborn. Then I stand and pull my duffle bag out from the dresser drawer and begin to stuff my clothing in to it.

TIFFANY

When I wake up in the morning I am confused because everything feels strange. I lie very still and wait. Massarat is pouncing on my hair. If she made a sound when she did this it would be 'pyong! pyong!' but she is as quiet as I am. Rainbow is sleeping in my armpit. My mom is not here. I feel a yucky feeling in my stomach when I think about her, like when I am really hungry or the opposite, when I have eaten a whole lot of jellybeans. I don't know where the ambulance took her. I don't know if she is lost now, or if I am lost, but one of us must be, because we're not together.

I know that I am in Suleiman's bed because the kittens are there, but also because I can smell his smell in the sheets. It smells good. I snuggle down deeper into the bed. But then I wonder where he is if I'm in his bed. I listen really hard but all I can hear are kitten sounds. Rainbow is purring and Massarat is licking at my hair, which is hardly a sound at all. What if everyone is lost? I jump out of the bed and run to the door and open it.

Suleiman is sitting on his green chair by the front door, feeding the pigeons. A few have fluttered away because of the noise I made, but the rest are singing their pigeon songs, which are just like lullabies you sing to babies.

"Good morning," he says.

"I thought you were gone," I say.

"I wouldn't leave you," he says. He gives me a pizza crust for the pigeons, so I rip it into pieces and toss it on to the parking lot. The birds fight for the crumbs, but in a friendly kind of way, not a mean kind of way.

I look at the door to my room, Room 5. It is closed. I wonder what's behind that door. Is my mom back inside sleeping? Is her throw-up still in there? Is someone new going to live there now because I can't live there by myself?

"Where's my mom?"

"She's very sick. The ambulance took her to the hospital. I have prayed to *Allah* that she gets better." He stops looking at the pigeons and looks at me. "To God, I have prayed to God. You understand, neh?"

I nod my head. But I don't understand, not really. I know some kids at school go to church and that's where God lives, but I've never been there, so I've never met him.

"So she's better now because you talked to God?" I ask.

"*Allah* has many beautiful names. *Al-Mujib* is the Responder to Prayer. I have asked. Now *Allah* can answer. Perhaps she is better."

"Maybe we should go check. At the hospital. Can we go there?"

But instead of taking me to the hospital, Suleiman takes me to the restaurant called Sadie's. He gets a cup of coffee for himself. My mom always puts lots of sugars and little creams in it, but Suleiman drinks it plain. I miss drinking some of the little cups of cream. But he gets me lots of other stuff: eggs, and toast with strawberry jam, and orange juice and a chocolate milk too. At first I am really hungry and I eat lots but then I start thinking about my mom and her throw up and how she fell down in it and I stop being so hungry after all.

After breakfast Suleiman takes me to a house instead of back to Nap-Away. He tells me it is his house. It has yellow flowers all around it and a fat tree near the front window and a blue door that is the colour of my mom's eyes. The house is such a pretty little house but it doesn't make Suleiman happy.

"It is too lonely," he says. He takes me inside and shows me all the rooms inside of his house. They are filled with lots of things, but no people, no cats, no dogs, no bugs. He shows me a room with a small white bed and a big squishy pink blanket on it. There are a few stuffed animals on the bed, and books on a bookshelf, and a toy box with Lego and puzzles and dolls in it. Suleiman tries to give me a stuffed animal, a floppy grey rabbit with a ribbon around its neck, but I don't want it. The room is waiting for someone to come and play, and to curl up in that little white bed and snuggle with the stuffed bunny. But I can tell it isn't waiting for me.

He opens the closet and pulls out some clothes. He shows them to me and asks if I like them, but I just shake my head no, so he stuffs all of them into a white suitcase and pulls up the zipper.

"Which things do you like?" he asks, pointing at the toys and books and stuffed animals. I squeeze my lips shut tight. "This, do you like this?" he lifts a doll up and tries to give it to me, but I keep my hands still. He picks up the floppy bunny again and pushes it into my hands. "Take it, take it," he says. But I drop it on the floor. I am thinking that Suleiman will be mad at me, but he just sighs and puts the bunny back on the bed so it can still do its waiting. Then he sits down on the bed so he can do his waiting. So we all wait for a little bit, Suleiman and the stuffed bunny and me, but nobody comes.

After a while I take Suleiman's hand. "She's not coming," I tell him.

"No," he says. "She is not coming."

"I want to go home," I say. "I want to go back to Nap-Away. I want my mom."

But Suleiman doesn't get up. He picks up the floppy bunny and puts it in his lap.

"She liked this one the best," he says. "See here? On the ear? The fur is all worn away because she used to suck on it when she was little."

"I want to go home," I say again.

"Yes," he says. "Home." He squeezes the little bunny tight against his chest. "I want to go home too."

ORI

Everything's quiet at the Nap-Away the morning after. There's a beige car in the parking lot, New Brunswick plates. A summer sun shining. A couple of pigeons roosting on the roof above Suleiman's door. I knock on his door, and next door on Iff's, but nobody answers. I pace around the parking lot, restless. Nap-Away sits, sags a little, resigned, like an old dog left behind, waiting for everyone to return. Steadfast.

I slump down in Suleiman's green chair. A woman wearing sequins and heels leaves Room 10, her red hair pulled up into a tight pony tail. A young mom, looks to be the same age as me, straps a couple of babies into a double stroller and heads eastbound along Kingston, one wheel of the stroller wobbling crookedly on its axle. Reminds me of Iff's little stroller. A guy with a crew-cut and a business suit pulls into the parking lot, gets out of a little red sports car. Disappears into Room 2. Brakes screech on Kingston Road, someone yells. The sun moves a little higher in the sky. I feel like I'm watching the earth rotate, the way the shafts of sunlight shift on Nap-Away's peeling yellow walls. A happy colour, like the goldenrod flowers in the meadow where Carter and I used to run in the summer when we were home.

I jump up and leave Nap-Away without looking back. Hop on the bus, find my way to the hospital. Sidetracked from my Carter-quest. I've started talking to him, as if he's with me.

"Remember the time you broke my thumb?" I ask him, as I wander through the hospital corridors.

Carter and I fought all the time. We wrestled on the couch, on the basement floor, once on the edge of the garage roof. Pinched soft parts of each other. I liked kicking him in the shins. We probably fought in the womb, kneeing and elbowing each other with our thin limbs, vying for space. Poking each other in the eye, just for spite. Most of it was fun. Not one time though, the time he bent my thumb back until the bone snapped.

It was early August. Lots of summer past, lots of summer still to come. Sticky hot and bored. We'd played Wild Things and Frisbee and a stupid nameless game with pinecones. We'd eaten a pack of raw hotdogs until our flat stomachs bulged.

We set out across the highway, through Mr. Ruggles' field, towards the schoolyard. There were a handful of kids there. The usual crowd, kids like us, who didn't go to art camp at the Y, or to soccer camp at the community centre, or to a cottage up north. Kids whose parents didn't give a shit.

Spratt was there. He was two years older than us. Thick chapped lips and piggy eyes. Orange hair, pale white skin with splotchy freckles. Mean, like the Ruggle's dog. Upper lip rippling to show his teeth.

"Hey," he said when we showed up. "It's the twins."

Carter looked at Spratt, long and hard.

"Yeah, it's us." There was something sparking in the air that day. A couple of the younger kids backed away. Like they knew what was coming already.

"Want to see something I found in the woods?"

Carter and I exchanged a glance. It was a dare, we both knew it. Hard to know if the dare was simply going into the woods with Spratt, or seeing the something-in-the-woods. Which was likely to be a maggoty dead raccoon. Or a Playboy magazine. I tightened my lips, nodded at Carter.

"Are you chicken?" Spratt asked, sneering.

"No, we'll go," Carter answered for us.

Spratt led the way. We followed him in a line, Carter, then me, then a couple of the older kids who hadn't run away: Mark, Suzy, a new kid that everyone still called 'new kid.' Spratt took us back across the Ruggles' field, veering west towards the ravine and the woods. There was an old shack deep in the woods. Every scary story we knew featured it. Dead Man's Shack.

Spratt made us go in one at a time. The new kid first. When the new kid came back out, he stumbled and fell to his knees. His skin was all waxy and white. Then he puked. Spratt laughed. Suzy backed away a couple of feet. Then a few more. Then she left.

"Are you a pussy like Suzy?" Spratt asked, looking at me.

"Nah," I said.

"I wanna go next," Carter said. He stepped forward and into the shack before anyone could stop him. Spratt shrugged. Followed him in.

When Carter came out, he grabbed my hand.

"Come on," he said. "We're going." His grip was tight on my wrist. His grey eyes were sparking black embers. He pulled me away.

"You wanna be a boy, but you don't got the balls for it. You're a sissy," Spratt taunted, leering at me.

"Let go!" I hissed at Carter.

"I'm not scared. I'll go in," I said to Spratt.

"Come on then. I've got something extra to show you." Spratt licked his chapped lips and winked at me.

Carter let go of my wrist, lunged at Spratt, swung a fist. Spratt ducked, sniggering. I darted forward, towards the door of the shack. But I wasn't fast enough. Carter flew at me, knocked me to the ground.

"I won't let you," he whispered.

"You went in. I need to go in too. Spratt won't ever let me forget it." I scrambled up from the dirt. Carter grabbed hold of me again.

"No one gives a shit what Spratt thinks," Carter said loudly. Started dragging me away. I swivelled around and bit him on the arm. He yelped, loosened his hold on me. I managed to twist out of his grip and bolt forward again.

When Carter caught me this time, he grabbed my thumb. Bent it back.

"You're not going in Ori," he said. And then he broke it.

I wiggle my left thumb.

What was in that shack anyway? Carter never did tell me. Spratt moved away. The new kid stopped talking. Or maybe he never started. But no one ever told me what was in that shack. I think I've imagined things way worse than what it must actually have been. Hard to know what nightmares are made of.

I continue trotting down the hallway. Peeking into random rooms. I don't really know how to find Iff's mom, which is why I'm just looking around and not asking. They must have a last name, but I don't know it. The wandering-strategy works, because eventually I find Iff's sister, Nikki.

"Hey," I say. She's wearing a blue tank top. Makes her eyes shine like glossy blue Smarties. I look down; my eyes meet her breasts. She's got no bra on and her top is a bit see-through. I can just see the perfect dark circles around the erect nipples. This flusters me even more than the crazy blue of her eyes. I keep looking down. Lower. Find her flip-flops. Cute toes. Shiny blue nail-polish on her nails.

"Where's Tiffany?" she asks. "I figured she was with you." I shake my head.

"Shit! Did the police take her?" I shake my head again.

"You forget how to talk?" I start to shake my head, then stop. Force myself to look up. Skip past the nipples.

"She's with Suleiman, the guy in the next room."

"K. Let's go get her." She spins around and heads down the corridor. Her flip-flops make a little slapping sound with each step. Thwack, thwack, thwack. I trot after her. She steps into the revolving door and I jump in with her. Pieces of our bodies touch. Elbows. Thighs. She smells great. Green apple shampoo and cinnamon gum. I take an extra sniff before we pop out the other side into the heat.

"How's your mom doing?"

"She's alive." Nikki says. Nonchalant. "She OD'ed again. Last time I was ten. That was before Tiff was born. She got her shit together after that. But here we go again." She spins herself around in a slow circle. It's nothing, a simple gesture, but it looks like a dance. Sidewalk's her stage, sunshine's her spotlight. "Back where we started."

"How'd you know she was here?"

"The hospital called this morning. She gave them my number. She was freaking out when I got here. She kept whispering to me about Tiffany, asking where the hell she was, but she didn't want anyone to know that she had no idea where her own kid was."

We get on the bus and ride back to Nap-Away. She sits by the open window and I sit beside her. She tells me about all the shit she went through when she lived with her mom. I tell her about Carter. She gives me a piece of cinnamon gum. I want to say stupid lame things to her, about how her eyes are like oceans, about how I want to dive in. Instead I just say they're amazing. She leans against me and laughs. Her bare arm is hot against mine. She's got three freckles in a triangle on her right thigh. I use my finger to connect the dots. Look into the blue. This time I don't look away. She smiles at me, then snaps her gum.

"Come on," she says. "This is our stop." We jump up and scramble off the bus. She leaps up on to my back and I give her a piggyback ride across the parking lot, swerving and stumbling and laughing. Moffit is waiting for me outside of Room 11.

I introduce them. Nikki's kind of flirty with him. I think she is probably flirty with everyone. Or maybe everyone is flirty with her, so she just expects it. Plays the game.

"I like your ferret," she says. It sounds like something more. She reaches up and runs a finger along Zelda's muzzle. Zelda perks up her head, coiling and twisting down from Moffit's neck. Nikki holds out her arms and Zelda winds her way into them.

I look at them from far away, as if I have just found both of them here, outside of my room. They're like Moffit's left shoulder tattoo, yin and yang. Incense and green apple, warm and icy, swirling black hurricane clouds and dry wheat stalks, tofu and Big Macs, hard brown muscles and pale soft thighs, stardust and a sliver of frosted moon. We stand in a little triangle, like the freckles. I connect the dots: he likes me, I like her, she likes some let's-get-matching-tattoos boyfriend.

Moffit tries to lean in and kiss me but I duck away. Instead he throws an arm across my shoulder. It weighs me down. I swivel my shoulder, slide out from under him. He quirks his eyebrow at me.

"What's going on?" he asks.

"Nothing," I say. Nikki watches me with those blue eyes. Smiles, like she knows what I'm thinking. What I want.

"Have you seen Iff?" I ask him. I tell him about the OD, the ambulance, the hospital. Suleiman keeping the kid.

"Nobody's been around," he says. "Why didn't she stay with you?" I'm wondering the same thing. Where is Suleiman anyway?

Nikki pulls out her cell phone, calls her mom. I can hear the screeching on the other end. Nikki ends the call, cuts her mom off mid-sentence.

"She's not a happy camper. She says you can't trust him. That he's into little girls."

"That's bullshit," I say.

"Whatever," Nikki says. She unwraps a new piece of gum, lets the wrapper flutter down to the ground. Offers out the pack to Moffit, to me. I take another piece.

"I don't give a shit about him," she says. "But I wanna know where he is."

"Where would he have gone?" Moffit asks.

"Probably to get something to eat. Maybe a coffee shop or the shawarma place. Or McDonald's? "

Moffit offers to stay at Nap-Away, in case they come back. He gets Nikki's number, punches it into his phone. Nikki and I head out down Kingston Road. I stop and glance back, see Moffit watching us leave. He's leaning back against the yellow wall of Nap-Away. They both look so loyal. Waiting for me to come back.

I skip forward to catch up to Nikki's shorty shorts and her long legs as she flip-flops away. "Wait up," I call out. She turns back, and smiles for me. I feel like a little kid, chasing after the ice-cream truck.

SULEIMAN

Over the last few weeks I have been fluctuating between two moods. One is a state of despair, and with it a heavy weariness; the other is a state of mania, in which I find answers, envision actions that spur me on. Despair and mania, like a bed and a staircase. I have been running up the staircase for hours now. Just like the other times, taking the kitten to Khadija, trying to go to Montreal with her, I find myself teetering at the top of a staircase to nowhere. All the action leads to nothing.

Today is the same. I have packed bags, one for myself, one for Tiffany; I have locked up the house; I have struck a deal at Zak's A-plus Auto, and made a down payment on a used Toyota hatchback; I have bought some snacks, some bottled water, and now I sit, with Tiffany at my side, ready to drive away from the parking lot of the No Frills grocery store. But, I think to myself. But.

First, I have forgotten about the kittens. There is no leaving without them. Not after losing Mini. Second, I have not considered that Tiffany might not want to go. In my mind I had pictured Amina, as she was last summer when we drove to Sandbanks: how excited she was, how she squealed when she saw cows in a field, how she wanted to stop at the Big Apple restaurant alongside the highway for apple pie, how she had sung a song about insects, over and over. Or was it spiders? No matter, Tiffany is not excited to go. In fact, she is reluctant, or maybe even frightened. She has stopped asking to go home; instead, she is silent. Her green eyes, as pretty as Khadija's emerald scarf, are wide with fear, the pupils enormous, like Rainbow and Massarat's when they stalk and pounce on each other. Her small hands are clenched together. And she is sitting so very still in the front seat of the car.

I inhale deeply, hold the breath, release it slowly. I find my way to God because this is what I have always done, all my life. *Al-Matin, Allah* the Forceful One, firm and steadfast. I consider. For a moment I believe that I must remain steadfast, loyal to the plan that I have begun to carry out. This is what it means to be unwavering. One must remain resolute despite misgivings. I breathe deeply again. But no. No. I have led myself astray. *Insha'Allah*, I will follow the path of right action. What craziness has brought me here?

"I have made a mistake," I say, looking at Tiffany. She says nothing. "I should not have taken you away from Nap-Away." She bites her bottom lip. Waits.

"I will take you home now." I nod my head. Inhale again. Yes, this is for the best. "We have to find out how your mother is. And the kittens must be lonely without you." Her lips twitch, turn up slightly. A not-quite smile.

"I must say one more thing to you first. I'm sorry. I did not mean to make things worse for you." I lean my head back on the headrest. I wish that Khadija were here, that she could hear these words, hear my apology. My mind begins to race. These words I have just uttered, they are meant for Khadija! This is what I must do: I must drive to Montreal so that I can say I am sorry. I try to remember. Have I ever apologized for how I turned away from her, how I blamed her? I know that I have felt remorse, told her that I have changed, brought her gifts as a symbol of my regret, but have I ever told Khadija I am sorry?

"I should go to Montreal," I say aloud. "To say that I am sorry."

"I want to go home," Tiffany whispers. "Not Montreal."

Two thoughts come to me at the same time. What if we go back and no one comes for Tiffany? What then? I realize I have made a mistake to steal her away, but what if there is no home for her to return to? At the same moment I think: what if we go back and Shelley is there, looking for Tiffany? How do I explain what I was doing? What if she believes I have kidnapped her? I don't think she would call the police, not with her own troubles, but it is possible. A tingle of apprehension tightens my chest.

I turn the key in the ignition, rev the engine and shift into drive. I must get back. I picture the Nap-Away waiting for us, just like *Al-Matin*, firm and steadfast. Yes, I must get Tiffany back to the one thing that is steady, unchanging.

TIFFANY

In my head I am telling myself the story of the two girls who live far, far away from each other. They both have kittens that they love. They are both brave and kind. They are both lonely and want to go home. I reach my hand in my pocket and grab my acorn, the one on a chain that Ori gave me, and squeeze it tight. I am trying to be brave.

I wish that I could go back to school. At school everything is always the same. In the morning we play outside until the bell rings and then we go inside and put our knapsacks in our cubbies. We sing O Canada with our loud voices, because Mrs. Lynch says we should be proud of our country. Each day she picks one person to wave the red and white flag with the leaf. Then we sit on the carpet and we do sharing time.

Once Jamal brought his hamster to school for sharing. Maybe I could bring Rainbow and Massarat to school one time. Everyone would be so happy to see my twin kittens. After sharing time Mrs. Lynch reads us a story. This is my favourite part of school. One time she even read us a chapter book that took us a lot of days to finish. It was about three kittens with wings. In books anything can happen. Stuff that's real and stuff that's not real. That's why I like them so much. And I like them because when you open them up it is like magic. If you don't open a book it just sits there, like a spoon on the table, or a carpet on the floor. But if you open it and read the words, it turns into something else. A whole other world is hidden inside, like the place where Winter lives, eating golden apples with the brave and kind little girl. I don't understand how that can happen. How can places and people and animals that aren't even real be inside of the words in a book?

After story time we get to do centres, like building a city with blocks, or lining up the plastic animals in a parade, or painting at the easels, or using magnet letters to spell words, or putting on a puppet show, or digging in the sand. Angel loves to build towers and Theo loves to knock them down. Then Angel stamps her foot and yells at Theo.

After centres we have snack time. I like when there are cookies shaped like bear paws and when there are strawberries. After snack time we sometimes go to the gym and play with hula-hoops or soccer balls or a big parachute and sometimes we go the library, or maybe our reading buddies come to the class. Then it's home time.

"I want to go home," I whisper to Suleiman. I can see Nap-Away in my mind, waiting for me to come back. Maybe it is missing me, the same way I am missing it. Maybe it is thinking that I ran away or that the wind picked me up and blew me away. Maybe Nap-Away is lonely for me.

Suleiman is driving me in his new blue car. It smells like cigarettes inside, which reminds me of my mom.

"Yes," he says. "I will take you home. Back to Nap-Away." He stops the car at a red light. He starts talking to the truck in front of us, or maybe to God, asking for secret things. I can't hear what he is saying.

"I am sorry," he says again to me.

"Me too," I say.

"Why are you saying sorry? You have been so good, so brave while your mother is so sick."

"I'm sorry I didn't like the bunny."

"No, you were right not to take it. It belonged to Amina, my daughter. I know why you did not take it, because you knew it was not yours."

"She's not coming back though. She's gone, like Mini, isn't she?" I ask.

Suleiman puts his big hand on my leg. It reminds me of the bear paw cookies at school.

"Yes," he says.

"Are they dead?" He nods his head for yes. "Did they go far away, to the place where you go when you're dead?" He nods again.

"I'm glad they are together," I say.

"That makes me happy too," he says. "Amina is in the gardens of paradise. There are beautiful green leaves above and flowing springs of clear water and ripe fruit hanging low on the branches. Everything she wishes for will be there."

"If my mom is dead," I ask, "will she go there too?"

Suleiman doesn't answer right away. Maybe he doesn't know the answer. Sometimes when he is thinking he rubs the bump on his eye. That is what he is doing now. He is driving and not talking and rubbing his eye with his thumb. Maybe it makes him feel braver, like how I feel braver when I rub the smooth part of my secret acorn.

"I don't know the answer," he finally says. "It is not simple. I am Muslim. I believe in *Allah*, so when I die I will hope to go to paradise because I have faith, and because I did the right thing." He pauses. "Right action is important. It is a struggle, every day, to do the right thing, neh?"

We must be getting close to Nap-Away now, because I can see the McDonalds. But there are a lot of cars on the road, so we are going slowly. Suleiman keeps talking.

"I have done bad things. But *Insha'Allah*, I will be forgiven. I must continue to try and do the right thing, just like you and your mother should try and do what's right. Even if she makes mistakes, she must still try to do the right thing the next time. But if she doesn't believe in God then there's a problem." He makes a funny sound, like a little bird saying tut-tut-tut. "Do you see?"

"No," I say.

Suleiman laughs. "It doesn't matter," he says. "You don't need to worry that your mother is dead. She is only sick. She is at the hospital. You will see her soon."

I wish I had something to give to my mom, to make her feel better. Maybe I will give her my special acorn.

ORI

I take Nikki to the shawarma place and Sadie's Bar and Grill and then she says we should try the McDonald's, so we head west along Kingston. It's making me hungry, all this searching at places with food.

"Maybe we should check the sub place first," I say. "And get some subs while we're there."

"Sure," she says. I'm guessing she's hungry too.

No Suleiman, no Iff. No Carter either. I pull out a fifty that Suleiman gave me a couple of days ago, to pay for our subs and chips. Nikki raises her pale eyebrows, whistles softly between her teeth. I laugh. While we eat I tell her the story of Zelda. Make it all tragic—living alone in the library for months, surviving on the spilled Cheerios and Goldfish crackers in the kids section. Practising her high-fives. Bravely waiting for rescue.

"You're weird," she says. But she's laughing. And her blue eyes are all sparkly, like the blue petals of the cornflowers growing behind the Nap-Away, lit up in the sunshine. We take our last bites and head out, leaving our crumpled wrappers and sub crusts behind, step back into the smog and heat. The sky is growing darker, and somewhere far off thunder rumbles. The wind whips Nikki's hair into her face. Her phone rings, some boy-band ringtone. It's so snug in the back pocket of those tight short that she has to wriggle her hips around to get it out. I want to slide my hand in there, walk along beside her, hand on her butt, like I once saw Carter do with Suzy Zammit.

"Is she there?" Nikki asks. Listens.

"What're you calling for then?"

She shrugs, hands me the phone.

"Ori!" Moffit says, all excited. "Joel just called."

"Joel?"

"Yeah, Joel, Mr. Black, you know, ukulele man. He just saw Carter!"

I grab Nikki's hand, start running. She yanks me to a stop, pulls off her flip-flops, so she can run barefooted. She's fast, with those long thin legs of hers. Like that slender African antelope, that races and pronks around on the Kalahari. The Dutch one, with the twisty horns. Can't remember its name. Carter would know because he made me watch a video of them. She flies along beside me, her blond hair streaming behind her, shimmering white and gold, white and gold.

"Where are we going?" she asks, breathless and laughing. Soundtrack, Florence + the Machine, "Dog Days are Over": all that running for your brothers and sisters. I run to the beat of the song in my head, leave everything behind.

We skid into the parking lot of Nap-Away. Moffit is waiting there. Big grin on his face. We do a crazy little dance together, hopping around and hugging each other. Zelda high-fives me with her little ferret paw.

"Where is he? What did Joel say?"

"He said that he saw Carter at a park downtown, at Queen and Church. He was just sitting on a bench. Joel tried to talk to him but Carter didn't seem to remember who he was. Joel's staying there, waiting for you. He said he'd try and keep Carter there. "

"I've gotta go there."

Nikki narrows her eyes at me. The blue disappears.

"What about Tiff?" she says. "What about my missing kid sister?"

I look down at her bare feet. The blue nail polish makes her toenails shine like sacred Egyptian beetles. I want to follow them wherever they go, keep looking for Iff even after we find her. But I need to run towards Carter. I can feel one hand, reaching out to Moffit, one hand holding on to Nikki's. I'm stretching, tangling, tripping.

"She's with Suleiman," I say. "He's a good guy. Despite what your mom says. She's safe, she's fine. We just don't know where they're at."

"Fine," she says. In a way that says it's so-not-fine. She bends over, wipes the bottom of her bare feet, slides her flip-flops back on. "Fine," she says again. She runs her fingers through her white-blonde hair and shakes it out. "Whatever. I'll go look for her myself." She turns and leaves.

I watch her go, think about my hand in her pocket, the freckles on her thigh, the way her nipples looked, trying to peek through the thin cotton of her blue tank top.

"Come on, let's go," Moffit says.

We dash over to the bus stop, to wait for the 102 westbound to Warden Station. Thunder rumbles close by, a low growling. I glance back as I get on the bus. In the parking lot a plastic bag gets picked up by the wind and swirls around, gets caught up in the black fence around Suleiman's mosque. A shingle rips lose from Nap-Away's roof and skitters down to the ground. As the bus pulls away, a single streak of lightning zigzags down from the sky. Nikki walks away alone along Kingston Road, her hair whipping around in the wind.

SULEIMAN

Our arrival back at Nap-Away is anticlimactic. I have managed to get myself agitated, preparing for confrontation, readying my explanation about where I have been, why I have taken Tiffany, but it has been needless. The parking lot is empty; no one answers at Room 5; there is no sign of Shelley, of police, of anyone. Even Yori is nowhere to be seen. The only thing to see is the sky behind Nap-Away, which is heavy and dark with grey-green clouds. The colour seems strange, ominous. The door to my room is swollen with humidity and hard to open. Once we are inside I see the kittens prowling around, their fur bristling, their pupils black and wide, their irises like little green halos.

I consider what to do next. Right action is important but cannot be achieved simply by acting carelessly. I need to set my intentions. First I must take care of Tiffany. I must make sure she has food, a place to sleep, safety and security.

Second I must take action to reunite her with her mother. Here, I pause. I know this is what Tiffany wants, but is this right? I'm not sure. I know that Shelley is not a fit mother. But is it right for me to judge, for me to interfere? I waver. Perhaps the right action is for me to call someone for help: Miranda, the social worker; the police; the Children's Aid; my imam. But each time I consider this, I can't seem to find the words to explain why Tiffany is with me in the first place. Perhaps instead, I should take Tiffany to the hospital, to find out how her mother is. Again, I pause. What if she is dead? What should I do then?

Perhaps right action involves waiting for events to unfold. But this feels like inaction. So my thoughts continue to spiral, around and around, searching for a place to land. What should I do? Who should I tell? Is anyone looking for Tiffany? Does anyone know I have Tiffany?

Yori knows. Where is Yori?

Instead of taking any action, I slump down in my chair. The inertia is back. The adrenaline that has kept me moving all day is gone. I am exhausted.

Tiffany stands in front of me. Her green eyes shine.

"Do you think my mom will come home soon?"

I sigh and shrug, like a teenager. I stand, open the door and look out. The rain is starting, falling in heavy drops.

"We will wait for the storm to pass."

Tiffany stands beside me, looking out.

"My mom loves it when it thunders and lightning," she says.

"My wife, too. She loves storms. They don't scare her at all." I feel an ache, pulling my abdomen tight. Khadija was never one to be afraid. I remember her giving birth to Ahmed, moving fearlessly towards her own pain like a warrior. And the way she strode through the blizzard, laughing, her black eyes burning bright. I miss her fearlessness.

"Is she dead too?" Tiffany asks.

"No, no, she is fine. She has moved away, to Montreal."

"Will you go there too?"

I consider. Of course I should go to Montreal. There is nothing left for me here. But I hesitate. How long can I chase after Khadija, when she has made it clear that she wishes to be away from me?

"I don't know."

The rain is picking up and I start to close the door. But wait. There is a young woman, alone, walking in the rain towards our rooms. Tiffany shrieks.

"Nikki!" She ducks under my arm and dashes into the rain. I step out after her. The woman swings Tiffany up, hugs her tight. Tiffany wraps her legs around her waist, clings to her. She carries Tiffany forward, towards me.

"Where the hell have you been?" she demands, glaring at me. I startle. For a second I think she is Shelley. But this woman is younger, just a teenager, now that I can see her up close. I shake my head, wipe the rain from my eyes.

"Who are you?" I ask.

"It's Nikki," Tiffany says. She slides down from the woman's hip, but keeps a hold of her hand. "My sister."

TIFFANY

It's a big thunderstorm, with lots of loud cracks and lightning that shines across the whole sky, making the dark go suddenly bright, like someone turning on the lights and then turning them off again, just as fast. After the lightning stops, Nikki lets me run around in the rain in the parking lot, which is filled with huge puddles that I jump and splash in. I wish that Orianthi were here so that we could play Wild Things in the rain.

When we go into our room I check to see if my mom's throw-up is still there, but all that's left is a wet spot on the carpet. After I'm all dried off and in my pajamas, Nikki knocks on Suleiman's door and asks if we can have Rainbow and Massarat in Room 5 and he says yes.

"What kind of name is that anyway? Massarat?" Nikki asks me. She is watching Massarat pounce on the wrinkles in the blanket on the bed. Maybe she thinks they are snakes.

"I like it," I say. "It means joy." I am lying on the bed and I can feel my eyes trying to close but I keep them open because I don't want to miss any part of this day, not now that Nikki is here and I know my mom is coming home tomorrow and the kittens are in my room.

Someone knocks at the door. I jump up and run to open it because I think it is my mom even though she doesn't ever knock on the door. It is Orion. Or Orianthi. I'm not sure if he is a girl or a boy today. He's all wet like he's been playing in the puddles too. He just stands in the doorway dripping. I think he looks like the lost dog from a picture book that Mrs. Lynch read to us at school.

Nikki stands inside the room looking back at him. She looks like my mom, because her eyes are all slitty and she is standing with her hand on her hip and not moving at all and not saying anything. Orion rubs his nose. That is how the kittens wash themselves, rubbing their little paws over their faces.

"Can I come in?" Orion asks. But he is not asking me, he is asking Nikki. I look at my sister. She makes us all wait. But then she says yeah, so Orion comes in. Nikki hands him a towel and he pulls off his hat and drops it on the floor and scrubs his face and head dry.

"You should go put on some dry clothes," Nikki says.

Orion nods, but he doesn't go. He leans against the wall and then slides down and sits on the floor. I want to tell him that he is sitting on the place where my mom did her throw up and that the carpet is wet there. But he is all wet already so I don't say anything.

"What happened?" Nikki asks. She sits down beside him. I sit back on the big bed and cross my legs. I'm not feeling sleepy anymore. I'm sort of hungry. But I don't say anything. I know that if I'm quiet I will hear more things because they will forget that I'm here.

"We didn't get there in time. He was gone." Orion puts his head down on his knees. He's wearing his red pants but they are all wet so they look darker, like the colour of purple grapes.

Orion makes a little hiccup sound and then shakes his head lots of times. All his shaggy hair flies around his face.

"I just need to see him," he says.

"It sucks that you didn't get to," Nikki says. Orion leans over against Nikki's shoulder. They stay like that for a long time.

"We met up with Joel. He said that Carter didn't say much. Talked about wolves. When Joel said that I was coming, Carter ripped a page out of his notebook and said to give it to me. Carter told him to ask if I knew what the wolves wanted." He reaches inside his pants, not in the pockets, but where the underpants are at the front, and pulls out a folded piece of paper. I bend forward and lean over so that I can see what is on the inside when Orion unfolds it.

It's a wolf. A wild thing kind of wolf. One that I don't think anyone could ever tame, not even with the magic words. It is the scariest wolf I have ever seen. I make a little gasping sound when I see it and Nikki and Orion both look up.

"Hey, Iff," Orion says. "I'm glad you're found." He smiles at me. His eyes are so grey, like the clouds in the sky just before the lightning flashed out of it. He folds the wolf over, so that its teeth aren't showing anymore and its black eyes are staring at itself.

"Where'd you and Suleiman go?" he asks.

"He took me to his house to show me Amina's room."

Nikki looks mad when I say it, and I think she is going to yell at me. But she doesn't.

"Tiff," she says. "He's not doing anything creepy is he? Like...maybe touching you? You know, like your private parts? Or getting you to touch him? Anything like that? I won't get mad if you say yes."

I shake my head no. "He doesn't do bad things. He showed me Amina's bunny. It doesn't have too much hair left on its ear because she loved it right off." I'm mad at Nikki for asking if Suleiman is bad.

"He told me about *Allah*. That's what he named God. About how you have to try to do the right thing so God will let you come to the place where Mini is, and Amina, where all the flowers and rivers are. Like how you told me about," I say to Orion.

"Whatever," Nikki says. "As long as he's not up to anything." She yawns. She looks cute, like the kittens. "Are you guys hungry?"

Orion leaps up. Shakes himself off.

"I gotta go get dry pants. Then I'll go get some food for us all. Maybe some KFC? I'll be right back," he says, looking at Nikki.

He leaves, but I hear him knocking next door, and talking to Suleiman. They talk for a long time. Then they laugh together and I hear Suleiman's door close. I can't wait for him to come back.

ORI

I've never had sex before. I'm pretty sure Nikki has though. No, I'm absolutely sure. It felt unstoppable. Hands and moans and wetness and slipperiness and trembling and gasping. Raw and relentless. Like a sharp breath in, held for too long, before exhaling. Soundtrack, "Howl" Florence + the Machine, wolf-like teeth raking across pale skin.

I want to have more of it. Want to climb up on the saggy roof of Nap-Away and sing about it. Like a caged and crazy yellow canary that's just tasted freedom. I want to find Carter and tell him about it. Late at night, whispered secrets. 'I never imagined….' I might say, and I'd tell him about the coldness of the bathroom floor against my naked skin, or the way I panted and bit my own lip. But I'm not sure I'd tell him everything, tell him about the way Nikki's thighs tightened, the way she writhed and squirmed underneath me.

I think about my fumbled attempts before. With Suzy Zammit back in middle school. Trying to maneuver her bra, to touch her breasts. With Mark Curtis-Meehan. His tongue like a snake's, flicking in and out of my mouth. With Moffit, all stoned and stardusted.

I sneak out of Room 5 in the middle of the night. Rain is dripping down from the edge of Nap-Away's roof and the sky is clear. Moon shining down.

I stop and stand there alone. Try to make sense of it all. Carter's wolf. *The wolves are real*, he had scrawled underneath the picture. Suleiman stealing Iff away. Nikki and her flawless freckled thigh. Moffit kissing me here in the parking lot, the stardust. Try to make sense of myself. Being Orianthi, being Orion, being Carter's twin. Wanting Nikki, loving Moffit, needing Carter.

A light shines out from Room 6. The door opens and Suleiman steps into the darkness. He looks up at the moon, looks out at the mosque. Sees me and beckons me over.

"You can't sleep either, with your troubles, neh?" he says. "Your brother, his wolves." I showed him the picture earlier, on my way out to get the KFC. Suleiman looks back up at the moon. "We all have our wolves, bringing us fear in the night."

We stand together, looking out at the night together, not speaking. Waiting for the wolves to howl.

"Ahhh, look," Suleiman whispers, breaking the moment. He points to the dark shadows at the edge of Nap-Away. A raccoon, pointy nosed and humpy backed, ambles out, followed by six kits. The little ones are noisy, all chittery and squealy. Ready to make mischief.

"She likes to parade them around, for everyone to see. They come to gather scraps. The bits of food that we toss away are like a feast for them." They circle around the dumpster, little paws splashing in potholed puddles.

"She's teaching them to climb up onto the roof. Every night is an adventure," Suleiman says. He pauses. "Come. We will go on our own adventure. I bought a car today." He laughs and gestures at a small blue car parked outside his room. I feel like I'll never need to sleep again, so I jump in. We drive east along Kingston Road and then all the way to the 401. Suleiman presses down on the accelerator and the car flies along the highway. I open my window, let my hand ride the wind, turn on the radio, crank up the volume. The music is mystical: chanting in a language I don't understand; drumming; a hypnotic steady beat.

Suleiman smiles at me. I realize I have heard him laugh many times, mostly a sarcastic laugh. But I haven't seen him smile, until now. I smile back. And we drive on into the wet night.

The sky is turning pink when we turn back towards the city. We stop to have coffee. Suleiman drinks it black, three full cups. I have pancakes, bacon, eggs, toast, orange juice.

"This coffee is not very good," he says, draining the cup again. "But still, it is coffee, neh?" His eyes are bloodshot and weary, he hasn't shaved in days, his shirt has sweat stains under the arms, dribbles of coffee down the front.

"Yori," he begins, placing down his cup, "I have to tell you something. I know you're a good person, that you're trying to do the right thing. You're hoping to help your brother. But you're also taking care of Tiffany, being like a brother to her." He stops and gestures for the waitress to fill his cup again. "I'm doing the same. I've lost my family, but I feel like an uncle to you, and to Tiffany. That's why I did something yesterday, something that I regret."

"I took Tiffany. I planned to run away with her." He shakes his head. "I wasn't thinking clearly. *Allah*, who is forever forgiving, will understand what I did. But it was wrong. *Insha'Allah*, I will not need her mother's forgiveness as well. I hope that she never finds out."

"I'm not so sure it was such a bad idea," I say. "Better she's with you than being dumped in foster care. She'd be there already, if it wasn't for you."

He takes a long slow sip of his coffee. Meets my gaze. Neither of us speak. I don't know what he's thinking. I'm thinking about all the foster homes we've lived in. All the crap that Carter and I've been through, with our mom, with our grandma, with our fosters. Stuff that we've seen, a couple that belong in Dead Man's Shack, like the time when we were seven and Carter called 911 because some guy with a hairy back and a gun was having sex with our mom on the kitchen table. I'm thinking about Iff's green eyes. What they've already seen, what they're still going to see.

"She has a family. She has a mother. *And* a sister," Suleiman says. "I didn't know about the sister." I look down at my crusts, stab one with a fork. I can't look at Suleiman and think about Nikki at the same time. I'm picturing my hands on her breasts, tangled in her hair, between her thighs. My heart does some kind of weird flip-flop. I can't wait to see her again. Have to hide a goofy grin.

"Her mother needs to get it together," I say. "And her sister," I look away, out the window, "isn't supposed to be a parent."

"True. But it doesn't make it right for me to steal a child away. I know it was wrong."

"Right and wrong don't always work the way they should. You make it sound so obvious, like we can always tell what's right and what's wrong. Most of the time it's just not like that. It's all muddy," I say. "Obscure."

"No, I disagree," Suleiman says. "We know the difference. It's just that we don't want to accept what is right and what is wrong. Or accept where they lead us, what they tell us about ourselves."

"Dude," I say. "It's just a fucking mess. The kid is five. She's living in a motel. Her mother's doing drugs, doing guys, doing her own shit. That's wrong. You let her go to Children's Aid, she goes to a foster home, where she's just another mouth to feed. She's nobody's family. That's the worst of it. You don't belong, no matter how much everyone pretends. You'll never belong. You're like those stray cats out behind the Nap-Away that nobody wants.

"Then maybe she's treated like crap, maybe beat up by another kid who's got nobody, got nothing, maybe something worse happens. Or maybe nothing bad happens, but she doesn't get to stay. So she goes to another foster home. And another. Her mother's gonna want her back, so she can't get adopted. Or nobody wants to adopt her, because she's not a baby anymore. Ok, so instead, you take her. Well, that's wrong too, isn't it? Kidnapping a kid."

I jump up. Shove my plate away. Kick the table leg with my boot. I turn to leave but I have no place to go. Instead, I swivel back to Suleiman.

"Or it's all right, maybe it all turns out great. She stays with her mama, the one that she loves, and her mama quits doing drugs. Or she goes to a foster home where she gets to live in a house with a tire swing in the backyard and no one's using drugs. Maybe they buy her a ukulele. Or you take her, give her all the love that you can't give Amina. There's nothing wrong with any of that, is there? Is there?" My voice is shrill. I give Suleiman's big arm a shove. He doesn't budge. He looks at me with sorrow.

"That's what I was thinking when I took her," he murmurs, looking down into his coffee cup. "That I could give her what I can no longer give Amina." He sighs. "You're right, everything seems muddy.

"Sit, Yori," he says. And I do. Like a good dog. "This is what's right. We should make sure she comes to no harm. Do you agree?"

He looks at me, long and hard. Everything is the same, his weary blood-shot eyes, his dirty shirt, but now he's like some kind of warrior or knight. Noble.

"*Insha'Allah*, she comes to no harm. But if she does, we'll try to protect her. This is what's right." He reaches his big hand across the table.

"No harm," I say. I take his hand and we shake. Make a crazy oath at sunrise in some no-name twenty-four hour breakfast truck stop.

SULEIMAN

I'm sitting outside of my room, on my green chair, watching Tiffany and the kittens play. I think of my breakfast with Yori, shake my head. It has a dream-like quality to it, the drive to nowhere in the dark, the endless coffee, the pledge we made at sunrise.

I look up and see Shelley walking across the parking lot. Tiffany sees her too and runs to her mother. She doesn't stop running when she reaches her, and nearly knocks Shelley over with her force. Her mother hugs her, holds her tightly against her body. I feel an enormous sense of relief. It was a good decision, to return to Nap-Away, to return Tiffany to her mother. I scoop up the kittens, scoot them back into my room, and return to my chair.

Tiffany and her mother walk together towards me. I'm not sure what to expect, so I wait instead of speaking. She sends Tiffany away, to find Nikki inside of their room, then turns to face me. She looks different. She has no make-up on, her hair hangs limply, and she does not narrow her blue eyes at me. I have not seen them like this, in the sunshine, so wide open, so direct. I'm taken aback by their intensity.

"I don't trust you," she says. "I don't get what you're up to. But I guess…" She shakes her head. "Let me try that again."

She reaches into her purse and pulls out a cigarette, lights it, and takes a long inhale. Her hands tremble, and I watch the cigarette vibrate in her grip.

"I thought you were being an asshole when I found out you had Tiffany. But I've had a bit of time to think about it. Things would be a lot worse off if the cops had taken her."

I wait. But she has no more to say. It is not an apology, but I assume it is meant to be one. And perhaps I don't deserve more of an apology than this, since I was, as she says, being an 'asshole.'

"Family is the most important thing. I didn't want to see her without a mother." This sounds like a truth. No, it is a truth, but it must also be a lie, according to my actions yesterday.

"I can't believe I almost died. I've gotta get my life back on track. I'm going nowhere. I've got nothing." She takes another shaky drag on her cigarette. "All I've got is Tiffany."

"You are lucky to have a daughter like her," I say.

Shelley narrows her eyes at me. This is more familiar, helps ground me. I know this Shelley.

"You're lucky too, you know. Lucky not to have the cops here, taking you away for kidnapping my kid."

I stand up, so that I can look down at her.

"I didn't keep her away from the police to help you! I did it for her. You were lying unconscious on the floor, maybe dead. Not because you are sick, not because you've got a disease, but because of the things you take, that you grab for like a child with candy. And Tiffany was here in the dark," I gesture at the parking lot, "crying, crawling on her hands and knees. She's just a child. She shouldn't have to worry for you, take care of you. You're her mother!"

I have more to say but I stop abruptly. Shelley is not arguing, she is not staring me down with those flat angry eyes. She is crying. I'm not sure what to do. I have no words to comfort her. It feels rude to turn away from her pain, so I stand there, hands at my side, and watch her tears slide down her cheeks.

She doesn't speak either, doesn't move, doesn't look away. The ash that is accumulating on the tip of the cigarette, which is dangling between her fingers, falls off and scatters in the summer breeze. The moment stretches on: the sun beating down, the stillness, the steady flow of her tears. I don't allow my mind to follow the paths that beckon it away. I stay present. I can't alter what is happening: I will not try to comfort her, but I will witness her tears, without faltering, without looking away. It almost feels sinful, like I am looking at her in her nakedness, a woman who is not my wife.

This one is suffering, I think, watching the next tear hesitate before falling over the rim of her eyelid. I name the next tear as well, and the next. Three sisters: suffering, sorrow, and shame. Ah, I know each of these tears well, like I know my own children.

Then I do something I thought I would not. I touch her on the cheek, gently, and wipe away the last tear with my thumb. So, I think, I can share the suffering of this woman who I have judged, who I have looked down on. I don't say it out loud, but I know that God shares in our suffering as well. *Al-Latif,* The Subtle One, who knows the delicate meaning of everything.

"*Insha'Allah,*" I say, "may we be free from this suffering, from this sorrow, from this shame." Her wet eyes widen. For a brief moment I think she will turn on me with anger, but she does not.

"I'm sorry," she whispers. I nod my head. A drop of rain, left over from last night's storm, trembles on the edge of the roof of Nap-Away and falls down with a tiny splat on the concrete between us.

I blink; Shelley looks up. Then she sniffs loudly and rubs the back of her hand under her nose, leaving a trail of mucus on it. She does not look back at me. Instead she turns away and leaves, opening the door to Room 5 and stepping inside.

I go back into my own room. I'm momentarily blind as I adjust to the sudden change of light. I step forward and stumble over one of the kittens, Massarat. I reach down and caress the kitten's soft fur. Massarat purrs in reply. I sit on the edge of the bed, holding Massarat against my chest. I feel like I am broken wide open, open to my suffering. I see that all my rage, all my grief, all my actions and decisions have been moot. Amina is still dead. Still dead, again and again. With God, but not with me. "We belong to God and unto God we return," I murmur, finding a well of consolation in the words.

Nothing that I do, nothing that I say, nothing that I *feel*, will change what has happened. I am fighting an endless, pointless battle within myself against what is real, against what God, the writer of destinies, has willed. She is dead. There is a great sense of comfort, knowing she has returned to God, and that I too, shall return, and be reunited with her. And oh, I am filled with gratitude for the gift of Amina, for my short time with her on earth, and the precious memories of her. Death has not ended our bond of love. Yes, I have sorrow from her death. But my *suffering*, ah, that is a different sister all together. My suffering is not because she is dead, not because she has returned to God. No, my suffering is because I refuse to accept that she is dead, refuse to accept Khadija's role in her death, refuse to accept how I have been feeling, how I have acted. I refuse to stand in stillness and silence and watch my own emotions unfold. The battle will end if I embrace God's will, just as I stood and accepted Shelley's tears. I did not try to fight against them, or to end them, or to deny them.

I sit, and I allow myself to feel the sadness wash over me. I don't allow it to lead me off into other thoughts; I don't allow it to make me jump up and take action; I don't battle against it with other feelings. The grief is immense, threatens to annihilate me, is too much to bear. Then it begins to change, like it always does, and I'm no longer sitting with grief, but with a slick and evil anger that has slithered into my heart. Maybe this anger will strangle me. It washes over me, floods me, swirls inside of me. But still I sit. My breath is ragged, but continues, a single breath at a time, one inhale followed by one exhale, as it has since that first moment when my lungs met air, released from my mother's womb. I sit and I breathe.

Amina is dead. There is grief. There is anger. Again and again I murmur the words, "We belong to God and unto God we return." The words anchor me, keep me from being swept away by the storm of feelings. Surely, after such hardship, there will come some ease. I will not always be clouded by this grief in my heart. I inhale, expel the air in a slow whoosh.

I stay there, Massarat curled in a ball on my lap, and breathe my grief and anger in and out.

TIFFANY

Nikki goes to the coffee shop and comes back with a box filled with donuts. I eat one that is covered in rainbow sprinkles and another one that is covered in shiny chocolate. My mom eats one of the plain ones. Nikki and I eat them in big bites, but my mom nibbles at her donut like she is a squirrel.

"Dad called," Nikki says, looking at our mom. "He wanted to know if you were ok."

"Whatcha tell him?"

"I told him you were home, that you were better. I didn't say anything about…" Nikki stops talking and looks at me. "He knows though."

"I'm gonna get clean Nikki," my mom says. "I swear."

"Sure," Nikki says. She picks up a third donut, a sprinkle one. She already ate two. She eats the top only, the part with all the sprinkles.

"Nikki let the kittens come over to play," I tell my mom. "When you were in the hospital."

"You really love those kittens, don't you baby?" My mom rubs some chocolate off my face with her thumb. Then she kisses me on the head.

"I loved Mini the most, but now I love Rainbow the most. She is the brave one. Suleiman says she is always leading Massarat into trouble."

My mom starts to put down the donut she has been eating but her hand is shaking too much so the donut flies out of her hand and lands on the floor. I jump off my chair and pick it up. I wait for my mom to do her swearing. She doesn't though. She reaches with her shaky hands for her cigarettes and tries to flick her lighter to make a fire but she can't do it. Nikki reaches over and takes the cigarette and lighter. She puts the cigarette in her mouth and lights it. She sucks on it and blows a puff of smoke up towards the ceiling, then she hands it to my mom. Now I am waiting for my mom to get mad at Nikki for smoking, but she doesn't do that either. My mom puts her lips around the cigarette and sucks in her breath. She blows the smoke out of the side of her mouth, away from me.

"Tell you what," she says, looking at me. "Maybe you can keep one of the kittens here. Maybe you can have the kitten for your own, for real."

My eyes feel like they are trying to pop right out of my head and I forget to breathe for a minute.

"Really?" I squeak. "Rainbow can be mine?"

My mom nods her head.

"But I don't want to clean up its crap," she says, blowing another puff of smoke out of her mouth.

"Nikki, I can have my own kitten come live with me!"

Nikki laughs. "Sweet," she says.

"Can I go ask Suleiman right now?" I am using my shouting voice. Mrs. Lynch would tell me it's not an inside voice, but I can't help it. I am just too excited.

"Sure," my mom says. I run to the door, but then I turn around and run back and hug my mom so tight. Then I hug Nikki too. I run back to the door and fling it open so that I can go get Rainbow and she can come and live with me forever.

ORI

Once upon a time, not so long ago, and not so far away, twins were born. Their big grey eyes opened to the world, and they begin to whimper, and then to howl together, in protest. They were skinny babies, with wispy dark hair that clung to their scalps, and thin ribs that clutched tightly around their hearts. They breathed in unison, these twins, their baby bellies rising and falling together, their chests fluttering and stilling. Each twin would only sleep if touching the other: a hand grasping a foot, limbs entwined, curled up together like newborn puppies.

The twins arrived into the world fatherless. Whoever their father was, he had slipped away long ago, long before there was even a hint of swelling in the belly of the mother. Not too long after their birth, the twins became motherless as well. There were many stories told across the land to explain how this had happened: the mother had abandoned them, left them on the steps of a holy place, or in a basket beneath a weeping willow; the twins had been stolen, taken away by the king's authority, despite the mother's desperate pleas; the twins had been spirited away in the night by the enchantment of a sorcerer.

But the story told most often, the one that most believed, was that the mother was taken, not the twins. By whom? Few liked to speak the truth out loud, but it was whispered that the mother had been taken by the grey wolves of the night. The grey wolves were feared across the land. Legend told that they only came for some and not others, but few understood who the chosen were or why they were taken. The grey wolves travelled in packs, on silent paws, sniffing and stalking through the night. Their fur was the colour of ancient mountains, their eyes burned a fearsome black. They were taller than the wolves in the forest, with broad heads and long muzzles. But unlike other wolves, the grey wolves of the night did not howl, and their silence made them all the more ominous.

The common people of the land feared the grey wolves of the night. They feared that one day the wolves would come for them, slinking through the fog. They feared what these silent wolves, with their clever black eyes and glinting sharp teeth, would do to them. But they knew too, that the grey wolves could do nothing to them. For if the wolves came for you, they did not hurt you, not with a swift rake of their bold claws, nor with their blood-stained teeth. The grey wolves of the night would not clamp their jaw down on you, severing an artery or snapping your neck. Instead, they would watch you with their burnt black eyes; they would stalk you through the dark corners of the city. The wolves would haunt you, haunt you until madness overtook you. By then you might believe that a wolf was gnawing through the muscles and tendons of your leg, exposing the bone, but the wolves were simply watching, silently watching the madness take hold.

So the people feared the wolves. But perhaps even more than the wolves themselves, they feared what the king's authority would do to them if the wolves came. A rumour spread that the twins' mother was imprisoned behind the great brick walls of the king's asylum. To protect her from the wolves the king's men would say, but few believed their words. They knew what happened behind those tall white walls. Some returned from that place and spoke of wicked spells and elixirs that left them reeling with terrible sicknesses; some spoke of rooms of white, the blinding whiteness of nothingness; some no longer remembered the speech of the people and spoke in meaningless sentences, or did not speak any longer. And some never returned at all.

Truth is hard to find. Perhaps the twins' mother was taken by wolves; perhaps in her madness she left the twins alone; perhaps the king's authority seized the babes and refused the mother's plea to kiss them farewell; perhaps all is true or none is true. But the simple truth remained that the twins were now motherless. So they became each other's mothers, and each other's brothers as well, hands entwined. If there was no one to love them, they would love each other, with a wild fierceness. If one needed protecting, the other was there, with ready fists and fiery grey eyes. And so they grew older and learned the ways of the world, always together.

One day, many years later, tragedy struck. The grey wolves of the night returned. A spring wind was blowing, bringing the sweet smells of budding lilacs, when the wolves arrived. They came on their silent paws, circling closer and closer until—

I slam my fist into Nap-Away's wall, just missing Carter's wolf, all gaunt and haunted, taped up on the wall beside me. *The wolves are real*, it whispers to me. Nap-Away shudders as the wall cracks, tiny fissures spreading upwards. A watershed of rage, flooding over. Fist to mouth, I suck on the skinned knuckles and start to cry, without making a sound.

"What do the wolves want?" I keep asking, but the answer stays hidden. My knuckles are throbbing. I need to find Carter, but I want to see Nikki. I feel like I have some kind of flu, but I don't feel sick. I feel hot, I can't eat, I can't sit still.

I dash across the parking lot to Room 5, bang on the door with my good fist. Iff answers, grinning like the Cheshire cat.

"Look," she says, pointing at her bed. One of the calico twins is curled up there, her tail wrapped around her body coming to rest at her nose.

"She's mine now. Really mine. She's not just coming to visit, my mom said she can stay forever."

We high-five. "Awesome," I say. "Which one is that?"

She gives me the 'duh' look. "That's Rainbow. Can't you tell?"

"Right, I kinda knew that. Twins get mixed up a lot, you know."

"Did you come to see my mom? She's all better," Iff says. I somehow managed to forget about Iff's mom. My brain is full of wolves. And Nikki.

"Yeah, I should say hi."

Iff calls her mom and Shelley comes to the door. She looks different. She looks like crap, especially her hair, which is hanging limp and greasy around her face, but she looks less icy, like she's melted a little. Like spring's coming.

"Hey," she says.

"Glad you're better." I say. There's some awkward silence. Iff is back inside, stroking her kitten. I shuffle around a little.

"Is Nikki around?" I ask, peeking behind her into their room.

Shelley shakes her head.

"I've gotta go see my housing worker tomorrow," she says. "I gotta get my act together, get outta this place. We weren't supposed to be here this long, it was just supposed to be temporary. We need a real place to live."

I pat the doorframe of Room 5. I'm thinking Nap-Away's about as real as it gets.

"You're gonna leave?"

"Well, yeah, of course, eventually. Maybe you could look after Tiffany for a bit tomorrow?" she asks.

"Sure. Will Nikki be around too?"

"I doubt it. She's gone home." She sighs, and reaches for her cigarettes.

"Did she leave..." I start to say. What, a love-note? Lame.

"Yeah."

I turn to go because I need to not be here right now. I need to go find Carter.

"See ya tomorrow," she calls out and closes the door.

I go back to the park at Queen and Church. It's not really a park though. More like the front yard of a church. Gothic-looking, ominous grey, crowned with pale green spires. Big archway over two heavy wooden doors. I go up the steps and touch the door, but I don't go in. The sun beats down, pigeons strut around on the wide walkway. No wolves, just a yappy little Chihuahua barking at the birds.

I look for them anyway, the grey wolves of the night. I circle around to the shaded side of the church, look for eyes glowing in the shadows. I check the mud for footprints, check for tufts of grey fur snagged on the rough bark of a tree. I look high up, checking for wolf gargoyles, peering down at me. I can't see them, but I know they are there, Carter's wolves.

"What do the wolves want?" I ask.

The church bells answer, ringing brightly into the summer. I pull out the page from Carter's notebook, the wolf sketch. The wolf is hunched low to the ground, his hackles raised, his tail brushing close to the ground, his ears flattened back. He's gaunt, with a row of thin curved ribs, like his heart is in the clutch of a dragon's claws. The jaws are snarled open, revealing rows of jagged teeth, a tongue that's unfurling like a whip. Something darker than blood trickles from his mouth in thick strands. I move the page around, the wolf's eyes follow me. They are pupil-less black hollows that seem to glow.

"What do you want?" I ask the wolf.

I feel like some deep truth is about to be revealed. I glance around, hoping for Carter to suddenly appear. Or the wolves. I listen for their silence. I hold the paper wolf against my chest, wait for my heart to open so that he can leap inside. I want to see the wolves, I want to be with Carter, to take his hand, lead him out of the woods. I want everything to reverse, I want to send the grey wolves of the night back to their fairy tale, to send the paper from Carter's notebook back to its tree, to send Carter back to me.

I study the wolf again, remembering Carter the last time I saw him. The way his lips curled back when he spoke. The darkness in his grey eyes, the way they burned wild. His notebook, filled with fangs, devoured dogs, claws shredding through the words.

Carter *is* the wolf. I touch his bristling fur, his fangs. "You're Carter," I tell the piece of paper. The wolves are Carter. When I find Carter, I'll see the wolves. No, when I find him, I *need* to see the wolves, see the darkness he's holding in, the darkness that's tearing its way out.

I look out again, see the shadow of the church falling across the park, the shadow of the trees stretched out across the grass, the shadow of a bicycle sliding past. If Carter is seeing wolves, it must be like both worlds exist, the real one and the shadow one, at the same time, in the same place, with no filter between them. The whole world pretends that the shadows don't exist, but they do, they do.

I can almost see Carter striding across the wide walkway towards the church steps, see the wolves shadowing him, see the wolf that is inside of him. The wolves are real. I know what the wolves want. They want to be seen. They want to be loved.

Back at Nap-Away Moffit's been hanging around Room 11 waiting for me. I grab hold of him.

"What's wrong?" he says. He rubs his hand across my back, tangles his fingers into my hair. I want to tell him about the wolves but I need to tell him about Nikki. Tell him some truths.

"I really like you Moffit," I say, pulling away so I can look at him. His eyes are so dark that his pupils seem to disappear in them.

"I know," he says. He quirks his eyebrow at me and half-smiles. "I really like you too. I've been thinking about what you should do. I figure you can't live at a motel forever, especially since Suleiman is paying for you to be here. And I'm guessing you're not going back home, wherever that was. So maybe you want to come hang with me?" He pauses. I take a shaky breath. This isn't how I planned for things to go. This is not the plan. Even though I have no plan.

"It's just a basement apartment. But there's lots of room. And you don't have much stuff," he adds, laughing. "Just a kitten and some well-worn boots." I grin, despite myself.

"You could start figuring out what you're going to do, maybe get a part-time job or something. Or maybe get some OSAP, go to school, take a writing class. Whatever. I don't really care what you do. I just thought we could, you know, be together while you do it."

"What about Carter?"

"Carter? Well, you need to live somewhere, whether you find Carter or not. And you need to have a life that's something more than just Carter."

"You're wrong. I don't!" But even as I say it I hear how stupid it sounds. Moffit doesn't say anything else. I have this sense of everything falling apart: my life of being Carter's twin, my friendship with Moffit, my thing with Nikki, which I'm starting to think maybe isn't a thing for her at all. Why didn't she at least say goodbye?

I take a shaky breath, but I still don't capture enough air. My heart is pattering like a hunted little rodent's. I run my hand across my torn knuckles.

"You're like Carter,' I say to Moffit. "You're like my brother."

He frowns, kind of smiles. Like he doesn't quite get it.

"What do you mean?"

I take hold of his hands, take hold of stardust.

"I love this tattoo," I say, touching each letter, leaping across his knuckles with a finger. "And this one." I slide my finger up to the words '*all good things are wild and free*' that are inked on the inside of his left forearm. "And this one." My finger jumps to the cow, wearing the flowered headband.

"I love how you've helped me search for Carter, how you bring me kale chips and Tofutti ice cream, how you taught me about stardust, how you played Wild Things with me and Iff.

"I love how you love me," I say. And I mean it. "I love you like I love my brother." I've never loved anyone like I love Carter. "I love you *like* a brother. Not a… a boyfriend."

"But…" he says, and it's the saddest little word.

Then he takes a step back from me. And another. His black eyes flash with something darker than sadness.

"But you've been pretending that you do," he says. "I'm not an idiot. I can tell when someone's not into me. And you've been acting like you're into me. Why would you do that to me?"

"I don't know," I say.

"Sure you do," he says. His words slice the air between us. "Sure you do, Ori."

"I didn't want to lose you," I say.

"Well you just did," he says. He turns to leave, then swivels back, steps closer. "We could've been friends you know. I would've been cool with that. I just thought…." He stops and looks around the parking lot. "That night when we were out here, in the dark, and we were spinning around, and there was stardust everywhere and we were kissing? And then later, back in your room? What was that all about?"

"You're like a part of me, like some other half of me, now that my twin-half is gone. I just… I just… I want to be with someone else."

"Who?" He asks. His voice is menacing. He grabs my arm. Nails digging in. "Who?"

"It doesn't matter. It's not about that. I like girls, that's all. It's not about you."

He laughs. A strange caw, like some scavenging bird. "You're kidding me, right? You're hoping to hook up with Iff's sister?"

I stay still. I don't nod, I don't speak. But I feel like my body is singing out the answer. Moffit shakes his head. Lets go of my arm.

"Good luck with that," he says mockingly. "She'll eat you alive." And then he's gone.

SULEIMAN

Massarat is lonely without her fearless leader. She is roaming around looking for Rainbow, meowing in empty corners, sniffing around the bottom of the door.

"She is gone, my little friend," I tell her. I whistle quietly, calling the kitten over. Massarat gallops to me, rubs against my leg purring. "You won't be lonely though. I'll still be here with you."

I imagine a different future for the kitten, one where Khadija saw her, admired Massarat's green eyes ringed with black, saw how the kitten was a way to bring us closer to Amina, thanked me for the gift. We would be together, Khadija and I, with Massarat between us, a fragile link bringing us back together.

But no. I shake my head. No, this is not how life was meant to unfold. This is imaginary, not based on what has happened, how I have behaved.

I pick up my cell phone and call Ahmed. He answers on the first ring.

"Ahmed!" I didn't actually expect to talk to my son, I was waiting to talk to an automated voice.

"Dad. What are you calling for?"

"I was calling to see if you are well, to see if your mother is settled in. To see how my family is."

Ahmed hesitates. "We're fine. Mom is...ok."

"I'm thinking of coming to Montreal. Not to bother your mother, not to interfere. I just feel I should be there. So that when the time comes..."

"Mom doesn't want to see you."

I pause. I know this already. Ahmed does not need to reiterate it. I know this truth, but still, I have hopes that it is not a permanent one.

"Ahmed, what should I do with the house?"

Ahmed remains silent.

"You're a man now. I see that. Together we should make some decisions. Do you think I should sell the house? It's too large for me alone. I have hope that Khadija will return, but maybe that's not realistic. And when you are done your schooling, you will come home, but even so, we don't need such a house, just for two."

Ahmed hesitates before answering. "It's a big decision," he finally says.

"I have been waiting and hoping for your mother and I to reunite, but I need to stop living like this. I need to choose a path forward. Insha'Allah, the day will come when Khadija will be able to think of us as a family again. But until then I am wondering what I should do."

"I don't think Mom will be able to decide," Ahmed says.

"No, I think this is a decision that we should make together."

"But it's my home," Ahmed says plaintively and suddenly he is a little boy again.

"Ahhh," I say. "It's my home as well. And Khadija's. And Amina's. But this home of ours is empty. So it is just a house. Perhaps it is the home of our past, neh?"

"I'll think about it Dad. I'll call you later."

"Fine. We can talk more about this decision. Ahmed, please tell your mother that I am…." No, I won't apologize through Ahmed. That's not a true apology. "Please say to your mother that I am thinking of her, as always."

"'K. Bye Dad."

I hang up the phone. How will I make this apology, if Khadija will not see me? She will not speak to me on the phone. I can't leave a phone message, it's not proper. A letter perhaps? This seems more permanent, unchangeable. A letter is something she can keep, something she can read again and again. I will be eternally apologizing. This is the right thing to do, I decide. But I have nothing to write on here at Nap-Away.

I pet Massarat good-bye and drive to the house. The first thing I see when I enter is Amina's picture in the hallway, the way that I left it, on the floor, facing the wall. I pick it up, hang it back up. Amina regards me with her sad brown eyes, her little smile.

"I have a kitten for you," I say to the picture on the wall. "Her name is Massarat. She is, as her name suggests, full of joy." I pull out my cell phone and scroll to a picture of the two calico kittens together. "This one is Massarat," I say, holding the phone up to Amina and pointing to one of the kittens. "It is hard to tell them apart. The other one, Rainbow, has a white-tip on her tail. And Massarat has the beautiful eyes. Do you see? They are lined in black."

"But I've forgotten. You have Mini, the little sister with you. So Massarat is here with me." I think that Amina's smile grows broader, that perhaps she nods her head.

"I am missing you always," I tell the picture. The sadness slithers in, constricts my chest. It wants to squeeze my anger out into the world. I stay still. I remember Shelley's tears falling, remember how there was nothing else in that moment. So I stay in this moment, allow the grief in, welcome it even. I look into Amina's eyes and breathe. She is with God. God is with me. This grief that tightens around me is a manifestation of *Al-Qabid*, *Allah* The Constrictor, who holds the rain back during the drought.

But God is not just the withholder, he is also the expander. The name *Al-Qabid* and *Al-Bassit* are inseparable when speaking of God. They are twinned together; God gives as he takes. There is relief after every difficulty; the rain will fall soon. After every hardship comes ease, so I must believe in God The Reliever as well. God who takes away with one hand and gives with the other. My breath comes easier, the tightening releases.

I kiss Amina's forehead, her cheeks, her lips. "Yes, I am missing you. Of course I am. How could it be otherwise?"

I turn and go upstairs to Amina's room. There is so much here that is no longer needed. Amina's clothes, her books, her bed even. And there is so much need out in the world, so many who are without. Here sits a wealth of things that are needed by others.

I take the clothes that are hanging and fold them neatly, empty the dresser drawers. In the basement I find some boxes and I pack the clothes into them, carry them out to the car. I can't do it all today, but I have started. I bring two things with me: the stuffed grey bunny, which I will keep, and a book filled with beautiful pictures for Tiffany. On the cover a great white horse with a golden mane is rearing up beside a small girl who holds his reins. I don't know the story, but the girl child looks brave. Brave and kind.

I am almost ready to leave when I realize I have not looked for some writing paper. I find a journal on Amina's desk, tiny flowers scrolled on each page. Her name is written inside the front cover, in large careful letters, but the rest of the pages are empty. I start to compose the letter in my mind, a confession of my sorrow. A wave of feeling floods over me, grabs me around my throat, cuts off my airway completely. I stumble back and sit on Amina's small bed, gasping. This isn't sadness, this is something darker, something trickier. For a moment I turn to my anger, let it swell up, like a mighty warrior. But no, I let the anger burn through me, and in the ashes I find something slicker, harder to hold. It is my shame. Ahh, this too, I think, this too, I shall allow, I shall welcome, as God would wish me to do. And so I stay there, holding Amina's small flowered journal in my hand, filled with my unwritten confession, with my shame and sorrow, my regret.

TIFFANY

My mom is smoking one cigarette and then another, and then even more. It's like she can't stop. There is a big cloud of smoke around her head that never seems to leave. She makes me go to the 7-11 with her so that she can buy more cigarettes. I ask if I can have a Popsicle but she gets mad and says to stop bugging her for stuff. Then she says sorry and buys me two popsicles, one chocolate and one banana. I like those flavours the best. Banana popsicles make me think of monkeys, laughing and swinging around in the trees, being silly. Their paws must get cold though, holding on to those frozen popsicles.

On the way home my mom tells me that tomorrow she is going to see our housing worker.

"What's that?" I ask.

"She's the woman who's gonna help us find a new place to live."

"Why?"

"Whatdya mean why? 'Cause we need a new place to live."

"Why can't we stay at Nap-Away?" I ask. I am starting to get a bad feeling in my tummy.

"It's a motel," my mom says. But I already know that Nap-Away is a motel. That doesn't help answer my question.

"But why can't we stay at Nap-Away? All my friends are there," I say.

My mom gives me a funny look.

"Suleiman lives there, and Ori lives there, and Massarat and the Grey One. And Ori needs to be my babysitter."

"Tiffany," she says, opening her new pack of cigarettes and pulling one out, "they're not friends, they're just our neighbours. Friends are kids your own age. Like at school." She lights her cigarette. "We're gonna move to a nice place. Maybe there'll be a playground, some other kids to play with. You'll make friends there."

"But I don't want to leave," I say. "I want to stay with Nap-Away. I want to stay! It's the first good place we've ever lived."

"It's a motel," she says. She is talking to me like I am stupid. I know that it's a motel. It's called The Nap-Away Motel.

"You're so stupid," I say. She looks at me with her eyes all flat and mad. She grabs my arm so that I have to stop walking and gives me a tiny shake.

"I don't need this shit from you," she says.

"I don't give you *shit*," I say. I have never said that word before. It's a bad word, even though lots of people say it. My mom says it and Ori says it and Nikki says it and kids at school say it, like Abishek who is in grade two and is a bully. When he bullies he sometimes says the f-word too. It feels bad to say it. But I am feeling bad, like how Max felt before he went to see the wild things.

We are standing on the sidewalk together and people are going past us. I am waiting for my mom to smack me for saying the shit word. But before anything else happens someone calls my mom's name and she stops looking at me with her angry eyes.

"Shelley, baby!"

It is my mom's new boyfriend, Tim. He is wearing his red baseball cap. He swats my mom's bum with his hand like there is a bug on it.

"Shell! How's my girl doing?" he asks her. She turns her mad slitty eyes on him.

"You nearly killed me the other night," she hisses at him. "That was some bad shit you gave me. And you took off, didn't even stay to see if I was ok."

"Ahh, don't be mad at me," he says. "I've got some new candy for ya. Whatdya say?" He slides his arm around her shoulder. "You look like you could use a bit of something."

My mom bites her bottom lip and chews on it a little. But she doesn't say anything to Tim.

"Come on, let's get high," he says.

She shakes her head at him.

"I'm trying to get clean," she says.

I don't really understand what they are talking about. It's like they are talking in secret words.

"Don't be such a drag," he says. "That's not what you really want, is it? I know what a girl like you needs." He leans in close to her and whispers something in her ear. She shakes her head. Then she looks down at me. I think she forgot I said the bad word and that we were in the middle of being mad at each other because she doesn't look angry any more. She looks scared.

"Come on, Tiffany," she says, grabbing my hand. It is all sticky from the banana Popsicle but she doesn't let go. She starts walking really fast and I have to run to keep up with her.

"Don't be like this, baby," Tim says. "Don't make me mad. You shouldn't be saying no to me." My mom doesn't say bye or anything, she just keeps pulling me down the street.

"I'll come by your place later," Tim yells.

My mom starts running. Even though I run as fast as I can I have trouble keeping up with her because she's going so fast. I try to look behind us because I think that Tim must be chasing us but I almost fall down when I do. I look ahead to where I can see Nap-Away, waiting for us to get there. We run and run and run to get away from whatever is chasing us and when we get home we are both panting like dogs in the sun. When we stop I look behind to see if Tim is still after us but there is no one there.

"Why did we have to run?" I ask my mom. Maybe it's like playing Wild Things. Maybe it wasn't Tim who was chasing us, but invisible things and we had to escape. It's sort of a scary game.

"I'm always running, baby," she says. "But I can't ever get away."

ORI

I've been cocooned in my room for hours, maybe days. Sleeping. The Grey One is pouncing around under my covers. He's engaged in a great battle against The Ten Toes. They take a last stand, then admit defeat, and flee. I jump from the bed, look out into the deserted parking lot. I'm Carterless and Moffitless. I feel like I've been marooned on a deserted island.

I go outside, mope around the parking lot for a while, hoping Iff or Suleiman will show up. I think about going back downtown, back to Queen Street to look for Carter again, to look for his wolves, but I don't want to leave Nap-Away.

I play with The Grey One in the parking lot for a bit, throw sticks for him, like he's a dog. He seems to get the game. Does some gnawing, some fetching. I try some names out on him: Mystery, Wild Thing, Smoke, Catsby, India, Wolf, Greyling, Theg-re-yone. He starts batting a little pebble around, pouncing on it then turning away and ignoring it before attacking it again. I call him over and he comes galloping. Maybe he is part dog.

Finally Suleiman shows up. I wave. Trot over to greet him. Wrap The Grey One around my neck, the way Zelda travels on Moffit's shoulders. If a ferret can do it, why not a cat?

"How are you? Where have you been?" I ask.

"I went to talk to a real estate agent. Maybe it's time to sell the house. But I can't decide. One minute I think I should, the next I think it is a terrible mistake. Even if Ahmed and Khadija returned, if such a thing were possible, even then, would we go back to this house?"

"Because of Amina?"

"Yes, because of Amina, and because of the things that happened after."

He looks down at our feet, his enormous sandals, my kick-ass Blundstones.

I reach up and stroke The Grey One. His fur is hot against the back of my neck. Makes me feel not so alone.

"I've been thinking a lot about the wolves, about Carter's wolves," I say. "I think they are part of him, you know? Like the dark part of him. Maybe there's some stuff that has happened to him, or stuff that he's done, that needs to be seen. Dangerous, wicked, angry stuff. Does that make sense?"

Suleiman reaches his hand up. I'm figuring he's going for his mole, his little worry stone. But instead he runs his big hand along The Grey One's muzzle, onto his back, around my shoulder.

"These kittens are growing so big, neh?"

"Yeah, he's kinda heavy." The Grey One's weight on my shoulder feels solid, like it's keeping me on the ground.

"I have a wolf too," Suleiman says. "Like the picture your brother drew. There is a wolf inside of me."

"What did your wolf do?" I ask.

This time he does go for the mole. He doesn't say anything. The kitten is purring in my ear.

"Was it Amina?"

"No," he says, shaking his head. "No, not Amina. Khadija. My wife. I was so angry, angry at Khadija for causing Amina's death, angry at my own grief, angry at myself for my lack of faith. How could I not have faith in what was meant to happen? How?" He holds his hands out wide, imploring. "I was nothing except for a terrible anger."

"What did you do?" I ask again.

He lets out a great breath of air. A garlicky whoosh.

"I blamed Khadija. I shouldn't have, but I did. I turned away from her. I became a person I didn't want to be." He moans. "*Insha'Allah*, I will be forgiven."

I reach for his hand. Hold it tight. I see his wolf, angry, scared, hunched behind him in his shadow, haunting him.

PART FOUR

SULEIMAN

The first words that I wrote, after opening the flowered journal to the first page, were *Khadija, I am sorry.* For a long time afterwards I didn't write anything else. These were the words that I had needed to say, that I had not said, and now they were written before me, indelible. I admired the words and all that they encompassed. I was sorry for so many things; each one of them was contained in those three words.

But of course it wasn't enough. So next I wrote: *I am ashamed.* It was much harder to write those words. The pen trembled in my hand and I fought the urge to place it down, to stop writing. Shame burnt through me, scorching my sense of pride, making my anger rise up again. I placed the notebook down and did not return to it for several days.

Today I re-read what I've written. "Khadija, I am sorry. I am ashamed." I laugh. It has taken me more than a week to write these seven words. I can see all that is contained in each sentence, but Khadija will not. I am not giving her anything with these seven words. There must be more that I can offer her.

I pick up the pen and take a deep breath. I feel like a school-boy again, like I am back in grade two, struggling to write in English, struggling to find a beginning to the story of my summer holidays. I am trying to tell a very different story, but the struggle seems no different. First I must tell Khadija how much I love her, how I have always loved her. I glance around the room. The bed is unmade, Massarat is curled up at my feet on the carpet, sleeping. Amina's grey bunny is dangling overtop of the TV. There is nothing here that reminds me of Khadija. I look down at my feet, holding my place in the world on the dirty carpet of Room 6. The carpet brings Khadija back to me. Not this worn carpet, but the blue one with golden threads woven through it. I am transported back to the night in our apartment in St. Jamestown. It feels like another life, unconnected to this one that I am living now.

How many times have I remembered that day, that moment of uncomplicated happiness? Have I ever told Khadija how I treasure that memory, how it sustains me, like air, like water, like God?

I bring the pen to paper and begin to write.

Hours later I stop, massaging my cramped hand. Now that I have started, the words are tumbling out, so many words that I can't catch them all. I will write more later, I decide. It is enough for now that I have started, that I have moved past the seven words.

I step out into the afternoon sunshine, blinking. I have not seen Tiffany today, nor Yori. I'm undecided about the rest of the day. I have been to the mosque this morning already. Perhaps I will go to the house and pack more boxes. I have been doing this every day, sorting and packing all the things we have accumulated over the years. Much of it seems meaningless now.

I could call Ahmed, ask about Khadija, talk to him again about selling the house. I should go to the pet store and buy food for the kittens. But for now I sit on my green chair, surveying the parking lot.

The door to Room 5 opens. I am expecting Tiffany, or her mother, but it is the older daughter, Nikki, who appears. Again, I am startled by the resemblance she bears to her mother.

"Hello," I say.

She looks at me with her icy blue eyes. She is chewing gum with her mouth open, smacking her lips and making the gum snap sharply.

"Hey," she says. She looks away but doesn't leave.

"How is your mother? Is she well?"

Nikki shrugs. Again, this shrugging, the language of the teenager. I translate: *What do you care?*

"And your sister?" Suleiman asks.

Nikki turns back towards me.

"Why do you want to know?"

"I care about her. We're neighbours," I reply.

"Well," she says, "they won't be your neighbour for much longer. My mom's got her name in for an apartment on Brimley. They'll be moving soon."

I feel as if she has just struck me. I clutch my fists, refrain from speaking. Tiffany will be gone. Why have I not thought about this before? Why have I never considered the possibility of them leaving, moving away? How could I believe that things would stay the same? Especially when I'm considering leaving as well?

Nikki pulls out her cell phone and quickly types a message with her thumbs.

"He shoulda been here already," she mutters.

I glance around the parking lot wondering who she is waiting for. I see Yori, getting off the bus. He saunters towards the motel, then stops abruptly. Yori is looking at us, at Nikki. I look back and forth between the two teenagers. Perhaps Nikki is waiting for Yori?

Yori comes forward to stand in front of Nikki.

"You're here," Yori says. He kicks the pavement with his boot, looks unsure. I sense unspoken things. I study Nikki's face but it is frozen, like an ice sculpture. I don't intend to, but I lean forward slightly, curious.

"Yeah, I came by to see Tiff," she says.

"You look great," Yori says. I look more carefully at Nikki. She is wearing very little: torn denim shorts that are too short, a white blouse with no sleeves, white flip-flops. I don't see her beauty, but I see how she radiates, how she shines like ice in the sun. Yori takes a step closer to Nikki, then reaches up and touches the white-gold hair. Ahh, I think, Yori believes he is in love with this girl. I look back at Nikki's face. But maybe she doesn't feel the same?

Nikki takes a step back, stumbling on her flip-flop.

"Can we talk?" Yori asks. "I haven't seen you since last week. Since…"

"I'm waiting for my boyfriend to pick me up," she says. "It's not a good time. You should probably get outta here." She glances at her phone, then shoves it back into her pocket.

"But, what about…?" Nikki looks at Yori scornfully, a look teenagers seem to have perfected. They are filled with contempt. It is their way of lashing out first, I think, rather than receiving the wounding.

"What, you thought we were a thing now?" She marks the word 'thing' with her fingers in the air, like quotation marks. She rolls her eyes.

"I just wanted to see what it'd be like," she says, "hookin' up with someone like you. It wasn't anything special." She snaps her gum again. "Besides, I would never date a he-she anyway."

I don't want to look at Yori's face. I remember the grief written on it after Yori found the dead kitten. I continue to look at Nikki, who is chewing her gum and looking out at Kingston Road. Perhaps I'm wrong, perhaps Yori doesn't have feelings for the girl. She doesn't seem worthy of Yori's attention. So I look.

But his face is as I imagined, a face wounded by betrayal.

A sporty black car turns off from Kingston Road, pulls up in front of them. A young man is driving, a single hand on the steering wheel, the other arm leaning out the open window. He has a look of brash confidence, much like Ahmed, an air of arrogance that has not yet been earned, but is there nonetheless.

"Hey, babe," he calls out to Nikki. She shakes out her blonde hair out and grins, then hops in the passenger seat. He leans over and pulls her head towards his, kisses her hard on the lips. Nikki waves goodbye in a vague way, without looking. Whether to me or to Yori or to Nap-Away is unclear. She does not look back.

I turn to Yori to offer some words of kindness but find nothing to say. Yori stays and watches the car leave, looking down Kingston Road long after it is out of view.

"Yori," I begin, searching for the right thing to say. "I wish she didn't speak so cruelly to you. I hope that—"

"Leave me alone!" Yori turns on me. His eyes are shining with unshed tears but his face is filled with fury. "You think you can fix everything!" He kicks the leg of my chair. "But you can't fix this, so just leave! Leave!"

I feel an exquisite ache in my chest. I turn away from him and go into my room.

TIFFANY

I wish that Tim, who wears his red baseball cap all the time, would stop coming to Nap-Away to see my mom. Every day this week he's come to see her but we couldn't run away from him because we were already home.

On the first day my mom told him to go away, but he didn't. He stayed at the door talking to my mom, leaning against the doorway with his big arm so she couldn't close the door on him. She didn't want him to come in but he started to get mad at her so she let him. He didn't say hi to me or to Rainbow. My mom and Tim did some kissing and stuff and then he left.

But the next day he was back. This time he brought beer with him and my mom didn't tell him to go away. She put on her lipstick and her tight blue top that is the same colour as her eyes. She did a lot of laughing with him and she touched his arms a lot, which is what she does when she likes her boyfriend. After he left my mom got mad at me for getting peanut butter on my bed. Then she got mad at me for eating all the peanut butter. Then she said we had to go buy more peanut butter but she couldn't find any money, so she got mad some more. After that she said she had to go get something from Tim and she left me alone.

When she came back she wasn't mad anymore. She was super excited and she was talking really fast and saying that maybe we would go and live with Tim, instead of living at Nap-Away. I don't want to go and live with Tim but I didn't say it because I didn't want her to change back to being mad again.

Tim is back again today. I wish he brought pizza this time because there is still no peanut butter and no cereal and no donuts and I am hungry. But he only brought himself and his red baseball cap. My mom says

I should go and see if Ori will look after me. But Ori isn't in Room 11 and Suleiman isn't in Room 6, so I take Rainbow on his leash and I go behind Nap-Away to my secret place where Tree is. Orion taught me the name of the tree. It's an oak tree, because it grows acorns. My special acorn on a chain is in my pocket and I slide it over my head so that the acorn hangs down against my heart. My antler branch is still here on the ground, hidden under some long weeds and old leaves and garbage. I pull it out and wipe off the dirt. If Orion was here he could make me a crown of leaves again. There is a plant growing through the fence that has pointy leaves and tiny red berries. I yank a big piece off and unwind it from the fence and try to tie it together into a circle. It's not as good as the crown that Orion made, but I put it on my head anyway. My hair holds on tight to the leaves and I can see a few berries out of the corner of my eye, hanging down in front of my face. I feel ready.

I touch the trunk of the tree and feel its magic. I look around to check if there are any wild things nearby and even though I don't see any, I say the words just in case: "Be still." And I wave my antler branch in the air. Everything is safe and quiet and good. I whisper into the tree and ask Mini and Amina to come out.

Mini comes first, a tiny black shadow that crawls under the fence. She hasn't grown any bigger at all. She is so small and sweet. She sniffs at Rainbow and Rainbow sniffs at her. They both start to purr and rub against each other..

Then Amina comes. She has her favourite bunny with her, the grey one with the ribbon, and she has an acorn around her neck, just like I do. She is wearing green pants that puff out around her like the parachute that we play with at school, and a green dress that matches the pants. There are golden lines all through the green, and she has on golden earrings too, and little white sandals. I didn't know she was going to be so pretty. She has such long eyelashes!

I feel shy but I can tell she does too, so I tell her about Rainbow and Massarat and The Grey One, who are all the brothers and sisters of Mini. She wants to know all about them, so I tell her all their different colours and how fluffy The Grey One is and how bossy Rainbow is to Massarat and how they all like to try and climb straight up the walls. She has a pretty laugh that sounds like a little bell. I ask her to tell me about her horse Winter and what it's like to go riding in the woods. She tells me that sometimes he goes so fast it is like riding on the wind. Every night she brushes out his mane because it gets so tangled and filled with leaves and sticks and burrs.

"My hair always gets tangled too," I say.

"After I finish brushing him, he tries to get me to feed him jellybeans, but they're not good for him so I only let him have them on special days," she tells me. "Mostly he should eat good treats, like carrots or apples." I tell her about the time Rainbow tried to eat pepperoni right off the pizza and she does that jingling laugh again.

"I might have to move away," I tell her. I want her to know in case I don't get to come back again. At first she looks sad, but then she smiles.

"I think we could still play together," she says. "I think the acorns are magic too, not just the tree."

We both hold on to our acorns and smile at each other.

"I'm glad we are going to be friends," she says to me. And I tell her that I'm glad too. We hug each other goodbye and she scoops up Mini and holds her tight against her chest when she leaves. I wave until I can't see her anymore.

"Goodbye," I whisper. And I think I can hear, from far far away, her little laugh that jingles like a tiny Christmas bell.

ORI

I return, again and again, to the steps of the church. I sit and wait and watch. I imagine the wolves, sitting motionless in the shadows, watching and waiting with me. Carter will come. Sometimes I whisper the words like truths. "Carter will come, Carter will come, Carter will come."

And then, one day, he does. I'm sitting on a park bench eating a hot dog from a stand on the corner. I don't even see him walk up, but suddenly he is there, sitting beside me.

"Hey," he says. As if we were expecting to find each other.

"Carter!" I squeal like a little kid, hug him close. Splurt a blob of ketchup-mustard mix onto his leg. He's skinnier than ever. Dirtier too. "I've been looking for you forever."

"I'm glad we found you," he says. He looks at my hotdog. "Can I have that?"

"Sure!" I laugh, hand over the half-eaten dog.

"I need to know you're ok," I say. "I talked to Joel from the ukulele jam. He said you were doing some crazy stuff. And he gave me this." I hold out the wolf.

Carter's grey eyes glint like sharpened metal. "Joel? He was trying to steal my energy, he was sucking it right out of me. I could feel it happening." He looks at me suspiciously. "I know what you're going to tell me, that I'm crazy, that it's in my head. Some kind of delusion. But it's not like that! It's more like science fiction, like science that no one understands yet. No one's working on this yet. I've started researching it. Maybe it has to do with mirror neurons, that's what I'm thinking. That's what I'm investigating now." He hands me the hotdog and pulls his notebook out of his knapsack, scribbles something in it.

"I'm having trouble talking, communicating, because I feel like I'm completely accessible, like my thoughts are broadcasting, but I'm completely misunderstood." He pauses and tugs at his hair. "I don't want to manipulate you, some people like that, it works for them, it's how they communicate, with the manipulation. It's like a game they play, but you're not like that." He tilts his head at me. "Maybe you believe me," he says, "but you don't want to tell me you do, right?"

I nod my head, give him back the last bite of hotdog. He doesn't sound any crazier than normal. He's always had theories, always talked about stuff that I didn't quite understand: nebulas, quarks, mirror neurons. But then I remember about the pencil in his heart. I steal a quick glance at his chest.

"Because then you'll feed my delusion, if you say you believe me. That's what they told you, right? But it's not a delusion, see? People are sucking me empty; they're messing with the connectivity of the social networks. My brain is too evolved. It's invisible what's happening, but I see it. Survival depends on art, on seeing what's real. I can see them, the energy vampires, trying to steal my brain." He laughs, abruptly. A bird-like squawk.

"I always talked way too much science for you," he says.

"No, that's ok. I just want you to tell me what's wrong."

"They're not real vampires, not like all that romance and twilight crap, I'm talking about predators, about people that feed off of your brain. They want to eat my thoughts and then discard me."

I don't know what to do with what he's telling me. Thought-eating.

"What about the wolf?" I ask, holding the picture out towards him again.

"The wolves!" He laughs sharply. "They're everywhere. Like pigeons roosting and shitting all over the city. Sometimes they sit like gargoyles, as still as statues way up-top a building, watching me. Sometimes they stalk me. They think they're being stealthy, but I can hear their nails clicking on the sidewalk behind me. I'm not an idiot. And I can smell them, they smell like dead meat; I can feel their mangy fur brush against me." He glances around furtively, lowers his voice. "They ride the streetcars, sitting in the old-people seats up front with their tails wrapped around their skinny legs, like they think they're special. They piss wherever they want, like dogs. Once I was in an alleyway and there was a wolf above me on a fire-escape and her pee came splashing down on me like rain. I felt it on my cheeks, all hot and wet." He touches his hand to my cheek, traces a line of tears. "They're always watching me, their black eyes are everywhere, and they flash their teeth at me, like the flash of a knife blade. I've kept track of them," he says, gesturing to his notebook. "It's all documented. I'm part of an experiment, you know. I went to a doctor and she messed with my brain. It's some kind of implant, some kind of device that draws them to me. Maybe with pheromones, you know?" He wrinkles his nose, sniffs twice.

"You want another hot dog?" I ask him.

"Yeah," he says. "I can trust you." We both stand up but neither of us move. I look him in the eyes. He scratches his tangled hair and averts his gaze, looks over my shoulder instead.

"Carter? Why'd you leave? Why didn't you take me with you?"

"I didn't leave you. I thought I could run away from them, but they've followed me."

"Who? Who are they?"

Carter scans the park, looks over his shoulders, left and right and left again.

"I had to leave you Ori. They said you'd do stuff to me, that if you found out..." He smacks his forehead. "Shut up," he mutters, "just shut up. Shut up shut up shut up shut up shut up shutupshutupshutupshutup." I grab his hand, squeeze it hard. He looks at it like he can feel the squeeze, but can't see what's causing it. "I thought I'd do something to you," he whispers. "Something bad. That they would tell me to do something bad to you." He swallows hard, looks like he might cry.

"Carter," I say. "Carter, it's ok. You would never."

Carter stares at me without blinking. "I'd chew your leg off."

"What the—? Like eat it?"

"Nah." He laughs, that crazy hyena cackle.

"For you, I'd do it for you. Like a wolverine." He grimaces, shows me his teeth. Chomps down. Not on my leg, just on air.

"Would you?" he asks.

"Chew my leg off?"

"No, chew mine off. For me. If I ever asked you to?"

"Why would I do that?"

He turns his head to the right, mutters something. Looks back at me. "Like, if I needed you to. Would you?" He steps towards me. "Ori!" He grabs my shoulders. His hands feel hot. My heart jolts. I feel an urge to squirm away, to bolt. He holds tighter. "You know, if my leg was caught in a trap, the kind with the metal jaws that clamp down on the bone. If I couldn't chew it off myself. Would you? Would you do it for me? Or if the shrews were in my foot, burrowing in it and infesting it. And I needed it amputated. Would you? Ori? Would you?" He looks panicked.

I breathe in, belly, diaphragm, chest, collarbones. Deep.

"I would." We lock eyes. His pupils are wide black orbs. Where's the grey? I slide my arms around his waist, pull him towards me. "I would. I would chew off your leg if you needed me to."

"Ok," he sighs into my neck, slumps forward. "Ok. That's good. That's what I needed to know. They told me you wouldn't."

"They're wrong, Carter. They're wrong." He stays against me. He doesn't smell that great. A sour, greasy smell.

"I'd do anything for you," I say. I keep holding him tight. "I've missed you." I have Carter back and that's what I've wanted, all these weeks that I've been searching. I've lost Moffit, I never had Nikki, but I have my twin back. And for just this moment, everything is sweet. Sweet like a ukulele riff, strumming me back home.

SULEIMAN

I'm seated outside on my green chair, writing to Khadija. Today I decide to tell Khadija how much I love the children that we made together, how much meaning they have brought to my life. Yes, Ahmed and Amina are like two treasures that we unearthed, shaped, polished, and cherished. I picture Ahmed changing through the years, growing from a helpless newborn into the man he is now. But Amina, her journey cannot be followed any longer. She is frozen forever as a five-year-old.

Should I try to explain my rage? Explain how the sadness twisted inside of me, like a strangling black vine, until all that could grow was anger? No, that's not what I want to write about.

Remember, I write, *how your belly grew so big with Amina? How you sat with that little blue teacup perched on your big belly, as if it was a shelf, and how we laughed and praised our new daughter for being so helpful?* I smile at the memory. Next time I visit the house I will look for those teacups. I will bring them with me when I travel to Montreal to take the journal to Khadija, I decide. I continue to write, trying to remember not just the great joys and sorrows but the simplest of things, the mundane details that turned into a day, a month, a year of life lived.

Amina wished to read so badly, because everyone else in the family could. Every night she sat with her books, trying. One day she brought you a book that Ahmed was reading and she followed the words with her finger, reading aloud to you, except the book was upside down. You did not correct her though, you just listened. She was so proud! I remember the smile on your face when you told me this story, how we chuckled together.

Ah, we both share such a love for our daughter. Ahmed, our first born, is like a tree, so sturdy and reliable, but Amina, she was like a wildflower, growing so unexpectedly in the midst of our family, something to marvel over, something delightful. I praise you and thank you for bringing her into this world.

I pause. A strange sensation bubbles up in my chest. It has felt tight for so long, locked in stone, but now the stone is starting to disintegrate into rocks, into pebbles, into soil. Soon, I think, joy will flower again. I picture a field full of bursting poppies and cornflowers, a dazzle of red and blue, their colours singing praises to the sun. I will bring some to Montreal, a packet of flower seeds to give to Khadija.

I glance up. Tiffany is skipping across the parking lot towards me. Held tightly in her fist is an already wilting bunch of dandelions. She stops in front of me, offers out the yellow flowers.

"These are for you," she says.

I extend my hand and take the bouquet. "Thank you, these are very lovely."

"They're my most favourite flower because they can be the sun and they can be the moon. And when they turn to moons, you can make wishes with them, like wishing on a star."

"The sun and the moon, neh? All of this in one small weed?" I chuckle. "And what would you wish for?"

Tiffany looks around the parking lot, up to the sky, over to the top of the oak tree, and back at Nap-Away. She steps behind me and gently pats the yellow wall of Nap-Away.

"I would wish to stay here forever."

"Ahhh," I say. "Ahhh. So it's true that you will be leaving, that we won't be neighbours any longer. And I'm leaving too, going to Montreal to be closer to my family." I pause. "I'll miss you."

Tiffany pats my arm. Then she leans forward and kisses my cheek, a kiss as soft as dandelion fluff.

Later, long after Tiffany has gone, I hear someone calling out to me. I lift my head from the journal. There is Yori, and walking beside him is his missing brother. They are alike in every way, as twins sometimes are. They are the same height, they stride towards me in the same manner, their hair is the same shaggy brown, their eyes, now that they are nearer, the same pale grey, a colour that reminds me of the pigeons, fluttering down.

"Yori, you found him!" I stand up to greet them.

"This is Carter," Yori says. Yori looks different beside his brother. Younger perhaps? No, that's not the quality. He looks happy, I can see that, but I've seen Yori happy before. No, that's not it either. I look at the brother, Carter. Up close I can see how they differ. Carter is skinnier, his face sharper and angled. He is dirtier too, his clothes, his hair, his hands. He is not looking at me, instead his head is turned away to the side and he mutters, as if Yori is there on his left. But Yori is not there, no one is there.

"I am glad Yori found you, glad that you are safe," I say to Carter. I smile at Yori. Then I realize what has changed about Yori. He no longer looks lost.

"They don't know you," Carter says. I'm not sure how to respond to this.

"I'm Suleiman," I say. I extend my hand. Carter's mouth twitches, once and again, but it is not a smile. He doesn't reach out a hand, so I let mine drop.

"You might be part of what's been happening," Carter says, then turns back to the left, as if listening to someone else. I look at Yori.

"I think his thoughts are a little messed up. Like maybe he hasn't been sleeping right. Or maybe he's on something," Yori says. "And he's kinda skinny—I don't think he's been eating."

I reach into my back pocket and pull out my wallet.

"You must get food, good food. Please, take it," I say, offering out a twenty dollar bill. "You must take care of him. It's obvious that he's struggling. At least he doesn't need to struggle for something to eat, neh?"

Yori steps forward and hugs me awkwardly, too tightly and too quickly.

"Thanks," he says.

"I am so happy that you have your brother back," I say.

"I'm not sure where he was living, but he said his roommate was bugging him, following him around and stuff. And that he couldn't sleep because of the animals. I don't know if they had pets or what. But I figured he'd be better if he came home with me," Yori says. He reaches his arm out and throws it across his brother's shoulders.

"Come on, Carter," Yori says. The two leave together, striding across the parking lot towards Room 11.

I sit back down and contemplate. Carter is not well, that seems clear enough. Maybe what Yori says is true, that he is lacking basic necessities: food, sleep, peace. Obviously something more is troubling him. He seems to speak to other beings that are not present, he does not seem connected to what is happening around him. No, that's not quite right. He seems to be not only connected to this world, but to another one as well. I wish that Khadija was here. She understood such things, had a way of seeing others deeply. She had a wisdom that I don't. When Khadija spoke, I often felt like a student, like she was my teacher.

I turn back to the journal, re-read what I have written. I want to tell Khadija about the things that are happening around me, about Yori and his brother, about what is troubling him. About Tiffany, and how she brings thoughts of Amina back to me. About my time at Nap-Away, how I have grown so fond of this rundown motel. About Massarat and the other kittens. But where should I begin the story, a story that is unfinished? I look around, at the row of doors marking the entrances to Nap-Away, at the parking lot, the blue spruce and the masjid next door, the pigeons roosting on the wires.

I will begin the story for Khadija there. An honest beginning, a humble one. I put pen to paper and begin to write again.

The pigeons are always close by. I have heard many others complain about them. Some in the city call them rats, rats with wings. I once thought of them in this way as well, but not any longer. No, not at all. Let me tell you of their colours, Khadija, the shimmering rainbow that is hidden amongst their grey feathers....

TIFFANY

Today my mom is super excited and happy. She is saying lots of stuff to me, about how things will be better when we move and about how she's gonna start fresh, she's gonna start over, she's gonna make everything right.

"You'll see, Tiffany," she says, lighting another cigarette, even though she just lit one and it is sitting in the ash tray making a river of smoke that goes right up to the ceiling. "I know I've gotta get my shit together, after what happened. I know that." She puts down the new cigarette and pulls her socks off.

"My feet are so hot," she says, scratching at them. "But here's the thing. I can't change if I'm staying the same, right? That's why we've gotta move. The doctor at the hospital said I should go to a program, detox or rehab or whatever. But that's not real, you know? It's not the real world. I need to stay real." She jumps up and does a weird little dance with her bare feet on the carpet, a fast pitter-patter, pitter-patter.

"Things will be different after we move," she says. "I promise."

"I don't want to live with Tim," I say.

"Tim is bad news," she says. She nods her head and then points her cigarette right at me. "Bad news. I knew him before, did you know that?"

"Before what?" I ask.

"From before, when I was in school, when I was friends with Tiffany. When I was Nikki's age." She goes back to her ashtray and picks up the other cigarette, so now she has one in each hand. "He did some really terrible things."

"Like what kind of bad things? Did he steal stuff?"

She puts her arms up in the air and spins around so that the two cigarettes make a smoky circle around her.

"Look at that," she says. "I wish I could blow smoke rings." She flops down backwards on the bed.

"Tiffany, I can't tell you what he did. You're too young to know about the kind of things that he did."

"Did he hit people?"

"Worse," she says. "Way worse." She rolls over on the bed, keeping the cigarettes up in the air. Then she keeps rolling over and over until she falls off the bed. She stays down on the floor, between our two beds, giggling. Lots of times my mom and I do silly stuff together. But today she is being silly all on her own, without me. Like she is the kid.

"I'll tell you a secret," she says. I think she is trying to whisper, but she can't make her voice be quiet. "He went to prison."

"What's prison?"

"Jail. You know, like in Monopoly. *Go to Jail. Go directly to Jail. Do not pass GO. Do not collect two hundred.*"

I don't know how to play Monopoly, so I don't know about those rules. But I know what jail is. We play a game at school that has jail. If you get caught by the cops you have to go behind the red ladder in the playground that takes you up to the slide. I know about real jail too, because Theo says his dad is there for stealing cars.

"Did he do killing?" I ask my mom. I think this must be the right answer because hitting is worse than stealing and killing is worse than hitting. But she doesn't tell me.

"Come sit with me Tiffany," she says, and she pats the floor beside her. She is still holding both of her cigarettes, but she is not smoking them. I take one of them away from her and put it in the ashtray and then I go back and take the other one away too. Then I sit down beside her.

"You're such a good kid," she says. She puts her head down on my lap. She has such pretty hair and it never gets any tangles in it. I like to braid it. Lots of times she doesn't let me play with her hair, but today she doesn't make me stop, so I start working on a braid at the side, over her ear.

"If I was a kid, I'd wanna be like you," she says. Then she starts to laugh, but just a little bit. Then she gets the hiccups. Then she starts to cry.

I don't say anything. I look at my mom, at how she is curled up on the floor without her socks on, crying. I am remembering what Nikki told me, when we walked to the library together, about how my mom was using drugs. I wish that Nikki were here.

I think my mom is using.

I keep playing with her hair, making lots and lots of braids in it, until her whole head is covered in them. She looks different. I wish I had elastics so that I could make them all stay in.

If we move, my mom says that everything will be different. I wish that some things could be different and some things could be the same. Mostly I wish that we could stay here, at Nap-Away.

My mom falls asleep on the floor and I scootch away because I really have to pee. When I come out of the bathroom Tim is inside of our room. I do a tiny scream because he was not there when I left.

"Where's your mom?" he says.

"She's sleeping," I say, pointing at the floor beside the bed. I wish that she would wake up because Tim doesn't ever talk to me, but he can't talk to her when she is sleeping.

"Like Sleeping Beauty," he says. He does a laugh that is really just the word ha! and then he walks across the room and gives her feet a little kick.

"You shouldn't kick," I say, but I only whisper the words.

"Why don't you get lost," he says. He walks back to the door and opens it. "Go on, get outta here. Scram."

It's almost nighttime but it is not dark yet. My mom leaves me alone sometimes, but not outside at nighttime.

"Mom?" I say. I bend down where she is sleeping on the floor and give her a little push. She makes a snoring sound and rolls over.

Tim comes towards me. I hop onto the bed so that I can go around him but his arm is fast like a snake and he catches me.

"Your mom and I have some talking to do about when she's moving in," he says, holding tight on to my arm. "So we need to be alone." He pulls me towards the door. I twist and wiggle and then kick Tim's legs. He laughs and opens the door wider. Then I bite his arm, and he yelps and lets go of me. This is something I learned to do from Theo at school.

"You little bitch," he says, rubbing his arm. He tries to grab me again, but I go backwards, away from him.

"Mom!" I yelp, but she doesn't answer. Tim comes towards me, like the kittens sometimes do when they are playing chase, really fast, and he grabs me by the hair.

"Gotcha!" he says, yanking my hair, so my head jerks back. I start to scream, but he claps his hand over my mouth. "Shut the fuck up," he says. So I stop screaming.

ORI

I want to feel better than I do. I'm not twinless; I've found what I've been searching for. So I should be feeling pretty swag. But I don't. I hear Moffit's voice mocking me: What's your plan, Ori? What's your plan? It's pretty clear I never had one. And it's pretty clear I need one.

Carter is pacing around the room, talking to someone else. I've been trying to convince him to go out and get something to eat but he won't leave the room. He's also doing some weird shit with his hands. Sign language maybe, or Bollywood hand dancing. Like he's trying to pull something down from the sky.

I reach into my back pocket, pull out the beaver postcard. It's almost in four pieces now, the folded edges are so worn. The quest is over. I can stop looking for Carter. So now what? We're not going back home to Foster Home Five in nowhere-ville. That's not home anyway. Home is wherever we are together, so Nap-Away is it for now. So if Carter is found and we're home, everything should be good. But it's not.

I decide a list is the way to go. Now that I can stop looking for Carter, I need to figure out what to do with him. So I need to know what's wrong with him, right? That makes sense. I grab a take-out bag from the garbage, rip it open. Flatten out the brown paper, start my list:

1)   talking to people that aren't there. Who are 'they'?
2)   not sleeping
3)   not eating
4)   pencil in his heart?
5)   wolves everywhere
6)   lighting ukuleles on fire
7)   saying things I don't understand

8)   dirty
9)   energy vampires

I look at my list. I know what it's a list of, but I don't want to say it, don't want to believe it. It's a list of crazy, is what it is. Carter's got some kind of crazy going on. It's not that I didn't know it. I did. I just wanted it to be different. Wanted to talk him off the edge of the universe, pull the pencil out of his heart, tame the wolves, make him better, like he was before. Better just because we were back together.

I glance over at him. He's crouched in a corner now, muttering.

I go over and touch his shoulder. "Carter?"

He looks up at me with hollow eyes.

"At night I hear the shrews in the wall, and when I wake up sometimes my mouth is full of them. I bite down and their tiny bones snap between my teeth. Their bones break into sharp shards like glass splinters and they taste like blood and their fur sticks to my tongue and makes me gag." He coughs like a cat with a hairball. "Their tails move around inside my mouth and I can feel their whiskers twitch against my cheeks, so I try to spit them out but they hold on with their nimble paws and I can't get them out. I thrash around and I claw at my mouth but it doesn't work. I can never get them out."

Shit, I think. Add infestations of nocturnal shrews to the list of crazy.

The Grey One skitters into the bedroom, pounces on some imaginary mouse. Who knows, maybe the mouse is real. Like the wolves. Like the shrews. Like 'they'. Carter looks at the kitten.

"Hey," he says, "you got your kitten back." Then he shakes his head. Frowns. Looks at me. "Is it real? Do you see it too?"

I nod my head.

"Yeah. He's kinda like the silver kitten, isn't he? Remember you wrote that song for me, played it on your ukulele?"

Carter looks like he might cry.

"I think my roommate stole it, my ukulele."

"We can go get you a new one tomorrow, ok?" He doesn't answer.

"Carter, can I take you to a doctor? Maybe see if there's something we can do to help you?"

"I went to see one already," Carter says. "She did something to me, to my brain. She said she could help me, but she messed things up."

"Did she give you medication?"

"It's an experiment. My roommate, Shae, he's the one who gives me the medications. It makes me do things I don't want to do. It makes the wolves come. It makes my tongue swell up." He sticks his tongue out at me, tries to grab hold of it with one hand. It keeps slipping back into his mouth. He keeps sticking it back out, grabbing at it.

"Maybe we could go back to her, but I could go with you. I could make sure that everything's safe, that nothing bad happens to you."

He stares at me. The tip of his tongue is sticking out. Reminds me of The Grey One, when he gets caught licking his ass, leg up in the air, little pink tongue protruding.

Carter's eyes are getting wide. Panic-stricken. He tries to back away, but he's in a corner. He does some scrabbling at the wall.

"They said you would say that," he says. "They said you would take me back, so the doctor could fuck around with my brain. She wants to strap me down, slice me open, dissect me. Take out my Brodmann's, seventeen, eighteen, nineteen. All of them!"

I back up, give him some space.

"Remember the shack, out in the woods, behind the Ruggle's? Dead Man's Shack?" I say. I hold up my left thumb, wiggle it at him. "Remember how you broke my thumb so I wouldn't go in the shack? Because there was something bad in there, right? Remember how you protected me?"

Carter cocks his head, turns to the left.

"Carter! You can talk to them later. It's my turn right now."

He startles. Looks back at me.

"I'll do the same for you," I say. "I will protect you. From whatever. From what's in the shack. From the doctor. From your roommate. From the wolves, the shrews. From them. Carter, I won't let anything bad happen to you. I promise."

Carter slumps back down on the floor, starts to talk.

"Now he is sitting on the floor. Now he is listening to Orion talking. There was a shack. The doctor might take him there. He knows that everything is incomprehensible. He is looking at his brother. He needs to be careful. Orianthi is looking at him now. He doesn't know if she is an imposter. The walls are starting to move, falling in towards him. He is listening, but he doesn't want to hear what they say. He is not real. He is dissolving."

"I tell way better stories than you, Carter," I say. I sit down beside him. "I can tell you what Carter's doing, what's happening."

Carter stops talking. Thumps his head back against the wall. I lean back beside him. Take hold of his hand. The Grey One comes over and joins us, curls up on Carter's lap.

***

THE BOY WITH FOUR GIFTS
AS TOLD TWIN TO TWIN

Once upon a time, not so far away, and not so long ago, there lived a boy who was not afraid of anything. Well, hardly at all, hardly ever, not really. The reason he was not often afraid was because he had four charms to protect him.

First, he had The Book of Everything. It was filled with wondrous things, dangerous things, mysterious things. In the book there were translucent jellyfish, black holes, venomous shrews, stardust, a map of the universe. The book was filled with knowledge and it made the boy marvel at the world, instead of fear it.

The second charm the boy had was a ukulele, an instrument with strings that laughed, that played songs filled with sunshine. Fear has trouble taking hold in the face of such joy, and the ukulele helped the boy from ever growing afraid.

The third thing he had was a pair of boots. His boots were solid and invincible. They had travelled through brambled thickets and dark forests; through the mud of spring, the long waving grasses of summer, the golden leaves of autumn and the cold snows of winter. The boots were trustworthy. They grounded the boy to the earth, letting him know his place in the world. The boots stepped through darkness without fear.

The fourth charm was not a thing at all, it was a person. The boy had a twin who was his sister, and also his brother, who loved him dearly and truly. Their love kept him strong and fearless. All his life he had held his sister's hand, which was the same hand as his brother's, as they faced dragons and demons and ogres together, fearlessly and undaunted. Three times the boy had saved his sister, who was also his brother, from mortal danger: once from the treacherous river, once from the wicked Spratt in the dark forest, and once from the evil lord Jepp, and three times back his twin had saved him from mortal dangers: once from the precipitous edge of Roof, once from the Zammit sorceress who had cast a spell upon him, and once from the jaws of the demon dog of Ruggle.

The boy had named his twin, and the gift of these names had given his twin power, and made his twin not afraid of anything, hardly at all, hardly ever, not really. For his brother the boy had chosen the name Orion, after the stars, and for his sister he had given the name Orianthi, after the sea. And for them both, he chose Ori, a name of great power. All throughout the kingdom and beyond, Ori was known, in many different guises: Ori and the myths of the mountain, Ori the black elf, Ori the divine, Ori the fearless dwarf, Ori the distant waystation for travellers, Ori the white guardian spirit, Ori the beginning.

One dark day something happened. 'They' arrived. 'They' were secretive; they lurked in dark corners, they whispered of evil things in the kingdom, they never left the boy alone. And he grew afraid, for the first time, truly and deeply afraid. And in his fear he began to run, and he ran and ran for many days and nights, through the moonlight and sunshine and rain, through the treacherous river and over the distant hills.

But when he ran, he forgot to grab hold of his sister's hand, which was the same hand as his brother's, and so his twin was no longer there to save him from mortal danger. And he forgot to put on his boots, so he lost his place in the world.

'They' followed. Wherever he ran to, 'They' ran too. When they found him, they destroyed his third charm, his ukulele, and its strings could no longer sing out into the darkness, and he grew more afraid.

He had only The Book of Everything to protect him now. He read it again and again, searching each page and every word, but despite all the knowledge it contained, nowhere could he find a way to escape 'They', nowhere could he find *anything* about them. It was as if they didn't exist at all.

Then 'They' brought forth the fearsome grey wolves of the night and the boy's fear grew as large as the longest night of the winter. He was filled with despair and hopelessness. All seemed lost.

But the boy did not know that his sister, who was also his brother, had followed him for many days and nights, through the moonlight and sunshine and rain, through the treacherous river and over the distant hills. He did not know that his brother, who was also his sister, was travelling through brambled thickets and dark forests wearing his trustworthy boots. Each step his twin took brought his boots one step closer to him. And each step his twin took brought a hand to hold one step closer.

Finally one summer day, when the sun was shining brightly overhead and a warm wind was whispering through the green trees, the boy and his twin were reunited. And so it was that two of his missing gifts were returned to him. He had his sister's hand, which was the same hand as his brother's, to hold as he faced the fearsome grey wolves of the night. And he had his boots, back on his feet, to ground him to the earth, to remind him of his place in this world.

"You can stop running," I say, holding tightly to his hand. "You can turn around now, turn around and face the wolves, the grey wolves of the night. They can't hurt you, Carter. They *are* you." I grab hold of the tabs on Carter's boots. Pull them off my feet.

"Here," I say, shoving the boots at him. "I've been wearing these every day since you left. So we'd be together. Like always."

He lets go of my hand to put the boots on. Which is good, because his hand was getting really sweaty. And his fingernails are caked with dirt. Like he's been digging in the earth with his bare hands.

"I missed you," I say. "I'm not me without you."

SULEIMAN

Through the thin walls, I can hear the sounds of sex: the squeak of mattress springs, a low rhythmic grunting, and a steady building moan. I close my eyes. A long time has passed since Khadija and I have been together like that. There had been one aborted attempt, a few weeks before we separated. Khadija had seemed willing at first, had in fact initiated it, but as things progressed she had become still and unresponsive. I hadn't wanted to look at her face, had pictured a far-away look in her eyes, even perhaps the glistening of tears, but what I saw was worse. My erection was shamed away by the blankness I saw in her dark eyes.

The moaning in the next room changes, become a harsher sharper sound, joined by the sound of the headboard banging against the wall. I picture Khadija's full breasts with their dark areolas, the pliable softness of her stomach, her smooth thighs and the triangular mound of curly black hair between them. I rub my thumb against my forefinger as I imagine caressing her nipples, seeing her arching towards me, encouraging me on. I miss the pleasure that I shared with Khadija. I stand up, shake my head, free myself from my rising sexual desire. There is a wild scream in the next room, then silence.

I step towards my kitchenette, wash my hands and face in the small sink there. As I dry my hands an unthinkable thought comes to me. I lurch forward, heaving, the sour taste of stomach acid rising into my mouth. *Was Tiffany also in the room next door?*

I wipe my hand across my mouth, splash cold water on my face. Shelley would not do such a thing, would she? But I can picture Tiffany, how she can stand so quietly watching, how her solemn green eyes take everything in. It is not hard to imagine, and it makes me believe it happened.

I step back into my room, pull on my clothes and step out into the night. I pound my fist on the door of Room 5. I hear an angry voice, then a murmuring. The door remains closed. I pound again, call out, "It's Suleiman, from next door."

I'm just about to raise my fist again when the door swings open. The boyfriend, Tim, stands naked in the doorway.

"What the fuck do you want?" he snarls. I step back. I have been struggling to control my own anger for so long now that I have come to think of it as something that only I have to contend with. Tim is clearly angry, and for the briefest of moments, I feel threatened. I almost laugh, recognizing this.

"Where is Tiffany?" I demand, stepping forward again. Shelley stumbles up behind Tim, clutching a sheet around herself.

"She's not with you? She must be with Ori then," she says, looking at Tim. "Is she, Tim?" she asks. Her words are slurred, high-pitched. She sways slightly, blinks her eyes heavily.

"Where is she?" I demand again.

Tim smiles, a lazy dangerous smirk. "How should I know? She's not my kid."

"Shelley, where is she? Is she here in the room with you?"

Shelley glances around, confused. "No," she says, but she doesn't sound convinced.

I hesitate. I'm relieved that Tiffany is not present, but where is she, if not in the room with her mother? She is not likely to be with Yori, not with the arrival of Carter earlier. And it's nighttime. I have seen her alone many times during the daylight hours, but never in the darkness, except for that one time. I glance at the parking lot, as if I might find her there again, fallen to her knees, but it is deserted. My chest constricts, my palms tingle. Something is not right.

"Did you see Tiffany earlier?" I ask Tim, but there is no answer. Instead the same slow smile, that is not a smile at all, slides across his face.

"Tim?" Shelley says, clawing at his arm. "What's going on? Do you know where she is?"

The smile vanishes. "Why the fuck are you interrogating me?" he says, looking at me.

My fists clench. My heart is thumping in my chest, spurring me on. "Because," I say, through clenched teeth, "I don't trust you."

Tim sneers. "I don't give a rat's ass what you think about me." He turns away from me, pushing Shelley back. She stumbles slightly and grabs Tim's shoulder. I'm about to follow, but my feet stop moving at the threshold of the doorway. I have a moment of clarity, realizing that I'm chasing after my anger when I should be looking for Tiffany. This man is trouble, but maybe it's true that he doesn't know where she is. And I'm wasting my time questioning Tim, when I could be asking Yori if he has seen her.

I turn and leave. I will check with Yori first. It's the obvious place to look. It is unlikely, but still a possibility. Halfway across the parking lot I look back at Room 5; maybe Shelley will come too. Instead I see Tim, pushing Shelley back until she falls to the floor, the sheet wrapped around her unravelling. I hesitate.

"Stop that," I call out. But the door swings shut and I can no longer see what is happening. Instead I hear a sharp yelp, the sound of a dog being kicked. I feel the quickening of my pulse, the tension in my muscles. I have made a mistake to leave them; I should go back, I should intervene.

I pause, listen intently. But I hear nothing more. My fists slowly unclench. Perhaps I misunderstood. Did Shelley fall back? Now I'm no longer sure. I shake my head. I'm distressed about Tiffany and it's causing me to overreact. Shelley has fallen and cried out, that is all, I tell myself.

I turn away from Room 5 and hasten to Room 11, to Yori. Tiffany will be there, I reassure myself, she has to be there. Because where else could she be?

TIFFANY

I am trying to make friends with the nighttime but it's really hard because of all the sounds I keep hearing all around me. I'm in my secret place behind Nap-Away. If Rainbow were here everything would be better, because she is a very brave kitten. She killed a bug yesterday, a big black one that was hurrying across the bathroom floor. I watched her do it and after she pounced on it and crunched on it, she played hockey with it for a little while, passing it back and forth like a puck between her paws.

Rainbow has very soft paws but very sharp nails. Sometimes she sleeps with her paws tucked around her nose, which makes her look very cute. Most of her paws are all white but one paw has two orange toes and another paw has a little black dot on it like a blob of paint. I like to stroke her paws when she is sleeping but she always wakes up when I do that and then she thinks it is time to play again.

I want my antler stick. I am scared to check for it on the ground in case, by accident, I find something else that is maybe squishy or maybe prickly hiding in the darkness. But even though I'm scared I crouch down anyway and start to feel around for it, because I know the stick will make me feel braver.

"Have you seen it?" I ask Tree, because all that I'm touching are weeds and branches and leaves on the ground, tangled around my ankles. I rub the back of my head, which is sore from where Tim yanked on my hair. I kick at the ground and my toe hits something hard. My stick!

I pick it up and hold it tightly in my hand. I feel a little better. The wood feels smooth and strong. I take a deep breath in and then I smack my stick against the wall of Nap-Away, as hard as I can. Smack! I keep smacking and smacking my stick and I start crying and my nose gets snotty but I don't even stop to rub it away. Smack! When I smack it one more time there is a big crack, and my antler stick isn't an antler anymore at all, it's just two broken pieces.

"Sorry," I whisper to Nap-Away, even though I know it's not hurt from all my smacking. I lean back against Nap-Away's wall, and for a minute all I can hear is my own breathing, zooming in and out of my mouth, and my nose, making sniffing sounds. Nap-Away holds me up, strong and brave, the way I wish I could be.

I pat my hand against Nap-Away instead of smacking it again. The wall still feel warm from the sun that was shining here in the afternoon. I sniff a little more, but then I hear a different sound. A scratchy squeaky noise that's coming closer and closer. Usually when I am scared I make a sound like a scream or an 'eeep', but this time I am so scared that when I open my mouth no sound comes out at all. My mouth is empty. When I open it again the same nothing noise comes out.

There is a lumpy shadow on the trunk of Tree with eyes that shine in the dark. It is too big to be a rat, too big to be a cat even, and I know dogs can't climb trees. It keeps coming closer, down and down, towards me. I can hear the sounds of scritching and squeaking, further up in the tree. I try to run away but my legs don't move at all. I feel like I am playing freeze tag and the lumpy shadow is 'it'.

It comes closer and closer and I scream and run, without making any sound or moving. When it moves from the tree to the top of the fence in to a patch of light from one of the back windows I finally see what it is. A great big raccoon! This is the first time in my whole life that I've seen a real wild thing. I have seen lots of pictures in books of wild animals, like wolves and bears, but I have never seen one for real. Not even at the zoo, because I have never been there. Theo went one time and he told me that he saw an elephant doing a ginormous poo.

The raccoon has shiny black eyes and a mask on her face and stripes on her tail. She lifts her nose, which is pointy, up in the air at me and I'm pretty sure she is sniffing me. I hope that I smell like a kid who likes raccoons. After she sniffs me she makes a grunting sound and then a whole bunch of little raccoons scramble down on to the fence. One-two-three-four-five babies follow behind. No, wait! There is one more who is chirping like a little bird, trying to cross from the tree to the fence. Six babies plus the mamma makes seven raccoons!

Mrs. Lynch, my teacher at school, has a hand puppet that is a raccoon. He is named Brambles. I'm not sure what that word means but I think it has to do with getting lost in the woods and eating berries, but lost in a fun kind of way, not a scary kind of way. That is something that raccoons would do for sure. When Mrs. Lynch puts on the puppet it is like Brambles is really alive. I can't wait to tell her about how I got to see a real mamma raccoon and her six babies.

They are leaving, climbing and balancing on the fence like we do with the monkey bars at school. I have to name them quick, before they are all gone. The little one at the end I call Chirp. I name the mamma Shadow. Then I have to name all the babies in between. I pick one to be Baby Brambles and one to be Acorn. The biggest one I name Oak. They have all followed their mamma away and I can only see their shadows now, and hear their squeaking noises. I haven't picked any M names yet so I name one Masker and the other one Miff, which is just like my name. It is a good rhyming name too, Miff, Iff, Tiff, Sniff. I decide that Masker and Miff can be the twins. Except maybe they are all twins. I'm not sure.

"Shadow, little Chirp, Acorn and Oak, the twins, Miff and Masker," I whisper. I stop to count on my fingers. I missed one, but I can't remember it. "Baby Brambles!" I do a happy little skip in the dark. I want to tell my mom about the raccoons, but I can't go back because of Tim, who pulled my hair and told me to shut the fuck up and pushed me outside in the dark. I wonder when my mom will remember about me and come find me and take me home. And then I remember what Nikki said, about how, when people are using, they forget about important stuff, like the kids they are supposed to take care of. Maybe I am lost and nobody even knows.

ORI

Suleiman is persistent. I tried to ignore his pounding fist on the door. Didn't work.

"Yori," he kept calling, "Let me in." Carter started freaking out. Muttering and listening intently, signalling the sky. Then finally in a voice filled with despair, Suleiman said, "It's Tiffany, Yori. It's Tiffany." So I opened the door.

"Tiffany isn't with you," he says.

"No, Suleiman, I've just got my brother here."

"She's gone. She's missing."

"What do you mean? Where's her mom?"

"She's at home. She's there with her boyfriend. But I think he's done something. I don't know. Shelley doesn't know where her daughter is. Is she here?"

We both look around. Like she might be here and we just don't know it. Dumb.

"Nah," I say, "I haven't seen her since I've been back."

"I have a bad feeling about this. Where would she go? At night? In the dark?"

Iff's not the kind of kid who runs away. She's the kind that freezes, like a terrified rabbit in long meadow grasses when the wolf comes.

He waits. I try to ignore the expectation in his face. "You must help me look for her."

I look back at Carter.

"Ori," Carter says. "Ori." Like my name means something else, something more. Like he's telling me the story of our life.

"Carter needs me," I say.

Suleiman's gaze travels to Carter, then back to me. I remember meeting him for the first time in the parking lot. Thinking he was kind of scary. Then seeing his big brown eyes, the long lashes framing them, thinking they were like cow's eyes, soft and peaceful.

"Carter will be needing you for a long time," Suleiman says. The words flutter around me, disjointed: *a long time a long time Carter needing you needing you* I grab at them, make sense of them. I thought I needed him. I've been looking for him because *I need him*.

"Ori," Carter says, "I can taste their blood."

"I can't," I say to Suleiman. "I can't leave Carter, not now."

Suleiman opens his big hands to me, palms up. "Yori," he says. "You made a promise."

Whose blood is Carter tasting? I wonder. The shrews? I lick my lips. Look away from Suleiman. Down to the floor. To my bootless feet, my mismatched dirty socks. I shake my head.

"Carter will need you for a long time, Yori," Suleiman says. "But it's Tiffany who needs you right now."

I don't look at Suleiman's eyes. Scuff my sock on the carpet. "*You* go look for her. She sometimes plays behind the motel, around the far corner," I say, pointing into the darkness.

Suleiman sighs heavily. I can feel his brown eyes looking right through me, like I'm transparent.

"Go look there first. And if she's not there, then I'll come."

I hear Carter scrabbling around somewhere in the room. Wonder if I'm lying to Suleiman.

"We made a promise that she would come to no harm. Nothing bad can happen to her. She must not be harmed. Do you understand? I can't let something bad happen to her!" His voice does a weird thing, like someone singing opera. I look at him, see his hands are in fists. That they're trembling.

"What's going to happen to her?" Carter whispers, sidling up behind me. I jump back.

"Shit, Carter, you scared me."

"What will they do to her?" Carter says again, his voice tight, like Suleiman's fists. He grabs my arm, digs his nails in, shakes it.

"No harm," I whisper to Suleiman. "No harm." But I don't know anymore what it means. How to stop harm from coming.

Suleiman looks at Carter, and his big fists unfurl, one finger at a time. Like his prayer mat, rolling out before him, revealing the beauty hidden inside. The moment stretches out, like light from distant stars, travelling through the universe, reaching out across the years. I hear someone else whisper 'no harm' in a soft voice, soft like The Grey One's fur, but I'm not sure if it's Carter or Suleiman.

Suleiman nods his head resolutely, breaks the spell. "You stay here, and I'll go look behind the motel, where you've suggested," he says. "*Insha'Allah*, I will find Tiffany there."

He walks away towards the edge of the building. It's darker than usual. No moon, and a couple of the parking lot lights are out. Across the parking lot the door to Room 5 flies open. I think I see Shelley, but just as suddenly she's gone and the door remains ajar. I can hear her shrieking at someone. Maybe Iff is there. Maybe Suleiman's wrong. I look back at Carter. Maybe everything's going to be fine. I step back towards my twin.

A scream rips across the parking lot. The sound is unearthly, an animal terror. It's coming from the open doorway of Room 5. My feet freeze. The scream has a twin, a second cry, long and harsh. The sound is an icy shock, like falling into a frozen river.

Suleiman is moving, faster than I thought such a big guy could, coming back from the far edge of Nap-Away. The screams keep coming. I'm still trying to process the sounds, but Suleiman flies back across the parking lot towards Room 5. He's maybe ten feet away when the door slams shut and everything is suddenly quiet. Spooky quiet.

I chase after Suleiman, swinging the door to Room 11 shut behind me, Carter inside. Skid to a halt beside Suleiman. I've only got socks on. Carter's boots are back on Carter. My left foot is throbbing from stepping on something sharp crossing the parking lot.

The door to Room 3 opens, someone peers out, looks around, and closes their door. In the distance, on Kingston Road, I see the bus pull to a stop and a couple of people get off. I have a weird feeling that nothing has happened. Or that Suleiman and I are in a different dimension than the rest of the world, where something terrible has happened but we are the only ones who know.

"You must call the police," Suleiman says. He thrusts his phone at me. "Call 911." He turns back and walks calmly up to the door of Room 5. I slide his phone on, punch in the numbers. Suleiman grabs the knob and tries to open the door. When it doesn't open he pounds his fist against the door, three hollow thuds.

"Wait! Suleiman, wait!" I yell.

"911. Do you need Police, Fire, or Ambulance?" a crisp voice responds.

"Yes," I say. "But no fire." I step towards Suleiman, grab his arm.

"We need help," I yell into the phone.

SULEIMAN

Al-Fattah, *Allah* The Opener, is the one who opens all the gates that are closed. It is an emphatic name, I think, with many meanings. To open something closed can be interpreted in many ways. But it can be simply this: that whenever a way is closed to you, you can remember his divine name, *Al-Fattah*, and ask Him to open it for you.

I speak to *Al-Fattah* as I raise my fist and pound it against the door to Room 5. If the door will not open, God may choose to open it for me. This is the simplest interpretation of an opening, but still, a possible one. Here is a closed entrance that I wish would open. I'm asking and hoping to receive.

How many other gates has God already opened for me? He has opened the gate of sustenance and provision, the gate of marriage and family, the gate of work, the gate of good health, the gate of belief, of the call to Him. He has opened my heart to faith, many times, when I have been struggling. He has opened me to knowledge, and even more so, to wisdom. And to gratitude. I remember living with Khadija in our high-rise apartment in St. Jamestown, Ahmed sleeping in a box, and the gateway to contentment, to thankfulness, being flung wide open. "Praise belongs to *Allah*. I am well. My family is well. I am happy." It was as simple as that.

Now, standing before the closed door to Room 5, I see another door opening. Here is an opportunity to take action, a chance to make things right. For many weeks I have been thinking about the things I've done wrong, the mistakes I've made: my smouldering anger at Khadija, my lack of faith during my time of hardship, my decision to steal Tiffany away. But here is a door to a different version of myself. With God's help, I will save Shelley.

These thoughts propel me forward, even though Yori is trying to pull me back, trying to stop me.

"You must let me," I demand, shrugging Yori's hand off of my arm. "I must stop whatever is happening in there."

I take a step back and then charge forward, barreling my shoulder into the door.

TIFFANY

When the screaming sounds finish everything is very quiet, like the quiet in our classroom the one time that Mrs. Lynch got mad and yelled at us. Even Theo was quiet when that happened. Screaming means something bad has happened. The screaming scares me, more than the lumpy shadow in the dark that was a raccoon scared me. In the quiet I creep forward so I can peek around the corner of Nap-Away. I feel like I am a secret, like a little brown mouse, sneaking around without making a sound.

It's dark in the parking lot, but I can hear yelling and banging from where my room is. I hold on to the corner of Nap-Away. I am shivering, like I do in the wintertime, but it is not even a bit cold outside. I stay close to the wall of Nap-Away and start creeping down the row of rooms. I count the doors as I go, Room 14, which is always empty, 13, 12, and 11, which is Ori's room. I look out towards my room. I am pretty sure that it's Suleiman banging on our door, and Orianthi who is yelling. That is what I think. But maybe I am wrong. I press my ear against the door to Room 11. I can hear someone talking inside. I make a little fist and I knock on the door, as quiet as a mouse.

"Orianthi?" I whisper. "Are you there?"

I look back to Room 5 and squeeze my eyes to see better in the dark. I decide that it is Suleiman and I am just about to run across the parking lot when the door to Room 11 swings opens.

Inside Room 11 is someone who looks like Orion. But it's not him. It's not Orianthi either. I stare at him and he stares at me.

"Are you real?" he asks. I nod my head yes. "Do you talk?" he asks.

"Yes," I whisper. He looks scared. Maybe he heard the screaming too. "Did you hear the screaming?" His eyes go really wide. They are the same grey eyes that Orianthi has, with little black dots splashed through them. When I look at his eyes I know who he is. He is Orianthi's twin, the one she has been looking for all this time.

I know a lot of things about him already. His name is Carter. He is the one who sent the beaver postcard and he is the one who drew the wolf. Carter is her little brother, but only because he was born seventeen minutes after she was. He likes to eat frozen pink lemonade from a can and he can walk on his hands. Orion told me he knows everything about animals and about the stars and about what is at the bottom of the ocean. Orianthi has been wearing his boots. I wonder if he will want them back now. I look at his feet. Oh, he already has Ori's boots on his feet!

"Are you scared?" I ask him. Carter wraps his arms around his body and squeezes himself tight. He nods his head yes.

"Me too," I say. "Where is Orianthi?"

"Sometimes she's here and sometimes she's not," he says. He shrugs his shoulders. "I don't know where she goes."

"Do you like her kitten?" I ask him. The Grey One is twirling around his ankles, rubbing his fluffy grey fur all over his legs.

"What if the wolves eat her?" he asks. I'm not sure if he thinks the wolves are going to eat Orianthi or if he thinks the wolves are going to eat the kitten. I know The Grey One is a boy, but maybe he doesn't know.

"Eat who?" I ask, just so I can be sure.

"I thought maybe there wouldn't be any wolves here," he says, looking around the room. I look around too, but I only see one kitten. Carter starts chewing on his lip, which is something kind of like what I used to do. I used to lick my lips all the time when I was worried. Then I got a big rash around my mouth. I hated it because Theo made fun of me and said I looked like a clown.

"Are they wild things?" I ask. His eyes seem to keep getting bigger and bigger.

"Yeah," he says. "They're wild, they're dangerous. I don't know why they follow me!" He grabs at his own chest and squeezes the front of his t-shirt into a crumpled up ball. Suddenly for the first time, I feel brave. I think it is because Carter is more scared than I am.

"I can tame them," I say. I am trying not to remember the picture of the wolf, which was the scariest thing ever. I take his hand and pull it away from the t-shirt. His hand is icy cold, like touching snow. He looks down at me and I smile at him. "Really," I say, "I can. Then they won't be dangerous anymore."

"Will they still be here?" he asks.

I am not sure what the answer is. Orianthi didn't explain that part. I decide that they have to stay, because taming them is different than sending them away.

"Yes, but they won't hurt you," I say. I wish I had my antler stick, but you don't really need that to tame the wild things. And it's all broken now anyway. You don't need the crown either. You just have to remember that you are Max.

I stand up really tall and I take a big breath in. I squeeze tight to Carter's hand. I feel all my brave shining up inside me.

"Be still!" I yell at the wolves. I don't see them, but I remember the drawing I saw of the wolf, with its terrible teeth and terrible claws and terrible eyes. "Be still!" I yell again and it makes all the wolves slink down onto their bellies and tuck their tails between their legs like they are scared little dogs.

I tug at Carter's hand.

"See," I say. "They can't scare you anymore now."

ORI

Suleiman collides with the door. It shudders in its frame but stays closed. He stands back and rubs his shoulder. I'm thinking he should try a high kick, like the cops do on the TV shows. Aim right beside the doorknob. Maybe I should do it. I look down at my bootless feet. Reconsider.

He looks up at the dark sky and his lips move. I'm guessing he's talking to God. Beseeching him to open the door. But then he shakes his head and stops talking to the gods. He looks around at Nap-Away, at the walls and doors and windows and the grey slumpy roof and he opens his palms to it.

"Please," he says, "I ask that I may enter." Talking to Nap-Away like it can hear him. All formal.

Then he gets ready to attack the door again. He crouches low, his eyes fixed on his target, his hands clenched into fists. Launches himself forward.

The door swings right open. As if it wasn't even locked. As if Nap-Away was listening and just invited him in. He stumbles forward, losing his balance and falling heavily to his knees. I was thinking we should probably go into the room like cops do. Like in the movies. Pausing and scanning for danger, signalling each other with stopped hands, a thrust of the chin, a quirked eyebrow. Tense and alert as we proceed forward. Except we have no guns. And after Suleiman tumbles into the room, I follow right after. I've still got the 911 operator on Suleiman's phone, but as I scramble into the room I drop the phone and then disconnect the call as I pick it back up.

I'm pretty hyped up. I'm expecting something nasty, so the blood on the sheets and carpet shouldn't be a surprise. Except it is. I guess because there's so much of it. The bigger surprise is Shelley, who is standing near the kitchenette. She looks like something from a horror movie. Dishevelled hair, knife in hand, blood on her clothes.

Suleiman scrambles to his feet. Shelley steps towards us, her knife raised, looking ready for a swordfight. It's shaking like crazy, vibrating like a chain saw. The whole scene is so friggin' crazy I want to laugh.

"He tried to kill me," she whispers. She uses the knife tip to point down at Tim, who is lying on the floor, blood all over his white t-shirt, looking pretty dead. I stare at him. I've seen dead before, dead kittens, dead dog, road kill, stuff like that. But never a dead person.

The three of us all stare at Tim, not speaking. He's not looking so good. His head looks loose, like he's a doll that's been tossed on the floor. And his trusty red baseball cap has fallen off, sits empty on the floor beside him. The inside rim is a stained, dirty white. His brown eyes are open, staring up at us. And his lips are pulled back, like that face chimpanzees make when they're scared, all their teeth exposed. His white t-shirt is sliced up, covered in blood. At the crotch of his jeans is a wet stain, seeping into the carpet below. He's peed himself. I shiver.

"He was gonna kill me." That's when I notice she's not just covered in blood, but she's bleeding. Her other hand is clutched around her stomach, and blood is seeping between her fingers.

"What happened?" Suleiman asks. Maybe he's a little disappointed about how this is unfolding. He was the brave hero, riding in on his white horse but the dragon has already been slain. By the damsel in distress.

"I pushed him. He fell. Conked his head."

"Then what?" I ask.

She raises the knife up. "Then I stabbed him, until he stopped." I guess she means stopped being alive. She waves her knife unsteadily in Suleiman's direction.

"What were you planning to do?" she asks. She laughs at him in a jeering kind of way, then starts to sob uncontrollably. Suleiman steps forward and slides the knife carefully out of her hand. She falls into him, heaving and howling.

"Hush," Suleiman says. "Hush. It's over now, neh?"

I'm not sure what I should be doing. I grab a towel from the bathroom, shove it against Shelley's side, where the blood is oozing. I look back at

Tim. I kind of know CPR. But I don't think it works when people are already dead. Right near his hand I see a pair of small socks crumpled up on the floor. Pink with white stripes. Everything comes tumbling down. Where the hell is Iff?

"Suleiman!"

He frowns at me, shakes his head.

"Suleiman, where's Tiffany?" His eyes widen and he releases Shelley abruptly. She falls to her knees, whimpering.

"Where is Tiffany?" he demands, looking down at Shelley. She looks around the room, wild-eyed. "What has Tim done?"

"He tried to kill me," she says in a slow monotone. "He said I was disrespecting him. Disrespecting him! What the fuck is wrong with him?" She is staring down at the towel I shoved into her hands, looking at the blood that has seeped into it.

"*Insha'Allah*, Tiffany is safe," Suleiman says. "But where is she?"

"Shelley, how do we get hold of Nikki?" I ask.

"Disrespecting him..." she mutters.

"What's Nikki's number?" I ask again. I give her shoulder a little shake.

"He's bad news. I shoulda known better."

"Perhaps you have Nikki's number?" Suleiman asks. He gives me an awkward look. "From being...friends."

I shake my head.

"I never asked her for it," I say. "Wait! Moffit has her number!" He put it in his phone that day I trotted away after Nikki, looking for Iff and Suleiman. I know Moffit's number. Spent a couple of nights in the Nap-Away phone booth at the corner of Kingston, whispering stories and secrets to him.

I punch his number into Suleiman's phone. I'm feeling shaky. There's no ground, everything is spinning around, colliding. Carter's here, Iff's gone, Tim's dead. I need Moffit to find Nikki to help Iff. Shelley's all stabbed up.

Moffit doesn't answer. No surprise. I've called him a few times, always get his voicemail.

"Moffit? It's me. I know we're not talking, whatever, but... I need your help. For Iff. Shit's happening. She's gone missing, and her mother's in trouble. She's been stabbed. Well, she stabbed someone too. I need to get hold of Nikki. Do you still have her number in your phone? I know you probably hate me, but still...Oh! And Carter's here!" I don't know what more to say. I tap 'end'.

"I'm gonna go look for her," I say. "She's gotta be out behind the motel." Because if she's not, where else could she be?

On my way to the back corner of the Nap-Away, I stop at my room. I get a bad feeling as I reach for the doorknob and open the door. The secret language of twins and all that. Carter's gone.

SULEIMAN

I am alone with Shelley, waiting for the ambulance, while Yori searches for Tiffany. She looks terrible. Her face is pale and sweaty, and the towel she is clutching to her side is soaked with blood. I go to the bathroom, grab a clean towel and bring it to her.

"You must press this firmly against the place that is bleeding," I tell her.

"He's the asshole, you know, not me." she says. She drops the blood-soaked towel on the floor, but doesn't reach for the fresh one. I place it in her hands, guide them to hold it against her abdomen. She sways gently from side to side, then stumbles forward. I catch her and help her to sit.

"I gotta get going," Shelly says. "I gotta get outta here. They can't find me here, like this. They'll take Tiffany." She looks around, panic in her eyes. "Where is she? Is she with you?"

I shake my head no. I look down at Tim, lying dead on the floor, wonder again what role he has played in Tiffany's disappearance.

"When did you last see her?" I ask.

"She was such a good baby. Nikki was a nightmare, but Tiffany was an angel."

I grab her shoulder, give it a little shake. "When did you last see her?"

"What was I thinking? People don't change. He's just a bad seed. Everywhere he goes, trouble follows." She winces and buckles forward. "And now look what he made me do."

Yes, I think, look. Shelley has killed someone. She will be imprisoned. Her daughter will be taken from her. So, I think, harm has come. I moan quietly, steady myself with a hand on Nap-Away's wall.

My phone vibrates in his pocket.

"Yes, hello?" I say.

"Ummm, it's Moffit. Ori just called me."

"Yes, yes. Yori says you can reach Nikki."

"Yeah," Moffit answers. "I've called her, she's on her way there. Tell Ori I'm coming, I'll be there in ten."

"Good," I reply, but Moffit has already ended the call.

Shelley is seated on the edge of the bed, muttering to herself. I step out to the parking lot, listening for the sound of the sirens. Where is the ambulance? It seems like a long time has passed since Yori called for them. I look back into the room, wondering how to explain what has happened, what my role in the events has been.

For a moment I consider what I would need to do to make this all go away. To clean the blood, to hide the body, to treat Shelley's wound without a doctor, to find Tiffany and reunite her with her mother, to do all of this before the police arrive. I snort. It would be ridiculous to even try such a thing. I survey the bloody mess in Room 5. Impossible. I have no role in controlling Shelley's fate. God will decide it, not me.

So, I think, change has been initiated. Shelley will go to the hospital; she will be held accountable for Tim's death. And what will become of Tiffany? Where is she?

I stand outside between the two doors of rooms 5 and 6. I feel agitated, like I must take action. What if something has happened to Tiffany? I try not to imagine it. I steady myself, draw a breath in. I will wait; I will not imagine something that can't be known.

There is an ambulance coming. Nikki is coming. Moffit is coming. *Insha'Allah*, Yori will return with Tiffany, unharmed. Whatever I wish for is not relevant. All will unfold as it should, as it is meant to.

TIFFANY

One time at school a firefighter came to visit our class. Her name was Kate. She had black hair and black eyes and she looked tiny and big at the same time because of all the firefighting clothes that she wore. She taught us stop-drop-and-roll. We got to practise doing it, which was a lot of fun. Theo rolled all the way across the classroom to where our cubbies are. She also taught us about hiding. She said lots of kids want to hide when there is a fire. Firefighter Kate said sometimes kids will hide in the closet or under the bed. But she said this was the wrong thing to do. She said hiding made it harder for her to find you and help you and to save you from the fire.

But I know why the kids who are in the fire want to hide. Hiding feels safe. When Tim comes over, Rainbow hides under the bed. One time Tim used his mean feet to kick at Rainbow. So Rainbow is smart to hide away. Shadow, the mamma raccoon, must hide her babies away somewhere, because I have never seen them before. She hides them to keep them safe from people who kick animals and run them over with cars.

That's why I'm hiding now. Same as Rainbow. Same as the raccoons.

ORI

Tiffany's not here, out behind the motel, not as far as I can see in the dark. I call out her name, softly, but only the crickets answer. I catch a glimpse of the raccoons, up on Nap-Away's roof, pattering across the shingles. Disappearing into a hole in the roof over Room 14, which is the last room of the row. Nobody ever stays in that room. Except the raccoons, I guess.

I turn to go back and trip over something on the ground, fall to my knees. For a breathless moment I think it might be Iff. Her little dead body dumped on the ground. But it's just a garbage bag, full of something soft and squishy. Foul smelling.

I scramble back to my feet and run around to the front of Nap-Away. There's an ambulance and cops and Suleiman standing solemn and still outside of Room 6, and Nikki, holding tight to a tall, burly guy, too old to be her boyfriend. A couple, standing just outside the open door of Room 3, watches. A body, Tim's I guess, lying on a stretcher, face covered. Shelley, covered in blood, being wheeled away on another stretcher, crying and reaching a hand out to Nikki.

No Iff.

I see Moffit, coming across the parking lot. I run to him, nearly knock him down. I didn't realize how much I had been missing him until now.

"Hey," I say, when he releases me from his hug.

His left eyebrow quirks up. "Hey," he replies.

I grin at him. "I'm glad you came."

Moffit shrugs, looks around at the chaos.

"Can I help?" he says.

"We can't find Iff. I thought she'd be somewhere out behind Nap-Away, you know, where we played with her that day? But she's not. And Carter's gone."

Moffit smiles a sad little smile. My face crumples up and I throw myself back against him, gulping back great big sobs. Soak a patch of his t-shirt with tears and snot. He's steady. Unfazed. I feel like I've come undone.

"Ori," he says, a couple of times. Rubs my back like I'm a little kid. Strokes my hair like I'm the ferret.

I pull away, rub my fists against my eyes. Shake my head so my hair flies.

"I don't know what to do about Carter, but we've gotta find Iff."

We go over to Suleiman, try and figure out when we saw her last. He gestures to Nikki to come over. I want to turn and run, to slink away into Suleiman's room. Then I remember that her mom's all stabbed up. I change from feeling bad for myself to feeling bad for her.

"I hope your mom's ok," I say, when we're face to face.

"She's pretty tough. She'll survive," Nikki says. She puts her hands on her hips and then cracks her gum. "It's Tiff I'm worried about. What's happened to her? Where is she?" She waves a hand at the guy she's with. "This is my dad." He looks a little like Tim. The baseball cap, bulgy man muscles, unshaven scruff.

"The police don't have much information. Shelley's not really coherent, and Tim's... well, dead," he says. He rubs a hand over his stubbly chin. Tugs Nikki tight against him.

"Either something bad has happened to her, or she's hiding somewhere. She's not the kind of kid who'd run away, is she Nikki?" I say.

Nikki shakes her head.

"I want to believe that she is hiding," says Suleiman. "That's a better ending to this day than other possibilities."

"Well we should be looking for her then," Nikki says, stepping forward, "instead of standing around."

SULEIMAN

I listen as Yori tells the police officers that there are many places to hide behind Nap-Away, on the other side of the fence where the used car dealership is. They leave together, the officers with their large flashlights beaming into the darkness. Nikki and her father have walked away from Nap-Away, out along Kingston Road. Nikki thinks that Tiffany may have wandered away, gone towards McDonalds. But I agree with Yori: if Tiffany had a choice, it would be to hide. I don't let my mind consider the other possibility, that she has come to some harm, that Tim, or perhaps some other man, has done something with her, something unspeakable.

I stay still outside of my room. I'm not hesitating, just taking a moment to pause. I'm thinking of Tiffany, of how she behaves, of how she listens, how she talks. I'm thinking of her stillness and of her spirit of goodness. I'm remembering the day she walked across the parking lot grinning, her t-shirt filled with kittens; the day she told me the story about a land far away where Amina and Mini lived together; the feeling of her small hand in mine. She is filled with such faith. It does not matter to me that it is not faith in God. She sees goodness all around her.

I wonder how things might have unfolded differently. What if I *had* driven her away to Montreal that day, taken her away from this motel, from her mother and her troubles, from this life that she was given? But no, that would have been stealing her from the path that she was meant to walk on. She will go forward, with braveness and kindness, forward through this hard, hard life she has been given.

I look at my car, think of my plan to leave, to go to Montreal. The flowered journal is full; I have finished writing my apology to Khadija. I won't leave now though, not until Tiffany is found, however long that takes.

Tiffany is so quiet, so still. Perhaps she has been nearby this whole time. Perhaps she is like Mini, the small, lost kitten who was close by, but so hard to find until it was too late. Where would Tiffany go that would be safe? I look to Yori's room, 11, then to my own. But no, we've checked the rooms already, and she is not hiding there. The mosque? But no, that would be something familiar to Amina, not to Tiffany. I sit down on my green chair, in the darkness, and close my eyes. Perhaps when I open them she will appear at my side, hoping to visit Massarat, or feed the pigeons.

Something brushes against my arm in the dark, a soft flutter, and my eyes startle open. A moth. It wings its way towards my blue car, sitting shadowed in the night. Ah! This is the kind of place where a child would hide. In fact, there is no better place. It is a place that will take her away from the screams in the night.

I walk over to my car, peer through the window. There are boxes piled up in the back, a cat carrier and a bag of chips on the front seat. And there is Tiffany, hidden under Amina's pink blanket, curled up on the back seat, asleep.

I quietly open the driver's door and climb into the car. I sit in the seat, looking forward through the glass. I fiddle with the keys in my pocket. I could just drive away. But I won't. I will wait for her to awaken, wait for the others to return. For now, for this moment, there is only the two of us, together in the darkness, as I wish it to be. *Alhamdulillah*, praise be to God, she has come to no harm.

TIFFANY

I wake up when Nikki pulls me out of Suleiman's car. At first I think she is mad at me. Then I think she is excited to see me. When she starts to cry I know that she's sad. Nikki never cries. She hugs me tight against her chest, squeezes me.

"It's ok," I tell her. I pat her arm. I look around. Something very bad must have happened, because there are a lot of police officers here.

"Is it because of the screaming?" she asks.

"No, stupid," Nikki says, "it's because of you." She pulls me away from her chest, and looks at me. "Where were you?"

I want to tell her a lot of things, about how Tim was a big bully, and how I broke my antler stick and found all the raccoons in the dark. About the terrible scream. About meeting Ori's twin, and taming his wolves. About hiding in Suleiman's car.

"Where's mom?" I ask. But I know the answer already. "She's using, right?" Nikki frowns at me, and I think she might yell, but instead some more tears run down her cheeks. She rubs her hand across her face, like how Rainbow cleans his whiskers with his little paw.

"Yeah," Nikki says. "Yeah."

 PART FIVE

ORI

Most days I walk around downtown for hours. Missing Carter's kick-ass boots on my feet, missing Carter's hand in mine. I'm always looking for him, always waiting for the day that he shows up again. Because we're tethered, still and for always.

Some days I hang out with Moffit. He takes me to weird little vegan cafes in Kensington Market, where nobody seems to mind a ferret on his shoulder. I spend a lot of time at the library at Parliament and Gerrard. Once, I went to the kid's section and found Maurice Sendak's book, *Where The Wild Things Are*. I flopped down on a beanbag chair and started reading it. Some little kid wearing rubber boots and yellow pajamas came and stood in front of me, sucking his thumb. Warm brown eyes, like a little Suleiman. No mama in sight. I read the book to him, like maybe ten times over. Showed him all the pictures. His eyes widened a couple of times. Then he left, right in the middle of Max leaving all his wild things behind, sailing away on his little boat. I wished him back. Wished I had yellow pajamas. Wished I could still suck my thumb.

I have a place to stay at Covenant House downtown. Didn't seem to be much point in staying at Nap-Away after Iff was taken away and Suleiman left. Well that, and also I didn't have any money to pay for my room with Suleiman gone. He took me out for breakfast before he drove off.

"*Fi Amanillah*," he said to me. "I leave you in *Allah*'s protection. I hope that we will meet again someday. I wish it to be so." Then I was alone at Nap-Away, hoping for Carter to come back.

It's not so bad in the shelter. Except they don't allow pets. Which sucks. Moffit's looking after The Grey One for me, until I can get a place of my own. I've snuck him into the shelter a couple of times though. When he's here he curls up on my shoulder and purrs in my ear. If I'm writing he leaps down and attacks my pen, especially if I'm writing fast. I've been writing a lot, making up stories for Iff, for Carter, for Suleiman, for Moffit. Wrote a story for The Grey One about the day he ate a bunch of bugs and puked up shiny black exoskeletons for hours. Moffit keeps saying I should take a writing class. Maybe. I know I've got to get my shit together. Make a plan. That's what they tell me at the shelter anyway. Get some skills. Get some school. Whatever.

Sometimes I go to the bus station. I sit inside and watch the screen that tells you all the arrivals and departures. Maybe I'll go to New York, eat pretzels on top of the Empire State Building. Or back to Oshawa, to find Stella and her weird-eyed dogs. Or Thunder Bay, where it's cold, so cold that that's all you can think about. Or Montreal, find Suleiman. Mostly I like to watch people saying goodbye.

I never got a chance to say goodbye to Carter, not the first time, and not this time either, but I got to say goodbye to Iff. It sucked. I wanted to scoop her up and keep her, put her in the front pocket of my skinny red jeans. Shrink her, like Alice in Wonderland. She'd be cute, sticking her little head out to look around, staying as quiet as a mouse.

Iff told me she talked to Carter. I don't know if that really happened though. She said he was scared of the wolves and that she tamed them, just like I showed her. *Be still.*

"The wolves can't eat him up now," she said. "He'll be safe."

Then she said he walked on his hands. "He has black freckles in his eyes, just like you," she said.

Before she left, I took the numbers off the door to my room at Nap-Away. Figured Room 11 would still be Room 11, with or without the numbers.

"We can each keep one," I told her. "You'll have one and I'll have one and that way we'll always be together." She tried to give me her acorn, the one on the chain that I made for her, but I didn't take it. I kissed the top of her head and said 'bye really fast and then ran away because I couldn't bear it any more. Because endings aren't like the fairy tales, where everyone lives happily ever after.

I've gone back to Nap-Away a couple of times, thinking that maybe Carter would come by looking for me. I asked at the office, hoping there'd be a note for me. *Ori*, it might say, *when I see the wolves I think about the magical kid with the green eyes, about how she wasn't scared of them. Once, I reached out and touched the smallest wolf, a grey one with moon-lit eyes. They said I should never, ever touch the wolves, but I did. I did!* And I'd fold up the note and tuck it into my back pocket. Pull it out now and again, think of Carter, turning towards his wolves. Think of him, wearing his boots. The ones that travelled far, through brambled thickets and dark forests. Think of him holding tight to my hand, even when it's not there.

But the last time I went the entire motel was surrounded by temporary fencing. Big notice board announced the condo-to-be. The parking lot was empty, the windows boarded up, like they were trying to hide Nap-Away's secrets. A flock of pigeons huddled together on the tired grey roof above Suleiman's room. Feathers all fluffed up. The leaves on the big oak tree had turned to rust. The wind blew and acorns rained down like little drums, and the pigeons all startled, clapping their wings as they took off. Whirled away like a cloud of smoke. I walked around the edge of the fence. Stopped by the dumpster. Saw Iff's pink skipping rope abandoned beside it, swirled into a little spiral on the ground. And a ghostly grey tabby, slinking around the corner of the motel. Maybe the mama cat to our kittens. I took one last look at Nap-Away, full of everything that was gone.

I still go to the ukulele jam on Wednesdays, hoping to find Carter there. Sometimes I just wait around outside, but lately I've been going in. I'm thinking maybe I'll get my own ukulele, learn how to play a few happy songs. Cheer myself up. Or play some enchanted little tune that'll pull Carter back to me.

Sometimes I go to the park at Queen and Church, get a hotdog, and sit on the bench where I found him in the summer. Last week, sitting there, feeding the pigeons some crumbs from my hotdog bun, I noticed something I hadn't seen before. On the first slat of the bench, written in black ink, the word Ori. Messy and jagged. But unmistakable. My twin, calling out my name.

SULEIMAN

I left Nap-Away five weeks ago. I drove straight to Montreal without stopping, straight to Ahmed's apartment. But when I arrived I didn't get out of my car. I sat, clutching the flowered journal in my hands, watching the doorway to the building, waiting to see Khadija. At five o'clock Ahmed arrived, striding down the street, large white headphones on his ears. Shortly after, the door to the apartment building opened again, and Ahmed reappeared, followed by Khadija. I leaned forward, my breath caught in my throat, straining to see her better, to catch the scent of her skin through the car's open window, to hear her voice, her sharp laugh. She seemed small beside Ahmed, and vulnerable. I watched them walk away from me, down the street and around the corner, out of sight. I remembered to breathe again, finally.

I waited on the curb, stepping quickly forward as someone exited the building so I could catch the door before it swung closed again. Three flights of stairs led to their unit, 308. I knew Khadija was not behind the door, but it didn't stop me from imagining the door swinging open, imagining the flash of her smile, the dark sparkle of her eyes, the soft touch of her hand on mine. I placed my hand on the doorknob, tried twisting it, let go.

The journal was warm from being held against my body, the cover slightly damp from the sweat of my hands. I wanted to place the journal directly into her outstretched palms, like an offering, but I knew that she would not reach out to me, that she would not want to accept it. I knelt and propped the journal up, right where the door met the doorframe. "*Insha'Allah*," I murmured, "she will be safe from harm." I turned to leave, looking back once at the journal, which looked small and insignificant. Tucked inside the front cover I have left a small packet of wild flower seeds.

I have settled into a nomadic life, driving my little blue Toyota for a few hours each day along sideroads and small highways, stopping eventually at a roadside motel to spend the night. Sometimes I stay for a single night, sometimes longer. I have no destination in mind, I travel where the road takes me, sometimes circling back westward again, sometimes going north. Yesterday I entered the province of Nova Scotia.

The kittens, Rainbow and Massarat, seem to like travelling. I had expected them to be restless, to claw at the windows or meow to get out. But when I drive, they curl up together on the rear window ledge, purring in the sun. They like the heat. When I pull over and stop, I lead them out of the car on their leashes, feeling both foolish and proud at the same time. A grown man, walking two kittens like they are dogs! But they walk well on their leashes; tails held high, soft paws padding confidently across the parking lot. Amina would not believe her *Baba* would do such a thing. Nor Khadija for that matter.

The car is less cluttered now than when I left. Things that I thought were essential have become pointless. Why am I travelling with silverware, I ask myself? If Khadija really wanted the blue teacups, would she not have taken them with her to Montreal? I give things away to people I meet at the motels, I drop things off when I drive past a donation bin, I throw things away when I realize they are useless.

I am stripping my life down to its bare essentials. I have a few changes of clothes in a small black duffel bag, along with a few toiletries. I purchase food and other necessities for myself and the kittens. Each morning I roll up my new prayer mat, a blue and gold one that I bought before leaving Toronto, and tuck it in the car, along with my Qur'an.

Each day is much the same. I pray, I drive, I eat and sleep, I care for the kittens. My life is filled with little, but I find meaning in each moment. I pet Massarat and feel the softness of her fur coat, the vibrations of her purr, the weight of her body, curled on my lap. When I eat, I do so slowly, savouring the taste and texture of each bite. My prayers don't feel obligatory; they are moments when my mind is empty and open, when I connect to the vastness of God. Driving, I watch the road stretch out before me, like an invitation that has no end. When grief or anger strike me, I don't turn away; I savour it like a bitter meal, allow it to fill me. Just like every other moment, it eventually ends, changes into something else. The grief comes less and less, and instead, I find myself filled with an enormous sense of gratitude for all that I have been given.

Sometimes, sitting outside of my motel room in the gathering darkness, I see Amina out of the corner of my eye. Or is it Tiffany? No matter, they are the same, both gone from me in this life, abiding only in my heart. But oh, how I miss her, in the stillness of moments like this.

TIFFANY

On the first day of grade one my teacher, who is named Miss Fisher, told us to draw a picture of our family. This is what I drew: a big house with yellow walls and a grey roof and lots of doors, except there was no grey crayon so I coloured the roof brown instead. Behind the house there is a big tree, and in the tree are seven raccoons. They are a bit hard to see because I coloured so many green leaves around them, and because I drew six of them very small.

Around the house there is green grass and lots of yellow flowers. I drew me and my mom and Nikki all holding hands in front of the house with Rainbow sitting in front of us. At the next door I drew Suleiman, sitting on his green chair, with lots of pigeons all around him, and Amina sitting on the grass playing with Mini and Massarat. Some of the pigeons look like rocks, because I forgot to give them legs. I coloured my skin brown and Amina's brown and Suleiman's brown. After I finished colouring him, I leaned over and smelled the picture. I thought maybe it would smell sharp and warm, like Suleiman does, but it just smelled like crayons.

When Suleiman hugged me tight to say goodbye, so tight that I couldn't even breathe anymore, I smelled his good smell and I told my nose to remember it, because I knew I wouldn't get to smell him again. He lifted me so high into the sky that I felt like I was flying. Then he swung me down and whispered some secret words to me that I didn't understand. They sounded like music, like a lullaby, but even better. I wanted to whisper special words back, but I couldn't think of any.

In my picture I drew Ori and her brother Carter at another door. He is doing a handstand and Ori is laughing. He sounds like a witch when he laughs, but a good witch, not a bad one. Ori is wearing Carter's boots, and Carter is wearing his boots too. The Grey One is sitting on Ori's shoulders, like how the ferret used to live on Moffit's shoulders. I try to draw the black freckles in their eyes, but it's too hard to make tiny dots with crayons. But I know that they are there, like the stars are always there, even if you can't see them.

After school Jane, my foster mom, which is like a mom that you borrow when you can't live with your own mom, picks me up. I show her the picture and she says she would like to come and live there too, and she asks if next time I can draw a door for her too. She has a dog named Sparrow, who is tiny and brown. I get to hold his leash and walk him home. His fur is all tangled and curly. His tongue hangs out of his mouth because he is old and missing a lot of his teeth. But he runs really fast.

At night, Sparrow sleeps on my bed, curled up at my feet. He makes very tiny whistling sounds when he sleeps, like music that is very far away. It makes me think of Amina and her jingling little laugh. Sometimes at night I pretend that Amina is sleeping with me and that we are twins. We both have no mother and no father, just like Ori and Carter. We hold hands and whisper to each other in the dark. I make up stories and tell them to her. We giggle together when Sparrow farts in his sleep. I like to tuck my toes under his little body because there is a warm space there, just the right size for me. I share it with Amina when her feet are cold.

ACKNOWLEDGEMENTS

A heart-felt thank you...

To the Toronto Arts Council and the the Ontario Arts Council for their generous financial support of my work, and to Jay Millar at Book*hug for the grant recommendation.

To Aimee Parent Dunn of Palimpsest Press, who gave me one of the best Valentine's Day presents ever when she responded to my query email the day I sent it and asked to read the full manuscript. I'm so grateful that she said yes. To Ginger Pharand for her sharp attention to detail in copyediting and to Dawn Marie Kresan, whose beautiful cover design captured the hidden beauty of Nap-Away. To Malak El-Tahry for her insightful and detailed commentary on the novel. My portrayal of Suleiman benefited greatly from her critique.

To Diaspora Dialogues for the opportunity to participate in their mentorship program, especially to Helen Walsh, Rebecca Fisseha and Zalika Reid-Benta, for her feedback on the manuscript. To author/mentor Andrew Borkowski for his insight and advice on the first draft of the novel.

To Marnie Woodrow, whose encouraging editorial helped me create a polished draft that I was ready to send out into the world.

To my Humber Games writing group—Doug Schmidt, Irene Fantopoulos and Phyllis Koppel—who have been a consistent source of encouragement and support right from the start.

To three teachers, none of whom read this manuscript, but whose guidance helped me write it: Wayson Choy, whose mentorship had a profound effect on my vision of myself as a writer; Donna Poulidis who helped me recover during a difficult time in my life, and helped me to set my *sankalpa* to write a novel and get it published; and Ginny McFarlane, who helped me discover my dream-path of becoming a writer.

To the many books that are a part of *The Nap-Away Motel*, some of them hidden beneath the surface, some of them found on the pages within. I'm grateful to Maurice Sendak's *Where The Wild Things Are*, for inspiring both Ori's and Tiffany's characters and to Carter's favourite books, Philip Pullman's His Dark Materials triology; *The Golden Compass* is one of my favourite's as well. To several books I read when I was researching mental illness, including *Rethinking Madness* by Paris Williams, *A Road Back From Schizophrenia* by Arnhild Lauveng, and *The Center Cannot Hold: My Journey Through Madness* by Elyn R. Saks. To the trans youth who told their stories in *Beyond Magenta: Transgender Teens Speak Out*, by Susan Kuklin. To *A Gift for the Bereaved Parent* by Zamir Hussain, for insight into an Islamic perspective on coping with grief.

To Grace and Virginia Kennedy, who spoke the secret language of twins; to David Newland for permission to use The Ukulele Benediction, and for the spark it provided in the creation of this story, and to Florence + the Machine for further inspiration. Their music and lyrics fuelled my imagination as I brought Ori's character to life.

To my sisters and my mother—I have been inspired as a writer by our shared love of reading and books; especially to Anna, who came through with some financial assistance for freelance editing. To my daughters: Chloe, whose fierce determination fuels mine, and Abby, whose steady courage reminds me to walk my own path. And to my dearest Linda, whose unwavering belief in me is astounding. Her loyalty and love have been a constant anchor in my life.

Finally to all the east end motels along the Kingston Road strip that inspired the creation of the fictional Nap-Away Motel.

ABOUT THE AUTHOR

Nadja is a writer and a veterinarian. Her work has been published in *Understorey, Room, Canthius,* and *The Dalhousie Review. The Nap-Away Motel* is her first novel. She lives in Toronto with her wife and their two daughters. Her author page can be found at www.nmlhazard.com.

PHOTO CREDIT: CHLOE HAZARD